I0590665

LIBERATION

THE BAD COMPANY™ BOOK FOUR

CRAIG MARTELLE

MICHAEL ANDERLE

DISRUPTIVE IMAGINATION

We can't write without those who support us
On the home front, we thank you for being
there for us

We wouldn't be able to do this for a living if it weren't for our
readers
We thank you for reading our books

LIBERATION TEAM

Thanks to the JIT Readers

Micky Cocker
James Caplan
John Ashmore
Peter Manis
Paul Westman
Kelly O'Donnell
Larry Omans
Peter Manis

If I've missed anyone, please let me know!

Editor
Mia Darien, www.miadarien.com

CHARACTERS & TIMELINE

Find the high-res version of the Kurtherian Timeline here:
http://kurtherianbooks.com/timeline_jeff/

World's Worst Day Ever (WWDE)

WWDE + 20 years, Terry Henry returns from self-imposed exile. The Terry Henry Walton Chronicles detail his adventures from that time to WWDE+150

WWDE + 150 years – Michael returns to earth. BA returns to earth. TH & Char go to Space

Key Players

- Terry Henry Walton (was forty-five on the WWDE)—called TH by his friends. Enhanced with nanocytes by Bethany Anne herself (Queen of the Federation), wears the rank of Colonel, lead the Force de Guerre (FDG), a military unit

that he established on WWDE+20, and now leads the Bad Company's Direct Action Branch.
- Charumati (was sixty-five on the WWDE)—A werewolf, married to Terry, carries the rank of Major, but is his equal partner
- Kimber (born WWDE+15, adopted approximately WWDE+25 by TH & Char, enhanced on WWDE+65)—Major
- Her husband Auburn Weathers (enhanced on WWDE+82)—provides logistics support
- Kaeden (born WWDE+16, adopted approximately WWDE+24 by TH & Char, enhanced on WWDE+65) – a Major
- His wife Marcie Spires (born on WWDE+22, naturally enhanced)—Colonel
- Cory (born WWDE+25, naturally enhanced, gifted with the power to heal)
- Her husband Ramses—Major, died on Benitus Seven, WWDE+153
- Kailin, Auburn & Kimber's son (born on WWDE+78)

Vampires

- Joseph (born three hundred years before the WWDE)
- Petricia (born WWDE+30)

Pricolici (Werewolves that walk upright)

- Nathan Lowell (President of the Bad Company

and Bethany Anne's Chief of Intelligence)
- Ecaterina (Nathan's spouse)
- Christina (Nathan & Ecaterina's daughter)

Werewolves

- Sue & Timmons (long-term members of Char's pack)
- Shonna & Merrit (long-term members of Char's pack)
- Ted (with Felicity, an enhanced human)

Weretigers born before the WWDE:

- Aaron & Yanmei

Humans (enhanced)

- Micky San Marino, Captain of the *War Axe*
- Commander Suresha, *War Axe* Department Head – Engines
- Commander MacEachthighearna (Mac), *War Axe* Department Head—Environmental
- Commander Blagun Lagunov, *War Axe* Department—Structure
- Commander Oscar Wirth, *War Axe* Department Head—Stores
- Lieutenant Clodagh Shortall, *War Axe* engine technician
- Sergeant Fitzroy, a martial arts expert and platoon sergeant

- Kelly, Capples, Fleeter, Praeter, & Duncan— mech drivers

Other Key Characters

- Dokken (a sentient German Shepherd)
- The Good King Wenceslaus (an orange tabby who thinks he's a weretiger, all fifteen pounds of him)
- K'thrall—a Yollin, used to be systems analyst on the *War Axe*, a warrior with the Bad Company
- Clifton—human pilot of the *War Axe*
- Bundin—a four-legged shell-backed blue, stalk-headed alien from Poddern
- Ankh'Po'Turn—a small bald humanoid from Crenellia
- General Smedley Butler – EI/AI on the *War Axe*, who they call the general
- Plato – Ted's AI from R&D
- Dionysus – the AI tasked to assist with running Keeg Station
- Paithoon – A Belzonian, escort for Kaeden & Marcie
- Bon Tap – a teal-skinned, silver-haired Malatian, a warrior in the Bad Company
- Slikira – Ixtali, four legs, a spider race, called Slicker, a warrior in the Bad Company
- Other Bad Company warriors: Tim, "Skates" Mardigan, Chris Bo Runner (Harborian), Jones, Einar, Gefelton, Eldis (wife is Xianna, a green-skinned alien woman)

CHAPTER ONE

Keeg Station, in the Dren Cluster

Terry pounded the bag. Relentlessly. It didn't make him feel better, but he didn't stop. Char ran through a series of leg exercises while Cory sat on a bench nearby, staring vacantly at a wall. They hadn't left her on her own since Benitus Seven. Her husband of more than one hundred years was gone, his body fired into space after a brief ceremony.

The blue glow had returned to her eyes, but the sparkle was gone.

Her parents struggled for normalcy, but it eluded them.

Aaron and Yanmei walked into the workout room. Yanmei approached slowly, holding her hands in front of her, almost in prayer. "Please join us, Cordelia," the weretiger said softly, kneeling to be eye level with her friend. "We seek to help you be at peace with the universe and prepare for our travel back to Earth."

"Earth?" Terry and Char asked at the same time.

Aaron intercepted them before they could interrupt

Yanmei, who continued to speak softly with Cory. The two women stood together and headed for the corner where the yoga mats were already laid out. Aaron held up his hand and smiled.

"Forever the teacher," Char said. He had taught Cory, Kim, and Kaeden back in North Chicago, long ago. He had been a teacher in China when he was taken and modified, turned into a weretiger. Aaron had made the most of it, sadly, until he met Yanmei, a weretiger who had been Terry Henry Walton's torturer, but that had been a different time and a different place.

"I am," Aaron admitted. "Ted has news. Some of us will be leaving soon for Earth, to take the IICS, as Ted calls them, and deliver them to our family and the powers that be."

"The Instantaneous Interstellar Communication System," Terry spelled out. "I expect Cory wants to talk with her kids, tell them the bad news."

"We want her to go with us, talk with them in person." Aaron wasn't asking. Terry and Char looked at each other and nodded. They would do anything to help their daughter through her depression and on the road to recovery. She would never be whole, but they wanted her to be able to live with her loss. Of all people, Terry knew what it was like. He'd hidden from humanity for twenty years as he learned to cope. His nanocytes had decided that he would live, even when he didn't care to.

"A change of scenery will probably help."

"Among other things, my friends," Aaron replied cryptically. "We will help her, with all that we are, because she deserves that and more."

Yanmei reached upward and then bent at the waist until she touched her toes. She slowly stretched downward until her palms were on the floor. Cory mirrored her.

Aaron excused himself and joined them, adjusting Cory slightly before assuming his stance. His long arms touched the floor before he finished bending. After a solid thirty seconds, they rose. Three iterations later, they lunged forward into the warrior pose. Cory slowly assumed the position. Yanmei reached over to straighten one of Cory's arms, rotating until her arm was under Cory's, supporting it. Aaron moved to support her back arm. They remained in that position until Cory's legs began to shake. They stood up and shook out before moving into a new pose.

In between poses, they didn't give her time to think. It was the first step on a long road, not to forget but to live a life as it had become. Move forward, one second at a time, one step at a time.

Char stood and stretched the tightness from her legs. She had overdone it, just like her husband. Terry rotated his shoulder, flexing, twisting, and wincing. After all the years and the treatments in the Pod-doc, it still gave him problems, especially when he worked out like a madman. He folded his hands in front and watched his daughter do something other than cry.

It had been tearing at his heart, because her grief was so profound, and there was nothing he could do about it. Terry felt the burden of life weighing him down, not able to shake the crushing mass. Char carried her own angst, every bit as great. No parent could watch their child go through what Cory was going through without having it grate on their very souls.

It gave them hope to see their friends intervene and slowly lead Cory onto the road to recovery.

Terry breathed slowly and deeply, licking his lips and picking up his towel. "What do you say we find Ted and ask how things are going?"

"We have dinner with them tonight. He might get suspicious if we talk with him twice in the same day."

"True," Terry agreed. "Then let's get changed and walk around. See if there's any color we can add back into this station."

"I know what you mean," Char said softly. "It's like everything is shades of gray."

"Fifty?" Terry injected lightheartedly.

"Don't you start with that." Char pushed Terry playfully, her purple eyes sparkling for a moment.

Normalcy. Maybe it wasn't such a distant thing.

After one last look at the weretigers working with their daughter, they walked away feeling much better than when the day started.

Spires Harbor

Sue and Timmons both stood with their arms crossed. They'd made their arguments, yet Shonna and Merrit looked skeptical.

"I thought we were pretty convincing, so what will it be? Moment of truth, bitches," Sue said, looking down her nose at the two.

"Why do we have to decide right now?" Shonna replied, putting her hands on her hips as she faced Sue. Timmons moved to the side, as did Merrit. If the Werewolves were going to throw down, they wanted to watch.

Shonna smirked first and Sue laughed. Merrit and Timmons harrumphed in disappointment. "Boys wanted to see mud wrestling, methinks," Sue intoned.

"Too bad, fellas," Shonna said softly. "Of course, we'll put on our project manager hats again. We need to contract the infrastructure required to build spaceships. I'm not sure it gets any better than that, but how will Char feel about it? I don't think taking her pack away will do anything to lighten her mood."

Sue and Timmons frowned. Ramses had been their friend, too.

"For the greater good," Felicity interjected, joining the werewolves on the observation deck of *Sheri's Pride*, looking at the beehive of activity surrounding the budding shipyard.

"We've all lost people," she said softly before speaking more boldly. "They were good people, but we have to move forward. The universe is expanding. We can sit back and watch, or we can grab that bastard and drag it in a direction of our choosing!"

"Damn, Felicity. What's got you so fired up?"

She smiled slyly. "Ted's home." She flipped her hair over her shoulder, looking smug as she turned and walked away.

Sue gave her the hairy eyeball. "You must be one hell of a woman, Felicity. My compliments! There was no amount of time that we were apart where Ted would return feeling amorous. One day or one year. He was always just Ted."

Felicity turned enough that they could see her blushing above a coy smile.

"Ladies! It's not a competition," Shonna said as she rubbed Merrit's shoulders. Timmons pulled Sue into a hug.

"Let the orgy begin," Felicity drawled as she walked away, adding an extra swing to her hips. The others stopped to watch her leave. Sue crossed her arms and scowled.

"Some people make a better fit than others. I don't want to think about a life without you," Timmons whispered, racing to the rescue before Sue despaired too long over something out of her control.

"You are right, you big, husky werewolf." Sue kissed him on the cheek. "We all have work to do."

Sue and Timmons shook hands with Shonna and Merrit to seal the deal. "I'll talk to Char," Timmons told them.

Christina strolled along the shopping deck. Marcie on one side and Kaeden on the other. "It's like you don't want me to shop, when you know I love shopping. Four shoe stores here and Felicity says that there will soon be six," she said without looking at either of them.

"We only want you to buy what we're selling," Marcie replied.

"And that would be?"

"Backstop us," Kaeden said softly. Christina stopped and turned.

"I've got your backs, but that's not what you mean, is it?"

Marcie moved around the werewolf to be in front of her standing next to her husband.

"General Reynolds wants someone to transform one of the regional militaries into a viable air-ground task force," Marcie said matter-of-factly. Christina screwed her face up as she contemplated the words.

Kaeden translated it into layman's terms. "A land army just in case someone is trying to be a dick. A show of force, that's not just show. And we know Dad's the right person for the job, but he can't be everywhere at all times. Back on Earth, Marcie, Kim, and I built up the FDG until it was a worldwide fighting force. But there was one drawback."

Christina crossed her arms, pursed her lips, tapped one foot, and waited.

"The enemy was the Forsaken. They made sure not to be wherever we were. It was a lesson in futility. We disbanded the majority of the FDG in favor of small tactical teams, and that's when we were finally able to engage them straight up."

"What's this have to do with me? I mean, I know you think I'm a one-person army, which is flattering, but training another army? I'm not so keen on that."

Marcie rolled her eyes and shook her head as Kae chuckled. When the couple composed themselves, Marcie answered. "We want you to assume my position in the Bad Company. You'll make a great deputy for Terry Henry. Kimber will take over the mech recon. Kaeden and I are taking over the expansion of the FDG."

"I thought Kurtz was doing that, with the other modified Pricolici?"

"Kurtz is a better tactical commander. He was always a front-line guy, but they need someone who's a little more recruiting, organizing, and strategy oriented. Plus, we want to step back from war for a little bit."

Christina's breath caught in her throat. She looked at her shoes. She didn't need more, but a new pair would make her feel better. When she looked up, she found Marcie and Kae watching her. "I can't blame you," Christina admitted. "Does TH know that you're leaving?"

"Yes, but he hasn't accepted it. That's where you come in. If he has confidence that you'll fill my shoes well, then he'll be more comfortable. All he can see is that his family is being torn apart by something he's been expecting to happen since we joined his war against evil." Marcie sighed.

"It's something we would do no matter what. Dad thinks he coerced us to join, but Marcie and me? We had two kids, a family, but we were denying who we wanted to be, and that was defenders of the oppressed. The one thing that has made the most sense in our lives is Dad's commitment to helping others. He always says that if you have the ability to act, you have the responsibility. We believe that. Few people are built for war. Humanity's basic instinct is to live more sedate lives. Travel for excitement, but return home at the end of a long day to a happy family, a good meal, and a warm bed. My parents have been killing themselves for as long as they've been alive to give others that life. The FDG is our chance to do that on a planetary scale.

LIBERATION

If we can help bring peace by crushing an enemy's army, then that's what we'll do."

"I'd say you fuckers were raised wrong, but my parents and their friends raised me to believe that, too. I get angry and in my—" Christina looked around to make sure no one was close by. "—Pricolici form, I want to shred them like cabbage."

"Step back from that and don't change form. As Terry's deputy, he'll need you to help him oversee the battle, but when the rubber meets the road and you're forced into close combat, the gloves come off and you crush your enemies," Marcie explained. Her lip twitched as the adrenaline surged. She clenched her fists.

Christina punched her in the chest. "I'm in. Let's go buy some new shoes to celebrate." Marcie smiled, not in humor, but in the way warriors did as they prepared to engage the enemy.

It was the confidence of someone who was more at home in war than in peace.

Christina smiled the same way.

Kae watched expressionlessly. He felt sorry for the clerk in the shoe store. *I think I'll wait outside,* he thought. Until Marcie and Christina each grabbed an arm and propelled him between them toward a store called Camper, a store brand taken from the fashion scene of old Earth's London. Kae groaned and frowned as the women sought a future addition to their wardrobes. Kaeden looked at their feet. They were both wearing shoes. *What the hell do you need another pair for?*

He didn't dare say it aloud.

CHAPTER TWO

Keeg Station, TSP's Fine Dining

Terry and Char stood in the corridor watching the flashing lights as each restaurant, bar, and store tried to attract customers through their signs and displays.

"It looks like Chinatown," Terry said. Char raised one eyebrow. As Felicity pushed for opening Keeg Station to the general public, the shop owners were attempting to expand their reach, and be successful enough to petition for more space.

"It looks like success, you mean. Capitalism at its finest. It reminds me of Kingston Town."

Terry agreed. "Better. It's the Kingston we grew to like. Vendors hawking their wares. They made everyone happy to be alive."

Char's face turned dark at TH's comment.

"Oh, shit. I'm sorry." Terry wrapped his arms around his wife and hugged her. He closed his eyes to be more present in the moment, more aware of her. She didn't sob, but he knew she was crying.

Again.

Am I heartless? he wondered. Terry's sadness was for his daughter. He missed those he lost in combat, but he considered it an honor to die in battle, especially while saving another. It was the epitome of sacrifice. *Glory to those who die in service to others.*

Someone tapped him on the shoulder. He turned to find Felicity and Ted standing there. Char leaned back, her eyes red, but recovering quickly thanks to the wonders of nanocyte technology. She smiled and hugged Felicity first and then she went for Ted. He tried to lean back, but she caught him and pulled him close. She made it quick.

Terry followed suit, but settled for shaking Ted's hand. Ted looked just as uncomfortable shaking hands as hugging. Terry chuckled and showed them to the maître d.

Felicity held up four fingers. A woman dressed in a long gown nodded and ushered the group in, giving them a private table in the rear shadows. Terry approved.

As soon as they sat down, Ted started to speak. The server stood there, ready to take drink orders, but Felicity stilled her with one finger.

"I'm sorry, TH, for all of it. I know you didn't bully me, even though I felt bullied, so I turned into what I detest. I'm a bully." Ted hung his head while Felicity rubbed his back. She looked at TH, her eyebrows raised expectantly. Char nudged her husband.

Terry looked to the server, who only shook her head. *Damn!*

"No one deserves to be bullied, Ted, no matter the reason, but I understand how you feel. I also understand how hard it is for you to talk about this. Know that you can tell me anything at any time. We'll work it out because the last thing I want, or any of us want, is for you to be uncomfortable. You made it possible to fight those bastards. The things you've done for us have made us all better. For that, I thank you, but we won't be hailing Ted. We all put our pants on the same way."

Felicity started shaking her head.

"We don't put our pants on the same way?" Char had to ask.

"No. He jumps, both legs at the same time, because it's more efficient."

"It is…" Ted mumbled.

"I'll take a glass of your finest dark beer!" Terry ordered loudly. The server wrinkled her nose in distaste. "You don't have good dark beer here?"

"Wine is best served with the meals in TSP's," she replied.

Terry looked like a stunned carp.

"He'll have the beer, but I expect since I'll be having a bistok steak, rare, that I'll go with a complementary red. What do you recommend?" Char asked.

"I want a bistok steak," Terry grumbled. "And a damn dark beer."

Felicity held up a finger. "We'll take a bottle of Asplesian Cabernet. Do you have anything that's more than five years old?"

"We have a ten-year old case, just arrived, Madam Director. Excellent choice showing a cultured palate." The server bowed slightly while watching Terry Henry. He tilted his head as he met her gaze. Ted didn't bother ordering anything as water was already at the table. He'd said his piece and was itching to get back into his lab. He folded his hands in his lap and started to fidget.

Felicity took it all in, astutely, as it had helped her throughout her adult life. Her ability to read people in order to better appeal to their sensibilities was legendary. Once the server retreated to the kitchen, she turned to Ted. "Thank you for sharing with us, my love. You have to eat first, keep up your strength, and then you can go back to your lab."

He stopped fidgeting as he looked her in the eye. He smiled and nodded. "Okay."

"And you." She looked sharply to Terry Henry Walton, but couldn't maintain her glare. "This isn't a place to order beer, you Neanderthal. Can't you order wine once in a while?"

Char laughed out loud. She brushed the silver streak of her hair from her face, tucking it behind her ear. "No. He absolutely cannot order wine. I think it's a genetic abnormality, although I'm sure there are clinical terms that apply."

"I like beer, what can I say?" Terry countered. "And I'm way behind. How long did I go without a decent brew? Although the reestablishment of Jamaica's Red Stripe brewery made me feel warm all over."

"We were always warm. It was the tropics." Char leaned away from TH, but held out her hand. He took it and smiled. Her purple eyes sparkled through the darkness of the restaurant's shadows. "It was a simpler time, too."

"Is this when you announce that Kae and Marcie are leaving us to do what they did back then?"

Terry pursed his lips and whistled. "I hadn't decided that they could go, not until this instant," he told them.

"Was there ever a doubt?" Felicity replied. Under the table, she put her hand on Ted's leg. He took it and caressed her fingers as he stopped rocking. "You don't keep people prisoner, TH. Just like Shonna and Merrit are going to lead the mineral extraction team. Between them and Sue and Timmons, we'll have Spires Harbor expanding to become the biggest shipyard in the whole sector."

Terry looked amused. "Do you hear yourself, the pride in your voice?" Terry asked. He leaned forward, bracing his forearm on the table. "I remember a time when the Mayor of New Boulder worked tirelessly to get a car running so he could take you for a cruise because you didn't like having to walk."

"I still don't," she answered, thinking back to the beater that smoked horrendously. But it was the best ride in town, a chariot that her husband provided solely for her. "And now, I'm excited about building a big shipyard in space. It's not too different from the dirigible factory we had in San Francisco. This isn't new, and make no mistake, Colonel Terry Henry Walton, this shipyard will build the nicest luxury passenger ship that will have ever been built so that Ted and I can travel the stars at our whim as we traveled Earth in our airships."

"Multiple Etheric power supplies for the Gate technology, the Instantaneous Interstellar Communication System, shields, cloaking, and everything else we will install on it," Ted said, perking up as he thought about the way ahead.

"You have Plato working on the design right now, don't you?" Terry asked. "You sly dog!"

Ted turned away to look for Dokken. Terry rubbed his forehead and closed his eyes.

When Ted couldn't find the dog, he continued. "The ship is already under construction, but on a not-to-interfere basis with primary contracts."

"You already have primary contracts?" Char wondered.

"We do." Felicity smiled broadly. The wine arrived just in time.

The server passed out the oversized wineglasses filled a third of the way. She held the mug of beer away from herself, grimacing as the head ran over the side and dripped onto the tablecloth. Terry took the mug with both hands and plunged his face into the foam to keep from losing more.

"Liquid gold," he said beneath a foam mustache.

"He isn't right in the head," Char told the young woman.

The server put a comforting hand on Char's shoulder, nodding in sympathy. The server didn't make eye contact with Terry. She caught herself before walking away. "Are you ready to order?"

Terry tipped the mug back and slowly drank while the others ordered. When it was his turn, he was still drinking. He threw back the remainder and placed the mug on the table. He used his napkin to dab at his mouth. "I'll have the bistok steak please, medium rare, with the orange tubers and greens, with a second steak on the side, please, also medium rare. And another one of these." He picked up his empty mug and handed it back.

"I don't know how you manage," the server told Char before taking the mug and walking away without writing Terry's order down.

———

Aaron, Yanmei, and Cordelia sat on meditation pillows as they faced the center of a small triangle. Each had their eyes closed as they chanted together, tones meant to calm the inner soul, repetition to focus the mind on the simple task at hand. They slowed on Yanmei's command until they finished.

"Open your eyes," she said.

Aaron slowly opened his as if waking from a refreshing nap. Cory kept hers closed as if afraid of the light.

"The world is out here," Yanmei said softly.

Cory blinked until she was looking at the weretigers. From Yanmei to Aaron and back again. "Thank you."

"We remember the past, but we have to look forward. It is the only direction in which our eyes point."

Cory nodded once without replying.

"Next event. A ten-mile run!" Aaron declared.

"Say what?" Cory blurted.

Yanmei's forehead wrinkled as she looked sideways at her mate.

"You know that I hate running more than anything. We run, because we need to run from our pain as much as run through it. Our destination will be where we started, but when we finish, we'll be different from the three who started the journey."

Yanmei looked at a picture on the wall of the workout room as she wondered where Aaron had come up with that bit of philosophy. It made sense to her, but she didn't know why. She had ten miles to contemplate it. She did the math in her mind and came up with a million trips around the station. *Must be off a decimal place or three,* she thought.

Terry had put the workout room off limits to everyone except Aaron, Yanmei, and Cory. They needed it without distraction and without well-wishers, people who were only trying to help but weren't.

The three left the room with Aaron in the lead. He stretched for four seconds and then started to run with a shuffling gait so he didn't smash his face into the overhead. Aaron was too tall for space stations, but he made do without complaint.

He was in the most foreign place he'd ever been but was more at home. He was doing what he was meant to do—teaching, mentoring, guiding a lost soul to help her find her way back to the world of the living. Yanmei watched his lanky form, adoring him the whole time. He looked back with love in his eyes. A match made in the caverns of Kentucky, where too many others died.

Even Akio almost died there, one of the most powerful of all vampires. From the ashes of evil bloomed the flower of life. Those who walked from the gaping maw of Mammoth Cave, including Terry Henry Walton and Cory, came away stronger. It was time for more of that.

Cory watched the weretigers as they looked at each other, an inseparable couple. She stifled the desire to cry yet again. They had shown her how to embrace Ramses's memory without seeing only his loss. She was alone but would never again feel alone. Cory rushed ahead, working her way in front of Aaron when the corridor widened. She sped up, running as only the enhanced could run.

Aaron changed mid-stride into a sleek weretiger. Yanmei changed too, shrugging out of her clothes to turn her fur free. Their yellowish-green eyes glowed as they loped alongside Cordelia. She reached down to bury her hands in their neck fur, feeling the warmth and softness that mirrored the souls within. Yanmei snapped at a passerby to give the trio more room as they ran along the curving corridor.

They continued running that way until Aaron thought he would wear the pads off his paws. Five miles sufficed, not ten, and they ended up where they started, with a lifetime of difference in between.

Aaron and Yanmei changed back into human form in the workout room, covering themselves with towels while Cory stretched.

"I think I'll go back to my room. I have to write a letter."

Yanmei's look asked the question without her having to say anything.

"To my future self, saying that each day will get better. Although I'll never forget, I know Ramses would be angry if I wallowed in misery. He lived his life to make me happy and I'll say that I never took that for granted. We had a great time. We have two incredible daughters. My next step is to go to Earth and find them. Maybe they'll decide to come back with me, but if they don't, that's their choice. Free will and all that. I'll support their decision and love them no more and no less than I always have." Cory cupped the weretigers' faces in her hands, her blue eyes sparkling at them. She held their gaze for a moment, then turned and walked away, head held high as she disappeared through the door.

CHAPTER THREE

The *War Axe*

Captain Micky San Marino scowled at his four department heads. Each of them looked at their laps, none volunteering to be the first to invoke the captain's ire, although it was a little late for that.

"What do you have to say for yourselves?" Micky demanded. Suresha held her hands up in surrender.

"There's nothing *to* say. It wasn't my department." The others glared at her and she resumed staring at her lap.

"Fine!" Mac declared. He was in charge of the environmental systems, but Micky was holding them all responsible because no one had stepped up to help. "We're still purging the system. The water supplies got into the ventilation, fouling the temperature sensors, so the auto-coolers kicked in and all of a sudden, it was snowing."

"It wasn't just snowing, Mac. It was snowing throughout the whole ship! My bed is under an inch of snow, as are the rest of my quarters and everyone else's quarters. What happens to snow when it melts?"

"I know, that's why we haven't raised the temperature, yet."

"And what are your teams doing to help?" Micky focused like a laser beam on Oscar Wirth, in charge of ship's stores.

"We, um… We…" he stammered.

"You built a ramp on the mess deck and were using trays as sleds."

Oscar rubbed his elbow where it was bruised. His ad hoc sled had gone sideways off the table, and he had slammed into the door frame. He acted as though his fingers in his lap were the most interesting things he'd ever laid eyes on.

"And you." Micky looked at Suresha.

His engineering department head looked around, finally pointing to herself in wonder. "Me?"

"Did I see a snowman down there?"

"Clodagh did a great job, don't you think? He even had a flower bonnet." Suresha smiled proudly until she met the captain's gaze. Suresha looked back to her lap for answers that remained elusive.

"Blagun?" the captain asked.

"I was outside working on the hull when it all happened. When I came back in, I immediately hit the shower. Thank goodness for the space heater in there."

Micky hammered his fist onto the table. The commanders shot upright and looked wide-eyed at their captain. "Is anyone doing anything about the snow?" he asked in a hard, measured tone.

The door to the conference room slid open and Wenceslaus strolled in, hopped onto an empty chair, then climbed onto the table where he flopped onto his side. Micky watched the cat lick a paw to clean his face.

"Smedley? Where have you been during all of this?"

"My apologies, Captain. I have been preoccupied with work tasks from Plato. Many of Ted's projects are coming to fruition, and the final details are most critical to get correct. Between the two of us, I believe we've nailed down optimal manufacturing processes and will be turning out miniaturized gate and communications technology in short order."

Micky leaned back, letting his chair support him as he kicked his feet to the top of the table. They'd wiped it down before he'd arrived, but the snow was on the floor, and numerous footprints showed. Cat prints joined the footprints in a testament to the traffic that had passed in and out of the captain's briefing room.

A gate engine on a shuttle pod that also had shields and could cloak itself. The immensity of the future lay before the Bad Company, but he was quagmired in a single inch of snow. He hung his head and decided to embrace the absurdity of the situation.

"You know what happens when you get snow, don't you?" he asked. No one answered. No one even moved. "Smedley, give me ship-wide broadcast, please."

"The comm is yours, Skipper."

"All hands, this is the captain speaking. The weather has created unsafe conditions throughout the ship, so I am declaring a snow day. Enjoy your day off. Captain San Marino out."

He glanced around the room before standing. "You four need to figure out how to get rid of the snow without it destroying any of our equipment. Now, go forth and do great things."

Wenceslaus rolled onto his back and stretched his paws in Micky's direction. The captain sauntered to the table and scratched the cat's soft belly fur. He picked up the good king, cradling him like a baby while he continued to scratch his belly. Wenceslaus settled in to the captain's arms and closed his eyes as if ready to fall asleep.

"Carry on," the captain ordered as he stepped softly through the snow on his way to the bridge, cat in hand.

"Nathan Lowell, you are a huckster and a charlatan!" Felicity said, smiling toward the screen. The camera didn't show that Christina was in the room, kicked back in one of the station director's oversized chairs.

The Bad Company's president looked at Felicity from his office in a remote part of the galaxy.

"You want to build a gate and open Keeg Station for commercial traffic. It's big, but not big enough to be a commerce hub. It's meant to be a secret station from which the Direct Action Branch can operate. Why do you want to blow their cover?"

"You don't think blowing up planets hasn't already revealed their existence?" Felicity stood so she could put her hands on her hips. She tossed her head to throw an errant strand of her newly platinum-dyed hair out of her vision.

"They haven't blown up any planets," Nathan countered. He stopped and pointed an accusing finger. "I've negotiated with you before and can tell when you're playing the emotion card. This is different. You've already started building the gate, haven't you?"

Felicity feigned shock and batted her eyelashes at Nathan. "I'm sure I have no idea what you're talking about."

"Those Dark Tomorrow fuckers tried to blow up Frontier Station 11. Once Keeg is on the map, they'll try to make their mark there, too." Nathan ran his fingers through an unruly shock of hair. It looked like he'd been awake for too long.

"When's the last time you slept, Nathan?" Felicity drawled softly.

"Too long ago. It's like the next crisis is the one that will tear the Federation apart."

"I don't think it's as fragile as all that," Felicity replied. "You are surrounded by good people. Trust them to help you and go get some sleep."

Christina wasn't able to see her father. She stood and hurried around Felicity's desk. "Holy shit, Dad! You look like crap."

"You kiss your mother with that mouth?" Nathan said with a smile.

"Every time I see her." Christina waggled her fingers and Nathan waved back.

"How are you doing?" he asked as his eyelids drooped.

"Better than you, clearly. I'll call you tomorrow. Felicity tells me that I know people who can help me get the bandwidth and the time, but for the life of me, I can't figure out who they are."

"Nathan," Felicity said, looking down her nose at the screen, "we're going to finish the gate and with a word from you, we'll activate it with a direct link to Onyx Station. We need this link and lifeline. We will become everything you need from the Direct Action Branch and more. We will be more than just self-sustaining, we will provide excess profit to the Bad Company's coffers."

Christina moved out of sight of the camera so she could wrap her hands around her throat and fake choking herself. Then she stuck her finger in her mouth and fake-gagged. Felicity tried to ignore her, but couldn't as she leaned close from behind the screen.

"Go get some sleep. We'll finalize the details later." Felicity clicked off before looking up. "This is the sexy stuff, dear, because this is about power. Not that your father is giving up any of his, but that we are mutually expanding our base, creating a need for products, filling that void, and then expanding further. You want to be a part of a dynasty? Well, this is how you build a dynasty."

Christina stopped goofing around and stood up straight. She studied the woman before her. "I see the wisdom behind it. On Earth, you did something like this?"

"Ted and I flew the skies in the greatest luxury possible. People held parties in our honor so they could get two minutes of our time. We will have that once again, dear. All it takes is building wealth. There's a lot of wealth in this universe." Felicity stood and walked to her window. Spires Harbor lay in the distance. "I've found that helping others is the greatest way to help yourself. Through new ships and upgrading old ships, we will help the universe to expand."

"What do you need from me?" Christina asked,

standing shoulder to shoulder with the director as they looked out the window.

"I need you to keep Terry and Char alive so they can keep everyone else alive, including my Ted. Whenever they go into battle, he'll go with them. If anything happened to those two, I believe that all we've worked for will come undone. There are few in this universe around whom things revolve. Bethany Anne and Michael are the key to all of it, and next are General Reynolds and your father. There are the Rangers, the FDG, that Ghost Squadron that no one talks about, and others, but Terry and Char, as much as they won't admit it, give people hope. As long as they live, they will bring a positive energy to our corner of the galaxy. You keep them alive!"

Felicity took Christina by the shoulders, gripping tightly, her blue eyes piercing.

"I understand," Christina replied softly. "I will protect them with my life, all of them, because that's what Terry's deputy is supposed to do."

"So that has come to fruition?" Felicity asked.

Christina smiled. "You know it has."

"I don't want you to think that I'm all-knowing. I am, but I don't want you to think it." Felicity laughed as she glanced back at the shipyard. "I like you a lot, Christina. You're one of us. Old school but new school. The inner circle. I'm glad you're here."

Christina nodded. She wasn't sure what to say. She one-arm hugged the director before leaving. She had a great deal of work waiting for her if she was going to fill Marcie's shoes.

"What is this thing?" Ted asked, miffed at being dragged to the hangar bay. The smallest of the Harborian frigates, looking long abandoned, sat on blocks in a far corner. Dionysus had to dispatch a maintenance bot to activate the lights in that section because they'd been cannibalized sometime in the past.

Joseph, Petricia, and Bundin appeared from behind the warship. "It is the next best ship in the budding Direct Action Branch fleet."

Ted's face twitched in confusion before he turned to walk away.

"Woohoo!" Ankh'Po'Turn yelled from somewhere within the vessel. After two clangs, three metallic screeches, and four bangs, the Crenellian strolled from the ship's open hatches.

Ted looked over his shoulder. "There you are," he stated the obvious. "I need you in the lab."

"This ship is going to be the fastest and best in the whole fleet. It'll be able to do things that even the *War Axe* cannot."

Ted turned around, walked to the ship, and started inspecting it from stem to stern. "Why are you working on this?" Ted asked while making faces at a torn fitting on the outside engine housing.

"Because Miss Cordelia asked me," Ankh replied simply, standing close and looking up at his mentor. "She needed a ship that would take her back to Earth."

"Why didn't she ask me?" Ted wondered aloud as he fixed the Crenellian with his gaze.

"Because she knew you were busy, but that you would drop everything to help her," Joseph interjected.

"That didn't work out because now that I know, I am going to drop everything, and we will have this ship operational and on its way in no time. Plato!"

"I installed two of the Etheric power supplies, just in case," Ankh stated, puffing out his small chest as he attempted to replicate the human gesture.

Ted held up three fingers. "Plato, bring a full complement of maintenance and service bots to the hangar bay, I will be retasking them from whatever less important job they are currently assigned to."

"Are you sure you should be doing that?" Joseph asked. Ted didn't bother with a reply.

"What can I do?" Bundin offered, his mechanical voice echoing off the deck of the bay.

Ted looked up. "Probably nothing," he said.

Bundin's tentacle arms drooped.

"Provisions!" Petricia declared. "If we're taking this ship back to Earth, we need to have supplies. Let's talk to Oscar."

Bundin waved his tentacle arms wildly as his stalk-head bobbed back and forth. He ambled toward the door leading into the station. Petricia winked at Joseph and followed Bundin out.

"We?" Ted asked.

"Of course, we," Joseph answered. "We're taking Cory to find her children."

Ted stamped a foot. "I can do that all by myself." He looked at the deck and shuffled uncomfortably until Felicity joined them. "Who else is going?"

"Anyone who needs to." Joseph held one hand in the other and waited patiently while Ted struggled with the ambiguity of the answer.

"I am not going, if that puts your mind at ease," Felicity told him. Ted smiled at her. "I want you to deliver those boxes of yours to our children so I can talk with them. I'm not saying to find our kids first, but you find our kids next. I miss my family, and now Marcie is going away, too."

"No..." Ted looked forlorn as he dragged the word out. Tears welled in Felicity's eyes, but she didn't let any escape. She blinked them away before composing herself. Ted sighed in relief.

"You do that for me, Ted," she told him.

"We will all do that for you. Sarah Jennifer, Sylvia, Terrence, Charlita, and Billy. We will leave no door closed in our search for them," Joseph declared.

Felicity smiled as she mouthed the names of her children. "You find my children and show them how to use that device of yours."

"It's an IICS, the Interstellar ..."

Felicity interrupted him by putting her finger over his lips. The muscles stood out in his cheeks from clenching his jaw so tightly.

"I'm sorry, my dear. You can tell me, but I won't remember any of those technical terms. That's not my thing. The IICS. I need one in my office, too, so I can talk with them whenever the spirit moves me." Felicity shimmied.

Ted's expression turned blank as he withdrew into himself. Felicity smiled at him. "I love you, Ted. Let me know when you're leaving so I can wave good-bye."

There was no benefit to remaining behind because Ted needed to be alone, disappear into his work in order to recharge. Emotions closed in on him. If they were in their quarters, he'd be able to better deal with it, but not here, not in the open.

"I'll help with the provisions," Joseph said at Felicity's nod.

Ankh and Ted remained behind as a small army of bots trundled toward the ship. Ted sat down where he was, in the middle of the deck. He closed his eyes as he communed with Plato. Ankh sat on the deck facing Ted. He joined the link with the AI and together, they built the project plan and started tasking the maintenance bots to repair and upgrade the small frigate.

CHAPTER FOUR

The *War Axe*

Terry, Char, and Dokken walked from the pod. Aaron and Yanmei had joined them. Two other pods with Bad Company warriors were disembarking. They strolled through the hangar bay and stopped. The second the hatch opened to the ship's interior.

Micky, this is TH, Terry said using his comm chip. *Is there something you didn't tell us?*

We thought since it was Christmas, we'd try to get in the spirit, Micky replied.

"It's not Christmas, is it?" Terry asked. Char shook her head.

"Back on Earth, it's July."

Micky, it's not Christmas.

Fine. HVAC is broken and we've been drying the ship out so the snow sublimates instead of melts. It's taking longer than we like but should have it all cleaned out in another four days. In other news, extra blankets are already in your quarters.

Ugh, Dokken grunted as he was first onto the snow-covered deck. Enough feet had walked through that a path was clear down the corridor.

"You're a dog. You're supposed to like the snow," Terry said.

Dokken stopped, turned, and ran. He jumped at the last minute. Terry instinctively ducked. The German Shepherd sailed by Terry. The dog's eyes shot wide as he tried to backpedal in mid-air right before crashing into Char. The two tumbled to the deck.

Sorry, Dokken apologized as he rolled off Char and into the snow. He stood and shook. Terry took a face full as he was stooped to pull Char to her feet.

She gave the hairy eyeball to Dokken as she stood before turning her attention to her husband. "What?" he stammered. "He started it?"

"That's how this is going to play out, huh?" Char reared back and threw the snowball that she had secreted in her hand. Terry turned his head as the snowball clipped a few errant hairs. He dove to the side, where the snow was untouched. He scooped up a handful but not quickly enough. Char landed on his back, driving him face-first into the deck, where she rubbed his face in the white mess.

"Uncle!" he shouted through a mouthful of snow.

"Smedley, is this your doing?"

"I can't imagine what you mean," the AI replied.

"You've been icing the corridors for months now, just to watch people take diggers. Are you conducting some bizarre study?" Terry wondered aloud, standing and brushing himself off. Char was also interested in Smedley's reply.

"I fear that I have been found out. With my ascension to

consciousness, I find that I get bored easily. I see how the crew comes together in various crises, and you should have seen them play! They were so happy, Colonel Walton. Right now, the captain is on the bridge with Wenceslaus sitting in his lap. And there's a snowman in the middle of engineering."

The warriors from the other two shuttles crowded the doorway, wondering at the snow within, waiting for the colonel and major to give direction.

"Well, General, I'm going to need you to fix this within the next couple hours. I like the ambient temperature to be above freezing because I've grown accustomed to life on the warm side." He smiled and wiggled his eyebrows at his werewolf wife. She blushed as she smiled back.

Dokken harrumphed and shook once again.

"As you wish," the AI said languidly, projecting through the speakers in the corridor.

The air vents kicked into overdrive, pulling air into them.

"How long has this been going on, Smedley?" Terry asked.

Music started to play.

"Smedley?" Terry asked above the sound of a calming violin concerto. "SMEDLEY!"

"I'm sorry, were you talking to me?" the AI replied, chuckling.

"I think we need Ted to dumb him down. He was so much nicer before," Char suggested.

"I'm still me," Smedley sulked. The music changed to a funeral dirge.

"I don't have the words," Terry said. He turned to the

group wedged into the doorway and gave the order. "Carry on."

They powered through, down the corridor, and scattered like quail.

"I miss Jenelope's cooking." Terry pointed a finger at his mouth as he rubbed his stomach.

"I married a twelve-year old." Char couldn't help but smile.

"About a million years ago," Terry said as he looked at the deck. He reached down and scratched Dokken behind the ears. "I can remember everything from before, but the twenty years was a blur, and then from the moment you and your pack chased me from the mountains is clear again."

"It wasn't my pack way back when." Char touched his arm, gently. She knew where his mind had gone.

"It's been such an incredible time, but it's a whole new life. Different from before and it feels like it's been better, and that makes me feel guilty."

"It seems better only because it's fresher in your mind," Char suggested.

"Will Cory take twenty years?"

"No. When your wife and daughter died, you didn't have anyone, only a world that was crashing down around your head. Cory has all of us. She has a stable home in which to stay grounded. She has everything you didn't have."

"It still sucks."

"I know, but it can suck a whole lot less." Char's purple eyes sparkled above a serious expression. She didn't like seeing her daughter in pain. It was frustrating and made her feel helpless, but it didn't mean that she wasn't helping.

"Let's talk with Jenelope." Terry took Char's hand and they walked slowly toward the stairwell. Dokken pressed against Terry's side.

Do you think she'll have any of the good stuff? Dokken asked.

"I think we're out. We're stuck eating bistok until we can get back to Earth and resupply."

Maybe you can bring some cattle out here. I like them better than bistok.

Terry ruffled the big dog's thick neck hair as they climbed the stairs, strolling from them in silence when they reached the mess deck. The snow was almost completely gone already.

Char smacked her lips. With the humidity near zero, she was drying out as quickly as the ship.

Thirsty, Dokken told them.

"Me, too, buddy," Terry answered through his cotton mouth.

The door opened to the mess deck. The tables and chairs were neatly arranged, clean, and empty. The snow was gone and it was starting to warm up inside. The clang of pots and trays from within the galley signaled that Jenelope was hard at work. The low voices sounded familiar. Char leaned around the corner to look into the kitchen.

Cory was elbow-deep in cutting up vegetables. Jenelope was at a table nearby working on a side of beef.

"Cory?" Char wondered. "When did you come over here?"

"Hello to you, too, Mom," Cory said with a slow smile.

CRAIG MARTELLE & MICHAEL ANDERLE

Char rushed around the serving counter to hug her daughter. Jenelope waved a wooden spoon at her.

"Wash before you touch anything in my kitchen! You've got dog all over you."

Hey! Dokken exclaimed in mock outrage. He worked his way into the kitchen.

"Get that mongrel out of here and tell him to take his dog, too!" Jenelope bellowed.

"My daughter…" Terry mumbled as he froze in place.

"What are you waiting for? The vegetables won't cut themselves up. Your hands won't magically be washed without using the sink. And you won't be out of here if you stand there like a Moai statue!"

I'm not his dog, Dokken said weakly as he slunk from the kitchen. *I smell beef. I want a steak. Rare, please. Eat more steak! Eat more steak!*

Cory laughed, lightly, with a small smile.

"Well?" Jenelope asked, pointing at the vegetables with her ever-present wooden spoon.

Cory held up her hands in surrender. "You better wash up, Mom. I'd be honored if you joined me."

Charumati walked to the sink, making sure not to touch anything on her way. As she was washing, Cory answered the first question. "I came over yesterday. Aaron, Yanmei, and Jenelope conspired to hand me back and forth until I had a way ahead."

Char finished and dried her hands on the kitchen towel at the side of the sink. She threw it over her shoulder as she returned to the prep cook's station. Jenelope pointed to the beef.

"Why don't you butcher that thing so we can get some

of it cooking. I already have the grill heating up. We'll sear it, then cook it just right." The chef raised her eyebrows and grinned mischievously.

Eat more steak! Dokken continued.

"Oh, hush! You'll get your steak, but this is the last that I was saving for a special occasion."

I'm going to get steak! Dokken declared. *Two please, obscenely thick and juicy, oh so juicy. I can smell it! I want steak!*

"For a sentient being, you're acting an awful lot like a dog," Jenelope said while puttering around the kitchen, moving from one stove to another, tasting and checking, dropping more spices where needed.

"I'm with you, buddy. A big old steak. I can taste it already." Terry took a seat at a table where he could see into the kitchen. Dokken scrambled to the top of the table and sat there, vibrating in anticipation as he watched Char start working on their dinner.

"Get off the table!" Jenelope ordered. "Who wants to eat their dinner where your butt's been?"

Dokken was done listening to anything that didn't have to do with a steak being delivered to his mouth.

"When Ted has his ship ready, they'll stop by and pick me up on their way to Earth," Cory said matter-of-factly, keeping her eyes on the task at hand as she worked her way through the stack of vegetables before her.

"Do you want us to go with you?" Char asked. Terry's ears perked up.

"No. You have things you need to do. It's my responsibility to go find and talk with Sarah and Sylvia. And if everything goes as it's supposed to, you'll be able to talk with all of us using one of Ted's IICS things."

"We'd like that," was all Char could say. Terry got up and headed for the drink station to fill a soup bowl for Dokken and a glass for Char. He delivered Dokken's first, holding it before the dog so he could keep his eyes on his future meal. He lapped wildly, splashing half the water onto Terry Henry.

"What the hell?" Terry put the bowl on the table. Dokken twisted his head so he could drink while still watching the kitchen. Terry tried to slink in to hand Char the glass.

"Wash your hands!" Jenelope shouted.

Terry downed the glass and hurried to the sink. After washing, he snagged a clean glass and filled it for Char. Two more glasses each and they were finally able to get back to work, Terry watching while Char and Cory sliced and diced.

Suddenly, Dokken found himself next to Char, his tail creating its own breeze because he was wagging it so hard.

"Can't you control that?" Terry asked.

Control what? Dokken replied, licking his dog lips.

"I love your dog," Cory said softly. Terry waited for it, but Dokken didn't say it. The shaggy German Shepherd looked at her.

Can I come to Earth with you? he asked.

"Of course. I'd like that," Cory replied.

"Me too," Terry agreed.

"Me three," Char added.

"One extra big steak for you, now get out of my kitchen, you filthy mongrels."

Terry kneeled to give Dokken a hug.

I thought I was getting two steaks, Dokken complained. Terry snickered.

"How about we take what we get and like it?"

Sheri's Pride, **Spires Harbor**

"I'm not sure about this," Shonna whispered, meant only for Merrit's ears, but the others heard.

"You wouldn't believe the change," Sue explained. "Sometimes, Timmons is a genius."

"Sometimes? I'm surprised you admit to it that often." Timmons laughed at his own joke, wrapping his arm around Sue's waist. She did the same to him as they prepared to enter *Sheri's Pride*.

Shonna and Merrit followed them in. The corridors were mostly empty as the majority of the work force was spread throughout the burgeoning construction project.

Sue let go of Timmons and walked in front as they approached two Harborians. The humans stepped aside and bowed their heads in deference.

"Carry on," she told them casually as she walked past. They nodded, but assumed the position a second time when Shonna appeared before them.

"What she said," Shonna told them. The two men hurried on their way.

"Did you use a bistok prod on them?" Merrit wondered.

"Werewolf," Sue replied.

"They think all women can turn into werewolves if they are provoked. They have the fear of the Were." Timmons grinned mischievously.

"Probably not a bad thing for them, as well as others we

could name," Shonna said, looking pointedly at Timmons and Merrit.

"We have the appropriate level of fear, have no doubt about that!" Timmons waved his hand in the air, the one that had grown back after Char excised it to establish her dominance.

"You were being a dick," Sue reminded him.

"And I paid for it. I'd like to think I'm better now."

Sue blushed. "Just a little," she admitted. "Where are we going anyway?"

"The command center. There's no longer a bridge since this ship will never fly again." Timmons held his hand over the pad and summoned the elevator. The doors opened immediately.

"Why doesn't the *War Axe* have an elevator for passengers?" Shonna asked as she strutted onto the elevator. "I could get used to this."

"Warships. Can't be bogged down with personal convenience and trash like that!" Timmons declared as the elevator moved smoothly upward. It slowed and the doors opened.

"Wasn't this a warship?" Shonna asked.

"Even a derelict entity like Ten knew that humans needed their creature comforts."

The bridge was in the middle of a reconfiguration with plastic sheeting covering an opening into the adjacent room. The set terminals had been replaced by interactive workstations, akin to what the ship looked like before Ten changed it to accommodate a single AI in control of everything. Half of the workstations were filled. When the staff saw the women, they stood and bowed their heads.

"Can I get you a seat?" one of the men said as he tentatively moved from what would have once been the captain's chair.

"Well done, Brice, and no, we won't be here long. Where's Tim?"

"He's escorting a group to Keeg Station on a liberty call."

"I'll be damned. Who determined that the Harborians could be loosed into the wild?"

"The director personally approved it."

"I think it's a good thing," Sue suggested before she draped an arm over Brice's shoulders. "When do you get to go and see that Rowan of yours?"

"I'm in charge, so I have to make sure all the others go first. We talk every night using the video communication."

"Young love," Sue sighed. Timmons held his hands up and shook his head.

"I can't remember being young."

Sue and Shonna rolled their eyes in unison. Merrit thought it best not to express his opinion.

"Let me show you what we've set up for the mining operation," Brice interjected. Timmons winked at Merrit, who blew out the breath he'd been holding.

CHAPTER FIVE

Keeg Station

"Put your backs into it!" Joseph shouted. Ted and Ankh looked sideways at him. The maintenance bots were moving the last of the gravitic shield emitters into place on the outside of the captured frigate.

"They don't have backs," Ted told Joseph. Bundin emitted a low rumble. It was how the Podders laughed.

Once the hardware was in place, Ted took the box that contained Plato into the ship. Ankh followed with a small toolbox. Joseph, Petricia, and Bundin waited outside.

"What is the ship called?" Petricia asked.

Joseph had a long and storied history on planet Earth. Ship names were not something that he took lightly.

"I was thinking something expansive, like *Chariot of the Gods*," Joseph said, spreading his arms wide.

"Chariot. Ramses was an Egyptian pharaoh, was he not?" Petricia asked.

"He was."

"*Ramses' Chariot?*"

Joseph nodded vigorously, finally putting his arms down. "I love that, Petricia! A testament and honor to our dearly departed."

"I suppose that means something important, beside the man who always treated me well. I like *Ramses' Chariot*, too."

"Do you know what a chariot is?" Joseph asked.

"It looks like a Harborian frigate, heavily modified to be one of the greatest ships ever flown within the universe," Bundin replied matter-of-factly.

"I'll take it. Let's check on the stores. I think, all of a sudden, Ted will announce that the ship is ready to go and give us two minutes to get on board and settled."

"It wouldn't be the first time," Petricia replied, casting a glance toward their luggage to the side of the ship. "Just in case."

"Do I need to get my stuff?" Bundin asked.

"Do you have any stuff?"

"I don't, but if I did, now would be a good time to get it."

Joseph nodded and slapped his friend's shell. Bundin's blue stalk-head weaved in a circle.

"Well?" Ted yelled from an open hatch. "I've been calling. We're ready to go, so let's go."

Joseph and Petricia jogged to their luggage while Bundin ambled to the hatch and squeezed through.

"You need to make these more Podder friendly," he told Ted.

"Maybe you can evolve into a box turtle and then you'd fit without a problem," Ted suggested.

Bundin stopped. "Interesting," he said before continuing. Joseph and Petricia toted their bags in behind the Podder.

"We know the way to our quarters," he said and took a sharp left when Bundin walked straight ahead. The billeting on the frigate was tight, with room for only a few dozen, and the doorways were too narrow for him to fit through. He'd been assigned to the cargo storage area as a place he could rest while being out of the way.

The galley was small, the bridge small, the engineering space small. Everything was small on board the frigate, except for the energy mounts used for the EMP weapon. Ted had kept those in place after he reverse-engineered the technology to confirm what they already had in R2D2's laboratory.

Joseph and Petricia looked at the bunkbeds in their quarters with disdain. "If this ship flies like I think it will, we won't be in space all that much." Joseph tried to sound confident and consoling, but Petricia wasn't buying it.

"Bunkbeds?" She rolled her eyes and stretched her neck from side to side. "The indignity of it all."

"You don't have to go, if you don't want. I doubt we'll be gone that long." Joseph didn't sound convincing. They hadn't been apart in a long, long time.

"Who's going to watch your back? If I remember right, Earth was a dangerous place, even on the best of days."

"I can take care of myself, but I have to admit, selfishly so, that I like you by my side, even if you're in a different bunk."

"I'll see what we can do about that," she replied. Frowning at their quarters, they left their gear behind and headed for the bridge. They stopped when they heard a commotion by the hatch that was open to the hangar bay.

"Felicity!" Joseph exclaimed and meandered down the corridor toward where she stood, blocking the hatch.

"Good morning, Joseph," she replied pleasantly before shouting, "I know you're in there!"

Joseph froze where he was. Ted pushed by, his face screwed up as he avoided looking at his wife.

"You weren't going to leave without saying good-bye, were you?" Felicity drawled sweetly.

Ted continued to look at the deck.

That's exactly what you were going to do, wasn't it? Joseph thought, trying not to laugh. Petricia took his hand and led him away before he could say anything out loud.

Felicity gave Ted a hug and quick kiss before walking away. Ted remained in the hatch, watching her leave.

Joseph had stopped. "Show's over," he whispered.

Ted raised his hand and waved, but she didn't see it.

"He really loves her."

"More than you'll ever know," Petricia said as she pulled her husband close.

Ted turned toward them. His expression was soft, but changed instantly to a scowl. "What are you looking at? Plato, open the hangar bay doors. We're leaving."

———————

Kimber and Auburn shook their heads as they looked at the new recruits. "This is the hand we're dealt?" Kim said, hands clasped tightly behind her back as she walked from one end of the single line of bodies. Most stood loosely, some looked around. A couple showed a modicum of military bearing.

"And your sorry asses are going to be elite Bad Company warriors?" Kimber told them. "I don't know if we can get there from here, not with this mob. What have we come to?"

Auburn dutifully shook his head and groaned as if being slowly boiled to death.

"And what the hell are you?" Kimber growled at the Yollin.

"Kimber, it's me, K'Thrall from the *War Axe*."

"What did you call her?" Auburn shouted as he moved close to touch noses with the warship's former systems specialist.

"I called her by her name. Is that not her name? I shall call her something else, just tell me. I admit, you humans are confusing as fuck."

Auburn snorted and turned away. Kimber kept a straight face. K'Thrall was right. They hadn't told them what to call her. She rubbed her temples before turning her attention back to the recruits.

"You will call me Major Kimber or ma'am. You will call him Major Auburn or sir. You will always say 'yes, sir' or 'yes, ma'am.' Unless the answer is no. Do your dumb asses understand?"

"Yes, ma'am," a smattering of voices said.

Kimber threw up her hands. "These are the elite? After the sounds of combat, I don't hear so good any more. You need to speak up. I said, do your dumb asses understand?"

"Yes, ma'am!" came the chorus. Kimber avoided looked at K'Thrall, who was shaking his head.

"Major Kimber, I think you're lying. Your enhancements from the Pod-doc would enable you to hear, even me when I talk like this." The Yollin's mandibles clicked as he whispered without moving his mouth.

"Auburn! Why don't you teach Mister K'Thrall about pushups?"

"Get out here, you sorry case of ringworm." Auburn snapped his fingers and pointed.

"I knew you could hear me. Do we really have to yell?" the Yollin continued to whisper.

"Yes! You have to yell. Now shut up and get into the pit!" Kimber screamed, spittle flying from her face. The four-legged Yollin shrugged and trotted to where Auburn was pointing. The cargo storage area had been cleared for new recruit indoctrination and the pit was a white-taped square on a rough deck.

K'Thrall leaned close to Auburn. "This appears to be another mistruth. How much of what I believe about the Bad Company is the truth and how much will turn out to be a lie?"

Auburn smiled. "Bear with me. Ignore this next bit, and then get into the pushup position." Auburn put his hands on his hips and spread his feet wide. "You worthless piece of dog shit! You will drop and start pushing the ground until I get tired!"

"If you insist," K'Thrall replied, disappointment clear in his voice. He struggled to tip his head back so his mandibles didn't get caught on the deck while he started to do his pushups.

"It's part of the process of tearing people down, removing their individuality, and turning them into a team, where they each get to blossom according to the strengths that they bring back to the team. You helped calculate the maneuver to throw us through space toward Ten's fleet. That wasn't a lie. Here? We can't train under live conditions because the noobs would get killed. Even experienced people can get killed in combat. Sometimes, the bullet has your name on it and there's nothing you can do about it."

K'Thrall stopped and held his position. "I understand. Sometimes there's a claw coming for you. All we can hope is that one of your teammates stops it before it gets to you."

"Exactly that, K'Thrall. That's what we're trying to do here. Everyone needs to watch everyone else's back, while stepping up their own game. When we go out there—" Auburn pointed toward the cargo bay door that opened to space. "—we risk all that we are. Every. Single. Time."

"I understand. I hope that I can make the grade, as it may be."

"Help us to bring this bunch around. God knows we need the people. There are too few of us and too many bad guys out there. We need this mob to turn into decent warriors, and then we need ten times more."

Auburn signaled for K'Thrall to stand.

"I will help you, Major Auburn, you and Major Kimber both."

"Thank you, K'Thrall," Auburn said softly before stepping aside and bellowing, "And don't do it again! Get your lame ass back in formation."

K'Thrall ran back, spun into his spot in the ranks, and stood at attention.

"As he is. Lock your nasty bodies at the position of

attention. Arms locked to your sides, hands are fists, heels together, and toes at a thirty-degree angle, and cut the shit! I see you squirming. I don't care if you have hooves, stand at attention!"

Christina strolled from the shadows. As Terry's deputy, she was now in charge of on-boarding and new recruit development. Kimber, Kaeden, and Marcie had the most experience, but two out of those three were on their way elsewhere. Christina didn't envy their task. Christina looked at twenty-five new recruits. Marcie and Kaeden were going to have to work with thousands, maybe even tens of thousands.

Kim and Auburn walked up and down the line, adjusting the recruits until they were in a marginally acceptable facsimile of the position of attention.

Kim marched smartly to the front of the new unit. "Platoon is formed for inspection," Kimber reported. She saluted and Christina returned it, smirking after Kimber wiggled her eyebrows.

Christina marched past her and headed for the left end of the formation, which consisted of a single row with twenty-five recruits, with half of them human and the rest from a variety of alien species.

"You're going to be working overtime putting together skin suits for this zoo," Kim said indelicately.

"Not at all," Auburn replied. "They're all spacefaring races so we'll modify whatever they use for suits. I think only one of them is incompatible as it's a ball. A globe that they sit inside. Can you see your dad if some goofy-assed recruit rolls up inside his clear ball?"

"No. We'd be responsible for giving him an aneurism,

and I won't do that. I expect you're already working on that one?"

"Dionysus is. I'm sure it'll be great."

Kimber motioned for Auburn to join Christina, who was already on the third person. She wasn't bothering to ask their names.

"Where are you from, Recruit?" she asked.

"Home World, ma'am," the man replied. Christina turned to Kim and Auburn.

"You were on one of the ships blockading Alchon Prime?"

"That's what I'm told, ma'am," the recruit replied.

"You didn't know you were on a ship?" Christina asked incredulously.

"I knew I was on a ship. I didn't know where we were or what we were doing."

"Are you okay answering to a woman?"

"Seems like that's all we've been doing since we were liberated, so yes, ma'am. You're not going to turn into a werewolf on me, are you?"

"Are you going to piss me off?"

"Most likely, ma'am," the recruit answered honestly.

Christina stepped back to better take in the entire group. "Listen up, you pack of meatheads. We have a month to train and a year's worth of information to cram into your pea-brains. How do you think we're going to accomplish that if all you're good at doing is pissing me off?"

One recruit raised his hand. Kim stormed up to him and with a few choice words, informed him not to answer questions that weren't questions.

"I'll tell you how we're going to do it. PT! Physical training. We're going to start each day with two hours of calisthenics, weights, cardio. You are going to be begging your mothers for breastmilk, but that's only the start of the day. Then the real work begins. Class, practical application, class, and more practical application. We have a section of the station reserved for your quarters, but you know what? We're not going to need them. You will sleep, eat, and work right here. This is your base of operations. You will keep it clean and orderly."

Christina nodded to Auburn, who stepped before the group. "Everything you need to turn this into a functioning barracks is against the back wall. Twenty-five of you means twenty-five different ideas in how to get it done. That would lead to one massive clusterfuck. We can't have that. Every military needs a chain of command. It makes things run more smoothly. Word goes down. Word comes back up. We live and die by the word!"

Kim and Christina wondered where Auburn was going with his speech.

"You first eight. Stop right there! You're number nine, dumbass, can't you count? You go over there. And then you last nine, you stand next to them. See how easy that was? Three squads. You, Yollin, stand up front."

K'Thrall pointed to himself. Auburn glared at him until there was no doubt. "You'll be the recruit platoon sergeant. You three at the front of the squads. You'll be the recruit squad leaders, just until we shove you out an airlock and put someone else in your place. He tells you what to do and then you tell them what to do. Everything you learn from this point forward is rooted in a single truth—logistics is king!" Auburn thrust his arms into the air, but no one cheered. They watched because they were ordered to watch.

"You four knuckleheads. Figure out how to arrange the barracks over there, out of the way of where we'll do most of our training. You have one hour to get everything set up. It should take less than ten minutes, but you're new and don't know anything. Heaven help you if you aren't done by then!" Kimber shouted.

"We don't have heaven in my culture," one of the aliens said softly.

"Shut up, hoof boy! Do what your squad leader tells you to do." Christina shook her head. K'Thrall walked quickly past the materials that had been staged in the corner of the cargo bay before bringing the three squad leaders together. Less than a minute later, they were issuing orders to their squads.

Ten minutes later, the cargo bay was set up with neat rows of sleeping bags, arranged by squad with small foot-lockers staggered head to foot to head.

The platoon formed up when they were finished.

Christina and Kimber weren't sure what to do. When they put the schedule together, they had planned on the activity to take a full hour.

"PT?" Kim asked.

"How about they get to know each other? They're going to be in tight quarters for the next month of their lives," Auburn suggested.

"Make it so, number one," Christina said in a gruff voice.

"You and your television," Kim said accusingly.

CRAIG MARTELLE & MICHAEL ANDERLE

"Your brother turned me onto it. Blame him."

"I wish I could, but he's heading to a different part of the galaxy."

"Are they already on the *War Axe*?" Christina wondered aloud.

Kim shrugged. The two women watched Auburn talk in a normal voice to the recruits, treating them like sentient beings.

"He's going to ruin them. They need to have a certain level of fear if we're going to train them," Kim said.

"If I have to, I'll go Pricolici on their asses. That'll make them beg for their mothers."

"Their first significant emotional event will happen after they've been asleep for what, two hours?"

"Sounds about right," Christina replied with a wicked grin.

CHAPTER SIX

Keeg Station, Hangar Bay

Kaeden and Marcie turned away from the shuttle pod. "I'm going to miss this place." Marcie gritted her teeth, but Kae looked unperturbed.

"We haven't been here long enough for anything. I don't feel like it's home. I'm more comfortable on the *Axe*." Kae shrugged and turned toward the ramp of the shuttle pod.

Marcie held out an arm to block his way. "Do you think we'll ever be back?"

"Ever? That's a pretty long time. We're going to Onyx Station and then who knows where. I think we've increased our long-term survivability by doing this. Mom and Dad stay right in the middle of everything. I'm afraid for them."

"And that's why they need to know that we'll be coming back, regularly. I don't want them to think that we've abandoned them." Marcie cupped Kaeden's face in her hand. He turned toward her, his expression troubled.

"They don't think that, do they?"

"They will if we don't give them a reason not to."

"Christmas is for family, right? We'll tell them that we're all getting together for Christmas each year. Give gifts, do the stuff that we haven't done before. Maybe start a new tradition." Kae smiled at his wife. "How do I deserve you?"

"Isn't that the universe's greatest question? I don't know, but you better keep working at it." Marcie looked into the pod where a few members of the Bad Company waited for their ride back to the *War Axe*, not to go to war but to go on liberty.

"We'll see them as soon as we get aboard and pick a date. Come hell or high water, we'll make it to wherever they are on that day. On a completely different subject, I heard that Clodagh built a snowman in engineering."

Kae let Marcie board first, picking two seats from the numerous empties. "I guess it snowed and was the ultimate winter wonderland."

"Is there any left?" Kae asked.

"No. I think your parents put a quick stop to that. Your mom likes it cold, but not that cold, and I think your dad likes it tropical."

"The Wastelands," Kae offered. "And Mom's a werewolf. Those two things changed him for life."

"For the better, undoubtedly." Marcie twirled her finger in the air. "Take us home, Smedley!"

"How about the *War Axe*, Colonel? Will that do? Ted has not yet worked through the installation of the power supplies and gate engines in the shuttles."

"What?" Kae exclaimed before clarifying. "Take us to the *War Axe*."

"Now that is something I can do!" the AI declared. The others in the pod chuckled to themselves. "I know, Kaeden, sometimes I take things too literally. As a new AI, I have my certificate, you know, proudly framed and hanging on my virtual wall. I have the burden of having to understand all things at all times. When I was just an EI, no such expectation existed. I miss the good old days."

"You were never just an EI, Smedley. You were and are my friend."

"Mine, too," Marcie stated. The others agreed with the sentiment.

"You are far too kind," Smedley replied as he sealed the shuttle, executed the pre-flight, and took off, flying quickly through the hangar bay's atmospheric shield. "We'll be landing in approximately forty seconds. There is no time for a beverage service, so please hang on for any final and erratic maneuvers."

Kae and Marcie looked at each other before gripping their jump seats with both hands. Without a single bump or jerk, the pod slowed as it entered through the massive doors leading to the *War Axe's* hangar deck. The pod aligned with the launch chute and assumed its position within, locking down on contact. The rear hatch dropped and they were free to go.

"Very funny, Smedley," Marcie said.

"I didn't say there were going to be any, but just in case. Welcome back to the *War Axe*. You'll find Terry Henry and Charumati on the mess deck."

Kae and Marcie steeled themselves as they headed out, stopping when they saw the Harborian Frigate taking a fair amount of space within the hangar.

A maintenance bot was working on inscribing the ship's name on the side.

"I would have never taken Micky for a cat guy." Terry leaned back, looking at his empty tray. Dark stains remained from where a finely cooked steak had once been. Dokken was flopped on his side, tongue hanging out of his mouth and laying on the table. Terry wondered how the dog had eaten it all. Jenelope had been exceptionally generous with the last of the beef.

Jenelope glared at the German Shepherd. For once, she'd joined them for an intimate meal among friends and family. She was never more than an arm's length from Cordelia, which allowed her to say the right thing and ask the right question, keep Cory looking forward and not back.

The door opened and Kae stormed in, looking around as if an enemy were near. "I smell steak!" he declared.

Marcie bumped him from behind. "You're blocking the door, Mister Steak Man, but I have to admit, they smell good."

"There are a couple that can be ready in a few minutes," Jenelope offered.

"Yes, please! And two beers."

"Take your beers and shove them ..." Jenelope stopped mid-sentence. "You know where, you cretin. Befoul my steak with beer. Maybe you'll get a microwaved bistok burger instead."

"Speak for yourself. I didn't order a beer and let me say

that you look marvelous!" Marcie grinned from ear to ear as she elbowed her husband out of the way.

"Flattery will get you everywhere, dear," Jenelope replied. The enhanced took advantage of their youthful looks when dealing with others. Marcie was one hundred and ten years older than the chef.

"And have mercy on the cretin. He'll be impossible to live with if he has to watch me eat steak while pulling a bistok burger from a microwave pouch."

"You could give him yours," Jenelope casually suggested while she got up and headed for the kitchen.

"Where did that nonsense come from? You usually have such common sense things to say, Jenelope. That there was crazy talk."

"I want him to know where he stands. Thanks for confirming that. Take your seats. I'll bring the plates to you."

Kaeden surrendered, raising his eyebrows when he caught his father's watchful eye.

"Don't look at me. I get that all the time, even though it is mostly undeserved." He turned to Char. She smirked back at him. "Welcome to my world."

"You can save the world, hell, save the universe, but when it comes down to it, we're all in line behind Dokken to get a steak."

I resemble that remark, the dog told them without opening his eyes or lifting his head.

"I still can't believe Clyde wouldn't drink beer," Terry said to no one in particular, eyes misting as he thought of his first dog after the world's worst day ever.

"I can't believe you called it beer," Char retorted, grimacing.

Cory's eyes darted back and forth at the banter. She cracked a smile. No one was safe from the sharp wits of her family and friends. She dug back into the remains of her steak, chewing slowly as Kaeden watched, smacking his lips as he waited impatiently for his own.

"Just one small bite?" he asked.

Cory looked at him and then to the medium rare bit on her fork. She swung it toward him before putting it in her own mouth.

"My wife and my sister are conspiring to starve me." Kae shook his head, but when he sat next to Cordelia, he put a gentle hand on her shoulder and smiled.

Terry leaned back to massage his stomach. "What are you two doing here?" he asked.

Kae and Marcie looked to each other, signaling with their eyes to speak. Neither would commit.

"You think I don't know that you are going to turn the FDG into a space army?" Terry pondered.

"Well...yeah," Kae muttered.

Ted burst through the door, his hair wild and unkempt. "Well?" he demanded, gesticulating like a crazy man.

No one answered.

Exasperated, he rolled his head and his eyes as if in agony. "We're ready to go. We can be back at Earth in a matter of hours. You may be talking with your grandkids and stepsiblings shortly after that." Ted looked at the group. No one moved. He threw his hands down in frustration and stormed off.

"I guess it's time to go," Cory said softly. "Sarah and Sylvia. I could see them today."

Her words carried the disbelief she felt. They hadn't parted on the best of terms, and she had never been sure why. She hadn't wanted to return and find her children angry with her. She preferred ignorance, but that was when she wasn't alone. Now, she wanted to be with them and learn why they felt the way they did.

Dokken stirred. Terry pushed the German Shepherd until he almost slid off the table. *I'm up. I'm up*, the dog grumbled. He rolled upright and promptly fell off the table.

"Serves you right for messing up my table!" Jenelope called from the kitchen. After bouncing off the chair, hitting his dog face, and flopping onto his back, he scrambled to his feet and shook his whole body. His tail started to wag as Cory smiled at him.

After you, he told her.

"Don't mind if I do. Smedley? Is my stuff in the frigate?"

"Your personal items have been delivered to *Ramses' Chariot* and stored in your quarters," Smedley answered.

"*Ramses' Chariot*," she whispered.

"A fitting name," Terry stated as he pushed back from the table and stood. "We'll see you off."

Char looked at the others. "All of us," she said, pointedly looking at Kaeden.

"But, my steak..." Kae pointed at the kitchen where Jenelope was on her way out with two plates. She stopped. Marcie looked longingly at her plate on which steamed a massive cut of beef.

"Really? Cory is going back to Earth and you two can only think of your stomachs."

"It's fine, Mom. I'll say good-bye here and with Ted's improvements to the frigate, we'll probably be back before we leave. I expect to see myself coming through that door any moment now."

On cue, everyone looked at the hatch. Cory laughed. Kae was closest and hugged her first. "Miss you already, sis."

"I know you do. As long as you have your TV and those god-awful movies you like so much, you'll be fine."

"You should try them. You don't know what you're missing."

She pushed him away so Marcie could move in for a hug. "If you find my half-brothers and half-sister, tell those fuckers they need to write more often. And use those words! Tell them specifically I called them 'fuckers'."

"I'm pretty sure I won't tell them that, but if we find them, Ted will give them one of his boxes. They can call you so you can tell them yourself."

"Tell them that I will!"

"Ted is going to make them call their mother first. After Felicity is done with them, you might want to go easy or they'll never call any of you ever again."

Marcie contemplated the idea. "You're probably right. I have to admit that I don't know them very well at all. We were already in San Francisco when they were born and raised. Little werewolves, my half-siblings. It would be nice to hang with them for a while. Maybe they can come back, if they want."

Cory nodded. *That would be up to Ted.*

She waved at Jenelope and headed toward the corridor with Dokken at her side and Terry and Char close behind.

. . .

Keeg Station

The emergency decompression klaxons echoed within the cargo bay, vibrating everything that wasn't welded to the hull. Flashing lights showed the stunned and semi-conscious.

The recruits had been asleep for exactly two hours. It was time. Kimber, Auburn, and Christina wore their ship-suits, hoods secure and positive air pressure intact. The main cargo door was cracked open and atmosphere was venting to space. Twenty-five recruits, twenty-five different reactions.

Only one looked to resolve the problem. Of the other twenty-four, eight were dutifully trying to get their ship-suits on and failing miserably. Six had run for it. Three toward the hatch leading to the station, which was auto-matically sealed during a decompression. They pounded on it helplessly. The other three were running in circles. The alien recruits hadn't panicked, but they didn't have shipsuits. They remained in their racks, trying to hold their breath.

Three recruits had been sleeping naked. Kimber groaned while Auburn shook his head.

Recruit K'Thrall, most capable of surviving a short time in space, had headed straight to the cargo door. He strug-gled against the wind as the air was being pulled through to space. The crack was miniscule, not enough to drain the compartment, but enough to get everyone's attention. The Yollin activated the manual override and closed the main cargo door. The klaxons stopped screaming, and the lights stopped flashing, plunging the cargo bay back into darkness.

"Get your asses into formation!" Christina yelled. Kim and Auburn ran for the ad hoc billeting area and rousted people. One recruit had managed to get back into his bag and fall asleep. The naked people were still naked. Christina turned on the lights, flooding the cargo bay. The recruits blinked and covered their faces.

"Get in formation! Stop fucking around," Kimber ordered.

K'Thrall smoothly moved to the front of the group. The squad leaders took their positions behind him, and the squads straggled in behind them.

Christina strolled in front of the formation.

"Excellent work, Recruit K'Thrall. You saved the platoon."

"Thank you, Colonel,"

"Shut up," she replied, slapping him on his carapace as she walked around him to stand before the second squad leader. "Why are you naked?"

"This is how I sleep, ma'am," the recruit said with an attitude.

"On your face, Recruit," she growled. He assumed the push-up position. "Did I say push-ups? Get down!" She stomped on the middle of his back, driving him flat to the deck. "Now worm crawl to the bulkhead and back."

He lifted to his elbows and knees and gingerly started to make his way forward. Some of the other recruits snickered.

"STOP!" she yelled. Christina kneeled next to the naked

man. "I said worm crawl, not low crawl. Stay down and get going."

"But the non-skid surface," the man whined.

Christina planted her boot on his back and pressed until he was flat. "Move!"

He pulled himself forward, one agonized centimeter at a time. She lifted her foot and looked at the platoon. They were frozen, statue-like. No one wanted to incur her wrath.

Kimber stepped into the breech. "Do we let a teammate struggle alone?" she asked conversationally.

"No, ma'am!" one recruited shouted and instantly deflated when he realized that he was the only one.

"Well then, what in the fuck are you waiting for?" Kimber asked, looking at the recruit.

"Ma'am?" he wondered.

"You low-life, shit-sucking no-loads have about three seconds to get on your faces and worm your way to the bulkhead before I start throwing bodies around."

The platoon became a mad scramble as they fell to the deck and started wriggling.

Christina winced at their exuberance. "STOP!" she ordered. "Get back in formation before you tear your ship-suits, or something less important."

She glared at the naked man whose red face and scratched body told his tale. He wasn't laughing any longer. The two other naked recruits, one man and one woman, breathed a sigh of relief at avoiding the self-imposed pain of sand-papering their bodies.

Kimber addressed the group. "What did we learn tonight, boys and girls?"

No one answered. K'Thrall turned his head to look down the platoon. When he turned back, he raised his hand. Kim pointed to him.

"If you want to be a warrior, you need to be ready to make war, no matter when, no matter where."

"Dammit, K'Thrall! You're stealing my thunder." Kim started to walk toward the platoon. "Bring it in."

The recruits formed a half-circle around her. Christina and Auburn joined them.

"What he said is the most profound thing you will hear over the next month. I want you to commit that to your pea-brains. Everything you learn, and everything you do, will go to that basic concept. A warrior must be ready, willing, and able to fight. No matter what. Now get back in your racks. Morning will be here before you know it. And get some damn clothes on!"

CHAPTER SEVEN

The *War Axe*

Cory hesitated as she looked at the name emblazoned on the side of the frigate. They'd even included a graphic of a chariot in the shape of a spaceship, with Ramses, larger than life, holding reins that led to a nosecone with flames dancing back past the ship/chariot. She reached as high as she could to pat it. She whispered words that no one could hear and turned back.

Her eyes glowed blue and sparkled from within the *Chariot's* shadow. She waved at her parents, who smiled and waved back. Dokken panted by her side. Cory grabbed a handful of the German Shepherd's neck hair and together, they headed for the short stairs leading into the ship.

I'll take care of her, Dokken told Terry Henry.

I know you will, buddy. I'm going to miss you. Terry screwed up his face in concentration as he used his chip.

Me, too, but we'll be back. I put my faith in Ted and this ship to carry us where we need to go.

"Son of a mother..." Terry stopped before he crossed the cursing line.

Char canted her head to look at him. "What did Dokken tell you?"

"Something like, all hail Ted," he replied.

The speakers within the hangar bay energized with trumpets blaring, followed by harps running up and down the musical scales. A chorus sang, "All. Hail. Ted!" The voices dragged the last word out for an annoyingly long time.

Terry and Char waited patiently. Ted reached out the hatch and waved, followed by the weretigers. The three squeezed back inside and the hatch closed.

"Smedley," Terry said calmly through gritted teeth. He clenched his fists until the veins stood out through his shipsuit. "If you ever do that again, I will dismantle you and jettison you from the nearest airlock."

"Fine," came the short answer.

Terry and Char moved to the side of the hangar to allow the large ship to move out. The frigate took up most of the empty space within the bay. It didn't attempt to turn around, but backed through the forcefield and into space. Terry and Char both waved again, wondering if anyone would see.

Terry's hand brushed against skin and he recoiled. Ankh stood next to them.

"How long have you been there?"

"The whole time," the Crenellian replied. Terry was sure he hadn't been, but Ankh wasn't prone to lying. Terry decided it was best to let it go.

He turned to Char and his heart stopped. Tears

streamed from her purple eyes, streaking down her face and dripping onto the front of her shipsuit. She didn't attempt to stop them. He did the only thing he could—hugged her and waited.

Ankh walked across the hangar bay and started digging into a delivery canister. It was different than the others wedged into the back.

The frigate had dropped it off, and Ankh was digging into it, which meant that it held special items from R2D2, the Queen's research and development section, customized by Ted.

Terry wanted to support his wife, but he also wanted to see if there were any new additions to his unit's arsenal. Char gripped his waist and rested her head on his chest. There was no end in sight. Terry started to breathe faster and shallower. He tore his eyes from the Crenellian and looked through the hangar doors where *Ramses' Chariot* angled away from them. A gate formed and the ship shot through it like a lightning bolt. With a blinding flash, the ship and the gate were gone.

"Was it supposed to do that?" he asked.

Char looked up at him, her eyes red and puffy. He caressed the side of her face. His breathing slowed and he forgot about Ankh.

Until the Crenellian started hammering on a piece of metal.

"Go. You know you want to."

"But you need me," Terry said as his eyes darted to the canister.

"I appreciate that you are being supportive. I'm going to

go to our quarters and lay down. Maybe watch *The Sound of Music* or something."

Terry smiled and pulled her to him, kissing her slowly. They delayed going their own way until the time was right. Char headed for the hatch leading to the interior of the *War Axe*. She stopped before going in to see that Terry was still watching her.

"It's Ted, of course that ship is going to have some pizzazz," she said over her shoulder.

Terry laughed as Char disappeared into the ship.

Now, let's see what kind of goodies we have.

Sheri's Pride, Spires Harbor

"What are we going to do with that stuff?" Shonna asked. The Harborian Destroyer's weapon systems had been removed and were floating free in space. In addition to the EMP weapon, the ship had a variety of guns and small missiles. It hadn't used any of its kinetic weapons against the *War Axe*. The Bad Company hadn't thought the ship had them and were surprised to find that it was heavily armed.

It was lightly armored, which they weren't surprised by. Ten didn't care about the human crew. If they were ejected into space, the evil AI could continue to fight the ship, that was, it could keep the ship engaged in combat. It needed the human crew to make repairs, but the AI was willing to sacrifice them and the ship to further its goals.

"Why didn't Ten attack us with the entire fleet at Alchon Prime?" Merrit asked.

"I think the original purpose was to eradicate all life on

the planet and then recover it, probably for mineral extraction or who knows what. Maybe Ten wanted more subjects to torture."

"I'm glad we kicked that thing's ass," Merrit stated.

"Ted kicked that thing's ass. And Ankh. Some of us just blew things up." Shonna looked away. As an engineer, she had an affinity for profound explosions.

"And most righteously so, I may add. When do you think that thing will be ready to take to the asteroid belt?"

"A couple days. There's already an unmanned fleet out there, but when we take Iracitus, then we'll get a good look at how big we can make this project."

"Iracitus? The ship has a name already? I always thought we'd call it something simple, like *Merrit's Awesome Mining Ship for Studs like Merrit.*"

Shonna didn't rise to the bait. "Iracitus is one of Plato's stepchildren."

"The ship already has an AI? How do we rate?"

"Maybe it's because Ted has little faith in us or maybe it's because Felicity asked. She wants this to be the biggest shipyard in the known universe," Shonna replied.

"A bit ambitious, but I like it. Who wants to do something half-assed? If we have an AI and then add in some minions... Oh, yeah. I like where this is going."

"We're not getting any minions." Shonna put her fists on her hips while giving Merrit the hairy eyeball.

"Of course we get minions. What good is being in charge if there's no one to be in charge of?"

"We will have co-workers. All of them male. I'll pick them out, so you don't have to sully yourself." Shonna smiled and returned to watching the progress on their ship.

"Wait a minute..."

Ramses' Chariot, Unknown Space

"I'm sorry to report that we didn't hit our target coordinates. Something pulled us off course," Plato reported to those on the bridge. The silence of the AI running through petaflops of calculations weighed heavily in the air. Cory, Joseph, and Petricia stood at the back of the bridge and watched the main screen. There were only three positions —the captain's chair, systems, and navigation—but only the captain's seat was occupied.

Bundin remained in the corridor, because it was too narrow for him to get through the hatch and onto the bridge.

Ted clenched his fists. His eyes remained unfocused while his mind worked closely with Plato to troubleshoot the issue and rectify the problem.

Cory tensed. She'd expected to see Earth and instead, the screen showed a series of flashing lights against an unknown starfield. Joseph draped an arm over her shoulder. Dokken stood against her leg on the other side.

"Relax. We have two of the greatest minds ever working on the problem. We'll be home in no time," he said softly.

"Home," Petricia pondered aloud. "I don't think of Earth as home. Not anymore. This seems so much more comfortable to me."

"A spaceship?" Cory wondered.

"Yes. I feel at peace while on a spaceship." Earth had not been kind to her, and she didn't miss it. As long as she was with Joseph and had her feet on a metal deck, she was right at home.

"Incoming," Plato reported calmly over the ship's speakers. "Shields are active and should hold against the first barrage."

"First barrage? What the hell is going on?" Joseph demanded.

"We appear to be in the middle of an alien fleet. They have not welcomed our arrival."

Ramses' Chariot began a series of maneuvers. The passengers watched the starfield twist and turn until the frigate's nose was pointed at a small fleet of ships.

"Ted?" Joseph said, voice rising in alarm. Joseph had been born and raised in the age of horse and wagon. He never shared his fear of getting blown to bits in the vastness of deep space.

"Please put your hoods up," Plato said cordially. Instantly, the humans responded, even Ted. Terry and Micky had drilled that emergency action into them until they could perform the routine in their sleep.

Which was exactly how emergency procedures were meant to be implemented.

The hoods sealed, the gloves wrapped around hands, and the bubbles filled with air.

"Ted?" Joseph repeated.

"We will cloak and maneuver in three, two, one." The ship jinked sideways and then turned back toward the enemy vessels. The alien fleet had increased their plasma fire into the location where *Ramses' Chariot* had been. Two missiles arced away from the biggest ship and raced past the *Chariot*.

Plato accelerated into the middle of the alien formation and stopped, holding position between the two largest ships.

"Plato?" Joseph asked, giving up on Ted.

"We cannot use our shields while cloaked, so it is imperative not to get hit by either energy or kinetic weapons. They are already changing their pattern of fire to blanket the area. The safest place to be is behind them."

"And they can't see us, not with their sensors or their eyeballs?" Cory wondered.

"Neither," Plato responded.

"What are we doing now?" Joseph asked.

"Calculations are almost complete. The gate engine is recharged. Through the next gate, we'll be in orbit around Earth."

"What happened? How did we get here?"

"An unfortunate intersection between gates and the Etheric. We're better now," Plato said confidently.

"I don't feel better," Cory admitted. "I feel sick to my stomach."

Joseph pulled her close. Dokken stuffed his hairy dog head into her hand. She ruffled his ears.

"Any idea who these aliens are?" Bundin asked. Joseph turned to look at the blue stalk-head and his four eyes. Joseph fancied himself an old English gentleman, so he didn't comment.

"We are collecting a great deal of data now. After we've gated out of here, we'll analyze the information."

"I like your priorities, Plato," Joseph replied.

"Gate engines online. Prepare to drop the cloak. Dropping cloak. Gate formed. And we're in," Ted said, more to himself than anyone else. He didn't smile. Establishing a gate in the middle of the enemy formation would have a catastrophic effect.

The flash extinguished with the gate as *Ramses' Chariot* went through. After that, secondary explosions erupted from the enemy warships as the energy wave swept over them. Plato collected the data until the instant the gate closed.

Disabled but not destroyed, the AI thought. *They shouldn't have fired on us. That's a lesson they'll remember, whoever* they *are.*

CHAPTER EIGHT

Keeg Station, Bad Company Recruit Training

"I don't think I've ever seen a slimier slimebag group of slimey slimeballs in my long life!" Christina droned.

K'Thrall couldn't help but look at his carapace. There was no slime. Once again, the sanity of human expressions eluded him.

"What are you looking at, Recruit?" Christina yelled, glaring at the Yollin. She held up a finger, calling for silence before he responded. She knew that he'd make her laugh. *You're going to be my aide de camp,* she thought, *as long as those knuckleheads we strapped to you don't get you killed. Then where would I be? We can't have that, so don't die, Yollin.*

Sergeant Fitzroy snuck up behind the platoon and banged a hammer against a pry bar. It had the intended effect. "Hoods!" he shouted.

Auburn's lip curled as he watched many of the recruits fumble with their suits. He knew that some of them were well acquainted with the shipsuit. He wondered how they had become all thumbs in no time.

"Stop," Kimber said. "Just motherfucking stop."

She stormed into the ranks and slapped the hands of those still trying to get their hoods up.

"Is there nothing that you can't turn into a dog's breakfast?" she demanded. The aliens looked around. They knew Dokken, but not the non-sentient version of the species. K'Thrall started to raise his hand again.

Kimber hung her head as she walked slowly to the front of the formation.

"Dad is so much better at this."

"As much as I might like yelling at people, I really don't," Christina said cryptically. "Bring it in, people."

The twenty-five shuffled their feet, hesitant in their movements.

"Here's the deal," Kimber started. "Back on Earth, when we trained new recruits, we did it Marine Corps style. Break them down, build them back up as one team, then train them to operate as individuals. It's how we were all trained. Colonel Terry Henry Walton did that better than anyone. We have tried to replicate his style here, but we're not on Earth and many of you aren't human."

Even the other aliens turned to look at K'Thrall. "What?" he shot back at them.

"As you were," Kimber ordered, signaling for quiet. "We're not him, and he's not here. So this is what we're going to do." She turned to Christina.

"We're going to tell you what needs to be done and then you are going to help us to help you to get there. Yesterday's billeting setup got us thinking. We can do it the hard way, or we can do it the way where you'll remember it best. Here are the things you have to commit to.

"First, the best way to implement emergency actions is through habit, which takes repetition. We will call for hoods twenty times a day until you can get them on in your sleep without waking up. Second, warriors need to be ready to fight. We will run combat drills, starting with simple hand-to-hand and work our way up. You have to know what everyone else is doing. There is no such thing as friendly fire, but there are teammates who have shot each other. That's not what friends do. Third, we are going to undertake operations that are hard. You need to push yourselves, always. When we're out there, if we don't get it done, people die. I won't have that on my conscience, so, my pretties, we're going to train and train hard, but all of us together. We won't be looking down at you, but shoulder to shoulder because we are all in this together."

K'Thrall raised his hand. Christina pointed to him.

"For the record, I've seen Dokken eat breakfast. For once, I know exactly what you mean." He turned to his fellow recruits. "It's as pretty as you guys trying to put on your hoods."

"Hoods!" Auburn shouted. He pulled his hood up, as did Christina and Kimber. K'Thrall looked away. They didn't have a shipsuit for him or some of the other alien races.

"Those of you who complete the training will be enhanced, using nanocyte technology from the Pod-doc. I know you all agreed to that as part of your enlistment documents. Understand that those nanos are your emergency medical treatment. We don't have a medevac, so if you get injured, we take care of our own until you can get back in the fight. We don't have the logistical footprint for additional bodies."

"Why not?" K'Thrall asked. "The *War Axe* has a capacity ten times greater than what's used. We have entire decks closed off to save energy."

Auburn looked critically at the Yollin. "More people means more people exposed to danger. Until they're trained and have some experience, we can't put them in harm's way. We just lost one of our own. I can't describe how much that sucks. Even though he was enhanced, the damage was too great. We couldn't get him back to the ship in time for the Pod-doc to save him."

"Why can't we use cryo-drones in support of the planet-side missions?" one of the humans suggested.

"Is there such a thing?" Christina asked.

"No, but this is the Bad Company. You are part of the greatest commercial enterprise in the galaxy. There are cryo-storage units and there are drones. I don't see why they can't be built and then sold to all the systems."

"What's your name?" Auburn asked.

"Mardigan, sir, but everyone calls me Skates."

"Come with me. We have work to do." Auburn took two steps before stopping. "Why is your hood down?"

"I didn't get it on during the last drill."

"Put it on," Auburn said.

"But we're going inside the ship," Skates replied.

"I'm not going to invest two minutes in working with someone if they're going to get themselves killed by being stupid and unprepared. We all go into combat. Me. I was never in the Bad Company, but guess what? When the shit hit the fan, I'm right there with everyone else, blasting away with the railgun. So Put. On. Your. Hood."

The man missed on his first attempt to pull it from his

collar over his head. And then the second attempt failed, too. Thirty seconds later, the helmet was in place and filled with air. He looked proud of himself. Kimber sighed and held her face in both hands.

"Pull it back and do it again."

"But I just got it on?"

Christina grabbed the front of the man's suit and lifted him into the air with one arm. "And this is why Terry Henry's way was most effective in bringing people on board. Listen up, you twatwaffles. If any of you want to do anything besides practice hood drills, you are going to get this dumbass to get his hood on in eight seconds or less. We'll wait."

She released Skates. He dropped to the deck and started to fall, but his fellow recruits caught him and shuffled him away. They formed a circle around him. One of the technically-minded explained how the shipsuit worked, something the others were paying close attention to.

Skates practiced a few times on his own. The others joined him. Up, down, on, off. Repetition.

Kimber uncrossed her arms and gave Christina two thumbs up.

"We won't regret doing it this way. We simply won't tell my father."

"He is results-oriented. He'll be good with the method, probably won't even care as long as the recruits are up to speed when they hit the hangar bay of the *War Axe*."

"Time's wasting, Skates, come on," Auburn declared.

Mardigan strolled boldly from the group of recruits.

"Hood," Auburn declared. Skates reached behind him and snatched the hood to pull it in front of his face, where

CRAIG MARTELLE & MICHAEL ANDERLE

it automatically latched and started to fill with air. His feet did not keep pace. His toe caught the deck's non-skid surface. When it finally pulled free, it slammed into the back of his first boot, and down he went. He hit the deck, his nose slamming into the front of his bubble.

The blood started to flow, the red smear trailed down the plastic. It flowed from his nose and over his mouth. He reached up to wipe it away, but his hand bounced off the bubble helmet. The recruits behind him shook their heads. Only a couple laughed.

"You got your hood up in five seconds. Well done, but now it's time to go. On your feet, Skates." Auburn didn't bother to help him up. He turned and walked away. Mardigan hopped up, waved to his fellow recruits, and started to run, stumbling. A single gasp came from his new friends, but Skates recovered and ran through the open hatch after Auburn.

His hood was still in place with the blood smear prominently in front.

The *War Axe*

"Drones?"

Ankh looked at Terry with a blank expression. He treated Terry's question as a statement, since to him, the drone that was taking shape beside the logistics canister was self-evident.

"How many do you have?" Terry changed his approach.

"This is the prototype. Smedley has already been given the production parameters so these can be produced aboard the *War Axe*. Four combat support drones will deploy with each shuttle pod," Ankh explained before returning to his work.

"But what do they do?"

Ankh stopped in the middle of what he was doing. He didn't show emotions like humans did, but his change in demeanor was very much like Ted's after he had been interrupted one too many times.

"They are armed with two railguns with ten thousand micro-projectiles per gun and four missiles. They are powered by the miniaturized Etheric power supply, so they also have a self-destruct explosive on board."

Terry rubbed his hands together as he drooled over the drone. Ankh went back to work. Terry Henry Walton walked away. The math was instantaneously in his head. Four per drop ship. Twenty-four combat support drones. Nearly half a million railgun projectiles and ninety-six missiles.

"How about that?" he asked, but no one was there. Kaeden and Marcie were going through stacks of manuals trying to decide what was best to use in training and equipping the Federation's combined arms force. Char was in their quarters. Micky was getting the ship ready to depart for Onyx Station. The snow was gone and everything was on track for the next phase of the Direct Action Branch.

Could they survive liberty? Terry wasn't sure about taking time off and letting his people scatter to the four corners of the galaxy, but he didn't have any choice. Each person needed to reevaluate their own reasons for being in the Bad Company.

He wanted everyone to let their hair down, not get

arrested, and return to Keeg Station refreshed and ready to deploy.

"Ten is waiting for us, make no mistake," he told the hangar bay. "And giving that thing time to prepare for us is chapping my ass."

Terry growled, deep in his throat like an animal. He closed his eyes and threw his head back. *We will need to beat Ten with brains not brawn. Ten is a master at getting under the human skin.* Terry let out a long, slow breath. He turned to Ankh on the far side of the hangar bay.

"We could all learn something from you, my small friend."

Terry's eyes automatically searched for the German Shepherd, but he knew that the dog wasn't there. He also knew that his hairy companion would never be his again.

"I wonder if Char will let me have a ferret?" he asked as he climbed. "A really big, smart one..."

CHAPTER NINE

Earth, *Ramses' Chariot*

The blue and green planet with the usual cloud cover filled the front screen. A blue stalk-head craned around the humans to see better.

"Is that your home planet?"

"Yes," Cory replied with a smile. "It looks so different from up here."

"That is a lot of water," Bundin replied. His tentacles held on to his stalk as he leaned sideways.

"Don't worry, Bundin. We'll be on dry land the whole time."

"Unless we take a dirigible," Ted interjected. "We've been gone less than six months. They know who we are. First thing to do is call Kailin, who is running the business. He'll know where everyone else is."

"Why don't we just take the frigate? It has gravitic drives and can fly within the atmosphere," Joseph suggested.

CRAIG MARTELLE & MICHAEL ANDERLE

"Right," Ted agreed. He chewed on his lip in contemplation. He'd relapsed to the technology he'd left behind, and it bothered him to have forgotten. Then he smiled, because of where he was now. "Plato, please disengage planetary defenses so we can transit to the planetary surface."

"Sending the codes now," Plato confirmed. "The transit window will open along a set flight path. Coordinates received. Engaging now."

The ship slid toward the upper atmosphere. They couldn't see the deadly interlocking and overlapping defensive layers circling the planet. A corridor opened immediately before the ship, along a one-time use path randomly assigned by the defensive satellites. It closed immediately behind *Ramses' Chariot* as it passed.

Dokken looked up at the humans. Their excitement was contagious. He didn't know what they were going to find on the surface, but clearly, the humans were looking forward to it. His tail started to wag of its own accord, picking up speed as they watched San Francisco get closer.

"That tickles," Bundin said, stepping away from the tail that was brushing back and forth beneath his shell. Cory scratched the dog's head, oblivious to everything else going on.

"Test, one, two, three, test, test," Ted said. Joseph leaned around him to see who or what he was talking to.

"I hear you loud and clear," Felicity drawled. Her face filled the front screen. "Ah! There you are."

"We are descending into San Francisco. I am counting on Kailin to know where everyone is and to make sure that we have landing rights to the dirigible fields throughout the world. I'll report back when I've found the kids."

Felicity opened her mouth to speak as Ted cut the feed.

"You know she was still talking," Cory said softly.

"She what? She was?" Ted said, looking up at the screen that now showed the final approach to the landing field north of Alameda. He shrugged and disappeared into a private conversation with Plato.

The frigate was smaller than the dirigibles plying the world's skies. Ted sneered as he looked at the airships. To think that he and Felicity were the envy of all because they traveled in such luxury. "Terrence, Charlita, and Billy, you better come home with me or your mother will be very angry with me. No, no, no. That won't convince them," Ted said aloud, arguing with himself to find the right words to tell his children. "The universe needs you. And your mother. The galaxy needs you. I need you to give your mother something to do besides me. No, no..."

Cory coughed politely as the ship settled onto the closely-cropped turf of the landing field. Bundin fought to turn around and headed for the hatch.

"You better let us go first, Bundin. These people are not used to seeing aliens."

"I take offense at that word!" the Podder declared.

"You're alien to them, stranger than anything they've ever seen before, and this ship is probably giving them fits. When we left, our departure was fairly quick and is an urban myth by now. Maybe they'll think we're the aliens."

"Aren't you?" Bundin asked.

"Thanks to the damn Kurtherians, I think we may be. Still, let us go first."

One by one, they jumped past the edge of Bundin's shell.

Joseph was first out. He stopped at the bottom of the stairs to breathe deeply. He took small steps, letting his feet sink into the grass as he moved. Petricia grinned by his side.

Cory stepped onto the turf and enjoyed walking on something other than a hard deck. This part of the greater San Francisco city-state didn't hold any memories for her. She had visited, but the airship facility wasn't special to her. She didn't want to go to the old naval station where they'd lived and raised their children, where she last saw Sarah limping away to catch a bus.

We raised them to be independent, she thought. *I can't be angry that they went their own way, can I?*

A small crowd gathered some distance from *Ramses' Chariot.* Passengers queuing for their airship from San Francisco, while others had recently arrived. Many stopped to look at the sleek ship parked between the dirigibles and its small but odd crew.

Bundin squeezed into the daylight. "It is nice to see the sun again. Do you have any caves that we can explore?"

"Terry Henry was tortured in a cave system that was rather extensive. It took us a while to dig him out."

Joseph stopped gawking at his old home and turned around. "Are you out of your mind?"

Ted looked around to see who Joseph was talking to.

"Akio and I almost died in there. Terry Henry almost died. Adams did die, and you stole a shuttle pod and were lucky not to get your ass shot down!"

Cory leaned into the conversation, pointing to her blue glowing eyes. "And that's where this happened. No,

Bundin, we won't go back there." It was also near where she met Ramses.

"This is a big planet. There has to be other caves." Bundin's stalk-head swayed as if in a tornado.

"We'll see what we can do, but not Mammoth Cave. Anywhere but there."

"We're going to Chicago," Cory whispered.

Joseph's breath caught. Petricia froze. Dokken started to whimper.

Joseph forced his head back and started to laugh. "And that's where we almost died again. Is there anywhere on this planet that something didn't try to kill us?"

"Jamaica?" Petricia suggested.

"Jamaica," Joseph replied. "At least this time, if anyone messes with us, we have a spaceship that will cause them no end of grief. We aren't the same as when we left."

"Maybe we can go see the Eiffel Tower," Petricia offered with a snicker.

"This tower is tall?" Bundin asked.

"Not anymore." Joseph continued to laugh while the onlookers stayed where they were, at a safe distance from the crazy people and their pet alien.

Ted worked his way around the others and assumed a laser-like focus on the air traffic control center, little more than a two-story shack in the center of the field.

The others followed, treading lightly on the soft grass. The smell of it filled their senses. The feel of it, so different from anywhere else they'd been since leaving. It felt like home, better, but not. The feeling remained just beyond their fingertips, where they were unable to grasp fully what their emotions were trying to tell them.

Dokken ran circles around the group. *I like grass,* he told them.

"You and every hippie from the sixties," Joseph replied.

I don't know what that means, but I'll take it they were a good bunch, not unlike German Shepherds.

"Not unlike them at all, Dokken."

Cory jogged into the grass after him, where they played a brief game of tag. Dokken's tongue flopped sideways out of his mouth. Cory's eyes sparkled in the sunlight as she played with him. Joseph and Petricia held hands, happy to see Cory smile.

"I think that I will wait in the ship," Bundin told the group. The eyes on his stalk showed him that he was not welcome.

"Probably not a bad choice, my friend," Joseph replied. "The people of Earth aren't yet ready to expand their minds with the possibility of an infinite universe populated with races like yours."

The Podder worked his way inside the hatch and watched the others leave before securing it, closing himself off from the outside world.

Ted continued undeterred. The group waited outside while he went in.

A man stood at a small counter. "Registration and landing fee, please," the man said without looking up.

"What? Don't you know who I am?" Ted asked.

The man's eyes dragged from the counter, up Ted's body, to rest on his face. "Nope."

"I'm Ted. I built this place. And I've returned with my spaceship. I need to see Kailin." Ted's lip curled and quivered.

"Who?"

"He runs this place. Where is your supervisor?"

"Off."

"I'll say," Ted retorted and stormed out.

The *War Axe*

"Prepare to get underway." Micky's voice echoed through the corridors.

"Intra-ship communications are closed," Smedley reported.

"Get me Spires Harbor, Smedley."

"You are connected."

"Spires Harbor, this is Captain San Marino. How are you today?"

"We're doing great," Sue replied. "I expect you want something. You're like that Terry Henry guy. You never call to make chit chat."

Micky looked at the ceiling and grimaced. *Chit chat.* "I'm sorry, I'll have to do better with that, but for now, could you please notify the shipyard to have the Harborian fleet ready to deploy upon our return?"

"All of them?"

"Terry wanted a functioning fleet, in case Ten throws a bunch of ships at us."

"Sounds like nine ships—destroyers, frigates, one battlewagon."

"Thank you, Sue. I'll owe you one."

"You and everyone else," she replied. "If you get beat up while you're out there, Spires Harbor is here to patch you up, good as new."

"That's your advertising hook. Good as new. Take care, Sue." Smedley closed the channel. "Clifton, whenever you're ready."

"Gate engine is charged. Executing. Gate is forming," helm stated as he went down his checklist. "Thrusters engaged. Easing over the event horizon. Next stop, Onyx Station."

The gate shimmered and the ship slipped through. After a moment of disorientation, space reappeared. In the distance, a massive station stood like a spindle, a beacon in deep space. The station was well lit and well attended. Ships circled it like bees around a hive, waiting for their turn to dock and deliver their materials. Hangar bays encircled the lower half of the structure. Some looked large enough to fit the *War Axe*.

"Are we docking inside?" Terry asked, incredulous at the size of the station. "Was it that big last time we were here?"

"It has always been that size, TH," Micky said as he mindlessly stroked the orange cat purring in his lap

"And this is where everyone gets off and scatters to the four winds." Terry pursed his lips, blowing out a long stream of air.

"Did they get that Dark Tomorrow stuff under control?" Char asked, eyeing the station as the *War Axe* closed.

"Nathan was comfortable that it was, but he's keeping us in the loop. He's got a couple different groups that he can put on the problem. I want to hear more from him about who these interstellar studs might be."

"What if they're women?"

"Stud muffins?"

Char shook her head and laughed softly.

"We better go see our folks off," Terry said and started for the hatch.

"Why?" Char wondered. TH stopped.

"I always send my people out with a pep talk." Terry looked at the deck and then the overhead as he contemplated. Once certain that he was right, he headed off the bridge. "Smedley, hold the shuttles until I can get there and say my piece."

"I better go and see what the current gonorrhea lecture looks like." Char nodded to the skipper and followed Terry out.

"I heard that! I'm not giving an STD talk."

"Not again, you mean!" she yelled into the corridor. "Thank God."

Terry was waiting at the top of the stairs for her. "I miss them already."

"I know. Me, too. Let's do what we need to do, have a good sendoff for Kae and Marcie, then get back to Keeg for the last of the new recruit training. I have high hopes for that group. Yollin, Ixtali, Asplesians, and a menagerie of other aliens along with the Harborians, who are almost alien." Char took Terry's hand, as they did when walking together.

The stairwell on the *War Axe* was wide, accommodating the hand-holding couple as they descended.

"It throws our mech plan out the window. We'll need independent designs for some of their body shapes. The Ixtali have four legs?"

"Four and two sets of mandibles."

"I feel like they should give me the willies, but they don't. It's the cantina scene in *Star Wars*, but this is real. If I'm drinking a beer, I don't care who's next to me. Just don't bump me or I'll have to take off your hairy alien arm!"

"I know you think that the bounty hunter shot first."

"All that matters is I'm willing to shoot first if someone points a blaster at my face."

"I would expect no less," Char conceded.

When they reached the hangar bay, they found the warriors and a few members of the crew waiting on their ride to Onyx Station.

"I heard they have a suite with a chocolate shower," Char stated abruptly, as Terry's steps had quickened at the sight of his people with crossed arms and tapping feet. He noticed Clodagh Shortall off to the side with one of the warriors. They were locked in a hug, faces smashed together.

Char slowed, acting as an anchor to hold Terry back. "What the hell is going on over there?" he asked, pointing at the couple while looking over his shoulder at Charumati.

"What do you think?" she asked with a shrug.

"But, he's a private and she's a lieutenant."

Char stared at her husband from beneath raised eyelids. "They are adults, and we're a private conflict solution enterprise. The *War Axe* is our ride to where we're going. She's one of the crew. So what, TH? Don't sap their fun because you're in a pissy mood."

"Why would you think I'm in a pissy mood?"

"Because you are." Char didn't elaborate before changing the subject. "Do you have any idea how much money you've made off Nathan because of your non-swearing?"

"I have no idea. I've been kind of busy," Terry replied.

"You could probably describe it as a few years of your salary."

Terry finally stopped trying to pull away. "What?" A smile slowly spread across his serious face. "You mean that I've got money? But I don't really care about that. We have what we need."

"Are you sure we have everything we need?"

"I'm now sure that you don't think so," Terry replied astutely.

"Terry Henry Walton, you lack a hobby."

"I'd love to play golf, but there aren't any courses out here. Aliens are such sticks in the mud."

The warriors continued to tap their feet as they waited. Some harrumphed, others coughed. Clodagh and Private Gefelton continued what they were doing without pause.

Char drew a canvas in the air with her hands. "Imagine, a brew pub with a golf course and batting cage simulator. A dancefloor with some music. Happy hour. Hot wings. And beer."

Terry blinked quickly to fight back the tears. "A brew pub. My own brew pub with a computer-simulated golf course using real golf clubs. That might be the best gift in the whole universe."

"It's not a gift. You'll have to pay for it with your money. I'm going shopping. And there's nothing to pay for, anyway. We need to talk to all kinds of people. I have appointments scheduled with a lawyer, an accountant, and of course, with a pub regarding a franchise."

"A lawyer?"

"Do you think that just because we're in space, we no longer have laws? This is business. You signed a contract with the Bad Company. We all did. Pull up your big boy pants and see if you want to run a bar."

"Pull up your frilly panties and join me!"

"You know they're not frilly."

"You got that right." Terry grabbed Char in a bear hug, picked her up, and swung her around. "What are we waiting for?"

He gently set her down before jogging to the impatiently waiting group. "BRING IT IN!" he bellowed, looking pointedly at the couple. They separated and joined the others.

"Liberty is about escaping the day-to-day grind," Terry started. "Go out and enjoy yourselves. Make the most of your time off, and then come back when your vacation is over."

"A month?" one of them ventured.

"Two weeks and meet back here at Onyx Station. Don't make us leave without you because we will, and then there will be hell to pay. Give me an oorah on three."

Terry counted down and the warriors cheered. It was their first real liberty since the Force de Guerre went to space, too many lifetimes ago, and became the Bad Company.

Kaeden and Marcie joined the cheer at the end before the group ran for their shuttles.

"Mind if we join you for the ride to Onyx?"

"Indeed." TH waved at them to follow as he headed toward the same shuttle he always used. Char nodded knowingly. "You can tell me about your goals for the army that you'll build."

CHAPTER TEN

Alameda, Earth

The factory looked the same. Just like the sky and the bay. Everything looked the same, but nothing felt the same.

"Have we been gone that long?" Petricia asked.

"Maybe we have. There's something off about this place. Ted? Can Plato sense anything?" Joseph asked.

Ted was storming toward the factory, a brisk two-mile walk away. "Uncle Ted?" Cory asked.

He slowed until he stopped, his head hanging and his chin resting on his chest.

"You feel it too, don't you?"

"Plato can't find anything. He continues to search and analyze," Ted relayed.

"But you feel it," Cory stated.

"I don't know what I feel."

Cory wasn't surprised at Ted's revelation. There were too many different emotions bombarding him. She put a gentle hand on Ted's shoulder. A soft blue glow appeared from between her fingers.

Ted remained still. When he finally looked up, his eyes were clear and his face relaxed. "Let's get to the plant and talk with Kailin."

"I'm looking forward to seeing my nephew," Cory replied.

"You not only have a gift, you are a gift, my lady," Joseph told her. Dokken barked and panted happily.

I couldn't agree more, the dog added. When he reached the pavement, he stopped. *Can we stay on the grass?*

Cory pointed to the massive buildings that housed the gravitic engine factory and dirigible construction facilities. "We cannot. We're going over there." She kneeled next to him to make it easier for him to see where she was pointing.

If that's where you're going, I'm going there, too. But we'll be back because our ship is here. Maybe we can cover the decks with grass. Ted could do it if he wanted to. Make him want to.

Cory chuckled. "I'll ask because it's important to you, but not now. We have some things to focus on first. I need to find my daughters."

Dokken nuzzled her hand. *Of course. I got distracted for a moment. It won't happen again. Shall we?*

The large German Shepherd trotted ahead, turned, waited for the humans to start walking, and then ran farther.

"The longer I'm here, the more it feels familiar. Maybe our lives aboard the sterility of starships and space stations have changed our perceptions regarding the chaos of nature." Joseph kept his eyes moving as he watched the world around them.

"Look, a dog," a rough young man said as he stepped

from the shadows. A group of his fellows appeared on both sides. "What's with the blue eyes, honey?"

"Get out of our way. We have things to do," Ted said gruffly, waving dismissively.

"I think you grossly underestimated what you've gotten yourself into. Leaving is your best option. Nothing else will turn out in your favor." Joseph looked into the mind of the young man, before exploring the minds of those around him. They didn't care. They were a gang and harassing people was the least of their crimes.

Dokken growled and bared his fangs. Ted sighed and shook his head. Joseph stretched his fingers and cracked his knuckles. He didn't want to see the others embroiled in a fight not of their choosing.

I will be their champion, he thought.

Cory cocked her head, looking confused. "Why would you do this?"

"We take what we want. Come on, boys. Kill that dog while I introduce myself properly to Miss Blue Eyes."

Onyx Station

Nathan Lowell's office was nondescript. "As president of the Bad Company, I would have expected something a little more opulent."

"Why?" Nathan asked as he stood to shake Terry's hand.

"To make sure you negotiate from a position of power," Terry answered.

"I always negotiate from a position of power." Nathan smiled easily and made his friends feel welcome. They took seats on a couch and in over-stuffed chairs. "We

CRAIG MARTELLE & MICHAEL ANDERLE

have a few minutes before your destroyer leaves for Belzimus."

Marcie and Kaeden looked at each other. "We thought that we'd be based out of here." Marcie stood and started to pace.

Terry appreciated her style; it reminded him of someone he knew.

"You will be, but like me, you probably won't spend much time here. What you'll be doing will be more hands-on until you have the feel of your front line leadership team."

"Are we going to have to earn their respect?" Kae asked. Everything stopped within the room. The fidgets, the pacing, even the breathing.

"There has to be more to your question," Nathan said.

"I don't want to have to beat anyone senseless, but are we going to have some ass-munching Klingon challenge me to a duel?"

Terry bit his lip. Char elbowed him to keep quiet.

"The army that you'll be building is made up of people who look and act human. But they most assuredly are not. I think you won't be surprised by the broad range of personalities you find on Belzimus."

"What do we call them?" Marcie wondered.

"Belzonian. Even the women. I guess that would be the difference between them and humans. You generally won't be able to tell the women from the men because they're hermaphrodites. Maybe that's why you can't tell them apart, because there is no apart to tell." Nathan checked his monitor to make sure it was off and he wasn't broadcasting. "They like to spread their DNA as wide as possible in order to ensure their species remains strong."

"What the butt-hugging nut-roll does that even look like?" Terry wondered.

"An orgy, or so I've been told," Nathan said, quickly looking away.

"Why does that matter?" Kae asked.

"You'll find that there's no jealousy there, not because of sex. They are still envious of position and rank and stuff like that, but not from what tends to distract humans the most."

"I'm starting to like the Belzonians," Marcie offered. "We transmitted our recommended organization chart based on what we'd seen. What do we need to change?"

"The only thing I saw was the reliance on existing structures. I believe you'll be better off if you move the leadership laterally, make them uncomfortable enough to learn the new way. If they stay in a position they think they know, they'll do it how they think they know it, if that makes any sense."

Kae and Marcie both nodded. "It does," Kae replied. Nathan stood and held out his hand.

"That's it, huh?" Kae said.

"That's it. Time to go." They shook hands, while Terry and Char waited by the door. After the hugs, Marcie and Kaeden strolled out. The door closed behind them.

"That's it, huh?" Terry parroted. "Better them than us. A legion of warriors who like orgies."

"A new chapter, TH. Marcie and Kaeden will be briefed extensively by Lance Reynolds, since they are going to be working directly for him from now on. They need to get there and get to work. Those people aren't going to organize themselves. We have too many places they need to go and too little time to get them there."

"I'd suggest the Bad Company's Direct Action Branch could fill in the gap, but we're spent, as you well know," Terry answered.

"I'm not going to do that to you. You went on a mission that I demanded you take, and then you lost one of your own. That was a high price to pay."

Terry and Char looked at Nathan without saying anything. They couldn't disagree.

"No buts. The power supply has a great value. In the end, no one will remember the price paid, only the cool toy that they'll soon take for granted."

Terry finally looked away. He saw a scuff on his boot. He licked his thumb and buffed it out.

"I hear that an All Guns Blazing franchise has just opened on Onyx Station," Char said.

"Your appointment with Rivka is in ten minutes, so you had best be on your way."

"How much money did you lose?" Terry asked. He sat up straight and listened intently.

"More than I'm willing to admit. You have defeated me, Terry Henry Walton. I thought you were completely incapable of controlling yourself. You're a Marine, for fuck's sake! Fuck, fuck, fuckity, fuck. Can't you hear those words forming in your mind, ready to explode with color and imagination from the mouth that has issued a million orders over the years? Give it to them hard and dirty, Patton said. You are this generation's Patton, TH. You want to fuck bomb the unwashed shit-suckers out there."

"I'm not Patton. I'd say that I'll take that in cash, but that's not how things work in this *Star Trek* universe of yours. Post the credits to my account, my friend. Tips are always appreciated."

"Tips? Don't bet against Terry Henry. That's the best one I have."

"Rivka?"

"She's recently arrived as an intern."

"An intern? You have got to be kidding me," Terry said.

"I know you wanted to say 'shitting me,' so let it out, Terry. Let the inner you blossom before us."

"No can do, Nathan," Char said, stepping between the two men. "His self-control is what's going to pay for the franchise. I don't want to lose that now, so we'll be off. But an intern? I hope she knows what she's doing."

"She's more than meets the eye. I call her the Queen's barrister, if that means anything."

Kaeden and Marcie returned to the hangar bay. They spotted a number of sleek ships as well as a wheeled vehicle. "Space-fighters and cars? I wonder who those are for." Kae pointed toward a cordoned area of the deck.

"It doesn't matter. Our ride is this way." Marcie motioned in the opposite direction.

"Clearly not one of Ted's shuttles," Kae lamented.

"He's had the technology up and running for a whole week now. It's going to take a long time to get out here."

"But we know people. Maybe we can get the FDG moved up the priority list?"

"Is that what we're going to call this group?"

"Do we get to name it?" Kae's lip twitched upward to form a half-smile. "I'll have to think on that one."

"Don't hurt yourself," Marcie quipped. "Something like the Etheric Federation Peacekeeping Force."

"We need something intimidating, but supportive, like Bad Guy Ass-Kicking Army."

Marcie stopped walking so she could more effectively roll her eyes.

"How about Power Rangers?"

"Big nope." Marcie started walking again. Kae stayed by her side as he continued to generate names in his mind.

"Army of the Etheric Federation, or Etheric Federation Peacekeeping Force."

"That's more like it. We'll see what the general has to say. I suspect that he has something in mind."

"You're probably right. He'll have a good reason for what he chooses as well, based on other factors within the Empire and the Federation."

"It might be the Queen's Army, you never know," Marcie said when they reached the shuttle. A uniformed guard stood at the hatch.

"Colonel. Major. I'll be your escort during your transit to Belzimus. My name is Paithoon. If you need anything at all, tell me, and I will acquire it for you." The man saluted by thumping his chest and dropping his hand back to his side.

"We'll need to learn your customs, so that'll start as soon as we reach the destroyer."

"The *Candied Moon* awaits."

Marcie and Kae both stopped dead in their tracks. "Our

destroyer is named the *Candied Moon*?" Kae stated the obvious.

"It is an honorable name."

"Does it terrify you to hear it?"

"Of course not," Paithoon replied.

"How about *Vengeance*? We need ships that people can rally around, not throw parties on."

"We love a good party," Paithoon said as his gaze drifted away.

"There seems to be a lot for us to talk about, Paithoon. The change starts right here, right now. The next party we throw will be when we're planting a flag where our enemy used to be."

"Sounds wonderful. Would you like me to start organizing that?"

"NO! I don't want you to organize that. It'll be a while before this group goes into combat. When that happens, we'll know what we need to do. Are you a fighter?"

"Oh, no. I'm in the protocol office. The fighters? Those Belzonians are wired differently. Weird bunch, those."

"Now you're speaking my language. Let's head over to the *Vengeance* and get this show on the road."

"I'm sorry?"

"You haven't spent much time with Earthers, have you?"

"None, sir."

"You'll learn." Marcie jousted with the man briefly, trying to encourage him to go first, but gave up and entered the shuttle.

"Somebody will learn," Kae whispered out the side of his mouth. "The *Candied Moon*? Holy flockenshnoogles! What in the big bone jobs did we sign up for?"

CHAPTER ELEVEN

Alameda, Earth

The street tough sneered as his gang spread out in a circle, outnumbering Ted and the group two to one. One pulled a long knife and angled toward the German Shepherd.

They don't have a clue. Dokken, if you'd like to take care of the punk leader, I'll dispatch those closest to me. If you could handle the man with the knife, Ted, I'd appreciate it. And Petricia, my love, I think those on your right side will run when all the others are down, but just in case...

Dokken didn't bother answering. He launched himself at the young man with all the speed in his enhanced body. The punk's eyes shot wide just before the dog landed on his chest. As they hit the ground, Dokken's jaws were locked on the man's throat, canine fangs digging in.

Joseph accelerated to vampiric speed to head-punch the five on his side. One after another, they didn't have time to move as the force of a sledgehammer drove their senses from them.

Ted lunged forward and grabbed the man with the knife. Ted snapped the man's forearm before picking him up by the front of his shirt and slamming him on the ground.

Petricia walked casually toward those on her side. One took a clumsy swing. Petricia easily dodged it and spun to back-kick the young man. He puked as he flew backward, landing and rolling to his side to cradle his assaulted abdomen. She followed through to elbow the next street tough in the head. He didn't have time to put his hands up to deflect any of the blow. His nose shattered, and he went down.

The last two ran. Cory frowned, anguish seized her. "Why?" she demanded. Dokken let go and hurried back to her. The punk leader struggled to take a breath through his crushed windpipe. Blood oozed from where Dokken's fangs had punctured the skin. The man started to flop on the ground as hypoxia set in. Without a final exhale, he stilled.

Cory started to go to him, but Joseph stopped her.

"I can help him," she pleaded.

"Not that one. I saw his mind. He was beyond help. There's hope for that one." Joseph pointed to the man with the exploded nose. Cory looked at the dead punk, nodded, and went to help the last man to fall.

Her hands glowed blue as she shared her nanocytes with their injured attacker.

"Any of the others?" she asked sadly.

"I'm afraid not," Joseph replied. He searched the faces of the fallen. "So young. What happened where people cannot safely walk the streets of the town that we built?"

Ted rubbed his hands on his pants as if trying to remove the stench of the knife wielder. He looked to the factory nearby. "I think Kailin will have the answers," Ted said.

Cory finished with the man, who looked at her with wide eyes. "Don't attack people anymore. It's a good way to get yourself killed. You'll find there's a greater reward in protecting those who can't protect themselves," Cory told him.

He ground his teeth together. When she rose to walk away, he grabbed her ankle. Petricia made a fist and reared back.

"Thank you," the man said and let go.

Onyx Station

A young woman approached. She wore a fashionable spacesuit. Terry wasn't sure whether it was armored or not. He resigned himself with the fact that she was new. Like her spacesuit. She approached, offering her hand.

"My name is Rivka Anoa, and I'll be working with you on your franchise contract for All Guns Blazing. Do you have any questions before we start?"

"We'd like to see the All Guns Blazing before anything else. Are you old enough to go in there? You look pretty young," Terry said.

"So do you," Rivka deftly replied. She was shorter than Char by half a head, with blond hair and hazel eyes offset by swarthy skin. "I'm twenty-five, I'll have you know."

"I'm not twenty-five, and I'd like to see what I'm going to spend Nathan's money on," Char said.

CRAIG MARTELLE & MICHAEL ANDERLE

"What are you, thirty-five? That's not that big of a difference."

"I think I'll be..." Terry stopped and started counting, ticking off his fingers as he went. "Round it up to one ninety. You know what that means! Somebody is going to hit the big two-oh-oh this year."

"Why?" Char rolled her eyes and groaned. "Why did you have to bring that up?"

"Because I need to throw you a surprise party," Terry said nonchalantly.

Char turned to Rivka. "Which way to the bar? I could use a drink."

"Follow me, please." She winked at Char before shielding her mouth from Terry Henry. "I can get a wheelchair for the old guy, if you'd like. I know you're not a year over twenty-nine. You look magnificent! I love your eyes."

Char loved the infectious exuberance of youth. "Lead on, Queen's Barrister. Wherever you go, we shall follow, as long as you're going to All Guns Blazing. If you're not, we'll find our own way."

They took an elevator to the promenade level, where Rivka held the doors for them to exit.

"This looks the same," Char said.

"All Guns Blazing is a brand-new addition to Onyx Station. One of the signature elements is the seven-by-twenty-meter window looking into space. It is made using proprietary technology that will be part of the contract. The beer vats and brewing system must be purchased through the Bad Company. There is no proprietary technology there, it's just beer, but the style of vats is unique and trademarked by AGB Enterprises."

"Stop right there, Barrister." Terry crossed his arms, puffed up his chest, and pushed out his biceps. "It's never just beer. There's an AGB Enterprises?"

"Of course. That's who owns the franchise rights and who you'll have the honor of paying a straight twenty percent of your revenue, not profit, to and who you'll also have the pleasure of buying your stock materials from. It's all in the contract."

Terry deflated. "Is there any room for negotiation?"

"None, but I will remain your representative for as long as the contract remains in force."

"What if you kill somebody and can't be a lawyer anymore?"

"That is a most bizarre question. Although barristers are often able to mete out justice under the Yollin Accord, we don't kill people. Should I be unable to continue my duties, for whatever reason, you will be provided comparable counsel from the firm. It's in the contract."

"We mete out some justice, too," Terry started, "but I expect it's a little different from what you do."

"I've heard about what you do. I'm not sure I'd be bragging about it."

"So what do you think we do?"

"Assassins. You remove people the Federation perceives as a threat to their power. You come in the dark of night. I'll tell you what, buddy, my door is locked and I can defend myself!" She pointed a finger at the two.

Terry and Char both stepped back, looking at each other in confusion. "That's not what we do. We've had exactly three missions so far. We ended a civil war on Poddern; we broke a blockade at Alchon Prime; and we closed an interdimensional rift and eliminated the Skrima, a race of demon-like aliens who had come through it."

"Oh. Okay!" she replied happily.

"Aren't lawyers supposed to take their clients without judging them, but more importantly, aren't lawyers supposed to research stuff, you know, get to the truth?"

"I am still new at this, but there are rumors about you and your Direct Action Branch. They're not pretty."

"What the hell?" Terry turned to Char. She shrugged and turned her head. "Is Nathan fu...messing with us?"

"I hope not," Char declared before her expression softened. "You look like you could use a beer."

Terry's ears perked up. "Could I ever. A nice and dark one. Cold. Big. And then another one that looks just like it."

"I think you're going to like All Guns Blazing. It's the most popular place on Onyx Station." They turned a corner and Rivka waved her hands as if making the bar magically appear.

There was a fight going on at the entrance. Rivka held her hand up, signaling for them to stop.

"Wait a minute," Char said. She and Terry pushed past the barrister and ran for the entrance. Half the Bad Company warriors who had arrived with Terry and Char were inside the bar, playing a drinking game. The other half were already drunk and trying to get in. The bouncers were having none of it.

"We've been here thirty minutes. How can they be drunk already? How can they be in a fight? How does crap like this happen?"

Terry grabbed the closest warrior and hauled him backward. The man tried to throw a haymaker as he swung around. TH dodged it and slammed the man on his face. Char rabbit-punched the next man. Terry kicked the third in the back of the knee. When the man started to stumble, Terry punched him in the top of his head.

The fight ended quickly after that. The bouncers were unscathed, standing with their arms crossed, watching Terry and Char with wary eyes.

"Form up, you knotheads," Terry growled at them. Six men and three women. All drunk and bruised. "You lasted a grand total of thirty minutes. That's not a record, so while you're confined to the *War Axe*, be comfortable in your knowledge that there are people in this universe who are stupider than you. How in the hell did you get drunk in thirty minutes?"

"A killer drink in one of the sub-level bars. The Supernova Hellspawn something or other," one of them mumbled.

"Get back to the *War Axe*. I will have Smedley track you and if any of you geniuses get lost, you won't be confined to the ship, you'll be in the brig. Don't pass go, don't collect two hundred dollars, and don't ever enjoy one minute of liberty for the rest of your natural-born days."

The group looked contrite until one of the women started puking. She remained at attention throughout the affair, leaving a splatter on the deck before her and a trail down the front of her shirt. The others started to giggle.

"You had best get back to the ship. Right. Now." Terry waved at them angrily. They turned and started to run, but they had turned in different directions. Two fell down, while all avoided the spew. They helped each other up, decided on a way to go, and dashed away.

"Isn't the hangar deck the other way?" Char asked.

"Yup."

Rivka stood to the side, covering her face to avoid the smell. Terry grinned at her. "Not our finest moment, Counselor. If you wondered about any night sneaking by steely-eyed ghosts, what you saw here today should put those rumors to rest. And you're probably thinking that we can't fight our way out of a wet paper bag. To the untrained eye, it may seem that way, but these people have been in combat for a long time. They're blowing off steam. That's all."

Continuing to cover her face while turning her body so she didn't have to look at the mess by Terry and Char, Rivka asked, "Maybe you can teach me a move or two? That was pretty good how you disarmed three of them in three seconds."

"But they weren't armed," Terry countered.

"You know what I mean," she huffed. She nodded to the bouncers, who waved them in. "After you."

Terry opted for seats at the bar, with his back to the window. He would look at space later. He needed to see the bar and understand the potential.

Rivka waited patiently as he inspected everything he could see, methodically looking from one point of the bar to the next.

"He's memorizing all of it."

"I'll transmit a complete portfolio of pictures. They come with the franchisee license."

"Sure, but he already has the whole bar committed to his eidetic memory. After one hundred and ninety years, you'd think his brain would be full, but it's not. Maybe when he gets to be my age..."

"I heard that," Terry said. "Nothing you can say will get a rise out of me, not while I'm here with this in hand."

The bartender handed over a perfectly-pulled pint, so dark, no light passed through the glass. Terry looked at it as if he were in love. He closed his eyes as he sipped it, keeping the glass close while he licked his lips and took another long, slow drink.

"I may never swear again," Terry suggested after he finished the beer and called for a second.

"Bullshit!" Char declared. "Once the bar is up and running, you'll be your old self. If you're going to drink the profits, I'll cut you off!"

"What?"

"Our bar. It's our bar. Not Terry Henry Walton's private watering hole."

"Ooh," Rivka said, pursing her lips and bringing up the contract on her pad. "I'll need to make some changes."

"Charumati Walton, co-owner, equally, if you please," Char said. Terry took a big gulp and coughed before smiling.

"It's every man's dream. I get to own a bar with my woman!" Terry declared loudly.

"For fuck's sake! What kind of barbarian is this turning you into?" Char leaned back on her barstool to glare at Terry.

"There's the woman I love. Co-owners in a wildly successful business enterprise, bringing entertainment, food, and drink to those who want to enjoy themselves for a brief period of time."

CRAIG MARTELLE & MICHAEL ANDERLE

"You two are weird," Rivka said without looking up.

Char stood and motioned for Terry to finish his beer, which he dutifully accomplished with little fanfare. "We're going shopping. Buzz us when you have the documents ready. I think All Guns Blazing is exactly what we need. And a new pair of shoes. Maybe an outfit to go with them. A purse, too. I almost never carry one, but who knows, especially if it's a good match for the outfit."

Iracitus, Dren Cluster

Shonna and Merrit stood on the bridge of the modified warship that they'd named after the AI that operated it. Iracitus expertly guided the ship away from Spires Harbor.

"Well done, Iracitus." The AI appeared as a human image on the monitor.

"Thank you. It's what I do."

"I expect there's a lot that you do," Merrit replied. He watched the stars fill the screen as the ship smoothly accelerated toward the asteroid field.

"Phase one is underway," Merrit stated.

"Phase two," Shonna corrected.

He looked askance at her and rolled his finger, signaling for a more in-depth explanation.

"Phase one was the unmanned ships and rough mining."

"I stand corrected. Phase two is where we build a processing facility in the asteroid belt, and then we'll reduce our need for long-haul cargo shipping by only sending refined ore between the belt and the shipyard."

"Exactly. Machines to build machines. A couple

humans. A few dozen Harborians. And that's it. I see watching a lot of movies."

"The important question is, did we bring enough popcorn?" Merrit asked. "First order of business, Iracitus."

"We will search for and select an optimal location for the processing facility."

"You already have some ideas, don't you?"

"I do. Let me show you what I have in mind." Asteroid maps appeared as flashes on the screen as the AI rapidly reviewed them.

"I'm lucky that I'm not prone to seizures," Shonna complained.

"Take care of it, Iracitus. We're going to our quarters."

"Sir?"

"We'll check in later," Merrit said firmly. They'd taken a small cargo bay and turned it into a luxury suite. Until they reached the field and deployed some of the equipment, they were forced to share their space with a small fleet of mining drones. The alternative was unacceptable. Standard quarters with bunkbeds.

It made them wonder how the others were fairing on the Harborian frigate...

CHAPTER TWELVE

Keeg Station

The two men looked at the computer screen. A three-dimensional model of a cryo-drone rotated slowly on the longitudinal axis before spinning on the lateral axis.

"Each of the drop ships can carry one of these?"

"Or a canister can carry a number of them. Once within a planet's atmosphere, with the Etheric power supply, they can stay airborne indefinitely."

"Micro-gravitic engines, but most power is in the cryogenic storage unit. What if they are in a suit or are an alien?"

Mardigan grumbled to himself. "We need to make it bigger. This one won't fit half of our people."

Auburn looked at the recruit. *Our people.* He wasn't the only one taking ownership of the unit.

"We'll turn it over to Dionysus to expand the frame and cryo-pod within. Time to get back to training. Good work, Mardigan." Auburn slapped the man on the shoulder.

"I can stay here and work with the AI on the redesign," he suggested.

"In the future, you'll have that option, but getting through recruit training is a rite of passage. Every member of the Direct Action Branch has to be able to fight, while knowing what the other warriors are doing. To get there, you have to train and train hard. Sorry, but it's time to rejoin the others. Take your lumps and wear them as badges of distinction."

"Yes, sir," Mardigan conceded, clearly unhappy with the choice. Auburn showed him the door. "Right." The recruit jumped up and raced out.

Auburn followed, thinking as he traversed the corridors of Keeg Station's lower levels. "How will you change when we open you up to civilians?" he asked the metal behemoth.

The soft hum of the ventilation and climate control system that kept the air fresh and at a constant temperature was his only reply. It would continue to serve the station as directed by Dionysus and the station's small maintenance team.

"I know. You'll go with the flow," he answered his own question.

Auburn didn't have to see the cargo bay to know what was going on. He heard the shouts and energetic engagement of hand-to-hand training.

Tim, formerly a mechanic turned Harborian guard turned Bad Company recruit, was circling the ring. His opponent was a teal-skinned Malatian called Bon Tap. His flowing silver mane swung from side to side as he labored to keep Tim centered.

The human worked his way forward, closing the distance. The Malatian saw an opening and charged.

Right into the trap that Tim had set. He sidestepped, grabbed a handful of the man's hair, and swung him around in a circle, slamming him head-first into the mat. Tim straddled Bon Tap from behind, wrapping an arm under his opponent's throat and pulling backward, twisting his head and straining his back.

"Enough!" Kim shouted. Tim released his grip, stood, and backed away. The Malatian slowly came to his feet.

"You need to cut that hair." Kim pointed and sneered.

"What? No. NO!" Bon Tap exclaimed.

Kim jerked back as if struck. "It's a liability in combat! We are warriors before all things. Because of that mop, you're vulnerable. Cut it or get the fuck out."

The Malatian's shoulders slumped and his head hung to his chest. He ran his hand through his long, silver hair as tears dripped onto to the mat. Kim wanted to punch him.

Christina stepped into the ring. "What's the issue?" she asked softly.

"In my species, only females have short hair. If I'm unable to keep my hair, I will forever be alone."

"Welcome to the Bad Company," someone said from the side.

Kimber was with her husband. She didn't know what it was like to be alone, but her sister had been shocked into that reality. She didn't wish it on anyone.

"I'm sorry," she whispered.

"What if there's an alternative?" the female recruit who'd spent the first night naked in front of her fellows suggested. All eyes turned to her. "We braid that shit tight.

It'll be a like a second helmet. He can let his hair down when he goes on liberty, which at this rate is what, sometime next year?"

Christina chuckled. The Malatian lifted his head. "I like you," he said.

"Fuck off, buddy! I'm just going to braid that metal shit you call hair."

He laughed and nodded. "Deal, but it's not metal."

"Shut your fucking pie hole and get over here," the female recruit ordered.

Christina slapped him on the ass so hard that he stumbled face-first into his fellow recruits. "Next!"

Onyx Station

Adina Choudhury stretched her neck from side to side as she led the way out of the White Orchid Spa tucked behind a promenade shop and sighed happily.

"Oh, I feel much better after that!" she proclaimed to the figure catching up with her. "Didn't I tell you a little bit of pampering would do us all some good?"

Captain Jack Marber pressed his hands against the small of his back and nodded. "You did indeed," he said. "They're very good in there. Months of backache from sitting in the *Fortitude's* crappy pilot seat—gone. We have to do this more often. I feel great!"

"Speak for yourself," moaned the Yollin following them through the door. "I still feel like I've gone ten rounds with a Ixtali kick-boxer."

He rolled his shoulders, the joints popping noisily,

causing the blood red raal hawk perched beside his right ear to let out an irritated squawk.

Jack offered Adina a sly wink. "Don't say we didn't warn you," he commented. "Lifeforms with exoskeletons shouldn't get massages."

"That poor guy," added Adina, her expression becoming serious. "I hope the damage to his wrists doesn't keep him off work for too long."

"I doubt it," said Jack. "Once the medic had finished bandaging the cuts and bruises on his hands, he reckoned the masseuse would be fine after a little physiotherapy."

"Well, he'd better not blame any of that on me," grunted Tc'aarlat. "I offered to go get the toolbox from the ship so he could really go to town on me, but he refused, saying he had a few dicks up his sleeve."

"I think you mean he had a 'few tricks' up his sleeve," corrected an amused voice from behind the group.

The trio turned to find a familiar figure approaching, arm outstretched.

"Nathan," cried Jack, covering his mouth to keep his voice down but taking the proffered hand and shaking it firmly. "Didn't expect to bump into you on this station."

"I'm here to drop off TH and Char," Nathan replied, gesturing to the two people with him. Both were laden with more than a few shopping bags. "They're due some vacation time, and I suggested they spend it here on Onyx Station."

There was a small buzz, and Nathan pulled his tablet from his pocket. "Excuse me, folks, I have to take this," he said, stepping away as his fingers danced across the screen.

TH nodded. "If I'd known 'vacation' was code word for

shopping, I'd have gone on a mission instead," he said. "Give me suicidal aliens and blowing up enemy ships over emptying my account for the privilege of sore feet and a dry mouth any day."

Charumati stuck out her tongue and narrowed her striking purple eyes. "Not my fault you're slow on the uptake!" she teased. "Only three more stores, then I'll let you go for a beer, or should I say, another beer."

"I'll need more than one if this is how you plan to spend the entire vacation," her partner chuckled. He turned to Jack, Adina, and Tc'aarlat, holding out his hand. "Terry Henry Walton, but my friends call me TH."

"Jack Marber," replied Jack as they shook, "and this is Adina and Tc'aarlat."

"I'm Char." The woman smiled, setting down her purchases to join in with the handshakes. "I'll be standing here all day if I leave it to my husband to introduce me."

"I love your hair!" offered Adina, gazing appreciatively at the silver stripe running down the length of the woman's glossy, dark locks.

"Thanks!" responded Char, running her fingers through the thick tresses. "TH says it's my way of making a statement. But I've no idea what that statement might be."

"It's your frequently stated commitment to never knowingly pass an open store without purchasing their entire stock," TH groaned. "You guys want to come and grab that beer with me while the ladies share shopping tips?"

"Beer sounds good," said Tc'aarlat. "And Mist never says no to a dish of muri meat, do you, girl?"

The scarlet-feathered raal hawk shrieked her agreement.

SKAWWWWW!

"Unfortunately, we can't," Jack said. "We have an appointment to keep on Damkin Prime. A few bad guys need fucking up due to their ongoing interest in buying and selling child slaves."

"That sounds even more fun than shopping." Char beamed. "Do you want a couple of extra fucker-uppers? TH is good with that cannon of his, and it might be useful to have a werewolf on your side of the equation."

"You're a werewolf?" croaked Adina, taking a small step back.

"As dangerous as she is beautiful!" TH said with pride.

"Looks like you two have more in common than just hair and shopping," Tc'aarlat pointed out to Adina. "If we go for that beer, you could learn more about— OW!"

The Yollin bent to his right, rubbing the spot where Adina's elbow had made contact with his ribs. "Gott Verdammt!" he cried. "How come a trained masseuse can't make a dent in my exoskeleton, but you can jab me like the horn of a charging bistok?"

"Practice makes perfect—and pain!" Adina snarled, readying her elbow once more.

"I think that's our cue to take our leave," Jack said. He shook TH's and Char's hands again. "Say good-bye to Nathan for us once he's finished his call."

"Sure will." TH smiled at the group.

"And good luck with your slave traders," added Char.

Jack glanced at Adina and Tc'aarlat as they glared

angrily at each other. "Judging by the mood these guys are in, I suspect it will be the bad guys who need the luck!"

Keeg Station, Dren Cluster

Felicity looked at the monitor on her desk. The system throughout the station was tied in with the IICS and since she was married to the man delivering the first batch to remote corners of the universe, she had exclusive access to the communication pathway.

Last time they used it, Ted had hung up on her. She wasn't amused, but it wasn't out of character for him. He had finished updating her and had already mentally shifted to the next task. She was surprised he closed out the link when he could have simply ignored her.

He didn't do it to be abrasive or to get under her skin. Being focused on the task at hand was at the core of his being. If he didn't consider it important, he didn't expend the mental energy.

Sometimes that could be frustrating. Felicity recalled the innumerable times during their marriage where something was important to her but not to him.

This time, he was taking an IICS to their children so she could talk with them. He had invented the technology, made it into something that mattered. It made up for all of the times he seemed distracted. Felicity was certain he had built it just for her, so she could talk with her children while also building an empire. Both were important to her.

And now Marcie was gone, too, but she could call her, depending on where they went, which she didn't know.

That chapped her ass. She was supposed to know everything.

"Where are you, Ted, and what are you doing? Our Terry, Char, and Billy will be the medicine I need," Felicity drawled. She looked to the monitor and then back out the window. Today wasn't a day to get any work done.

CHAPTER THIRTEEN

Alameda, Earth

"Kailin? I don't know where he is. No one knows. He took off four months ago. The guy in charge is called Timmons."

"No, his name is Thompson. That's what it is. We don't see him much either. He mostly stays in the office."

The man tried to point, but Ted was already headed for the stairs. He knew the way.

The others nodded as they passed. Dokken forced his way between the man and Cory, watching him the whole time. The dog lagged back, making sure no one came at them from behind.

"Now I *know* something is wrong," Joseph said over the noise of the factory.

They plowed up the stairs, forced their way past a secretary, and burst into the office. Ted was furious. The others weren't happy either.

"Who the hell do you think you are?" the man yelled before seeing who it was. "Ted?"

"Where is Kailin?" Ted demanded.

"Gone. He resigned and left," the man replied. Ted walked around the desk. The man called Thompson backpedaled until he hit a seam in the carpet and fell over. Ted grabbed him by the lapels of his cheap suit jacket and pulled him upright.

"Why would he resign?"

"I don't know. Too much pressure, maybe."

Joseph looked over Ted's shoulder and reached into Thompson's mind.

"Pressure from you and your cronies. You threatened to destroy the plant if he didn't leave," Joseph said.

Ted picked the man up and flung him across the room. He hit an I-beam with a sickening crunch and slid to the floor, a growing pool of blood surrounding his head.

"I'm not sure it rated that," Joseph said. Ted didn't give Thompson a second look.

"We need to call Kim and Auburn and see where their son might have gone. In the meantime, we're going to Chicago. We'll land wherever the hell we want. They need to know that we're back."

"They don't need to know that we're not staying," Joseph replied.

"No. They don't need to know that. I will get answers. We won't leave until Cory finds Sylvia and Sarah and I find Terry, Char, and Billy and give them an IICS so they can call their mother."

Ted stormed from the office. The wide-eyed secretary dove out of his way. Joseph, Petricia, and Cory walked past, sullen and lost in their own thoughts. Dokken sniffed the body before carefully pulling a piece of beef jerky from the man's pocket and trotting after the others.

Ted never slowed. He took the steps two at a time on his way down. He walked through the factory like he owned it, which he still did. The rest never apologized as Ted pushed people out of his way. The workers decided it wasn't worth trying to detain the man like security was requesting.

Security! They never needed such people when he was running things. The thought of it galled him.

Ted stopped once he reached the parking lot. *Ramses' Chariot* descended, getting close to the vehicles, but not touching them before the stairs descended to the pavement. Ted climbed up and went inside. The rest never hesitated.

"Saves us a hell of a walk," Joseph said as Petricia entered in front of him. Cory followed with Dokken running up the stairs last. The German Shepherd could still taste the jerky. He wanted more, but he wanted to find Cory's daughters first. If they smelled anything like her, he could lead Cory to them. They only had to get close.

And then he would ask for more jerky.

Keeg Station, Dren Cluster

In space, day and night had no meaning beyond what was created artificially. Humans built Keeg Station, and it ran full-time operations, but personnel worked according to the human clock, twenty-four hours with a set eight hours of so-called night.

Although it was foreign to many alien cultures, they

quickly adapted. Being spacefaring meant never-ending change. It was the only constant in the universe.

The lights had been turned down in the cargo bay and the recruits were in their racks. It had been a long, hard day. The leadership team expected them to sleep well.

"Should we hit them with a significant emotional event?" Christina asked.

"Tonight?" Auburn asked. His face said 'no.'

"Let them get their beauty sleep. Maybe tomorrow morning, rock their world an hour early."

"To what end?" Auburn wondered. With the shift in training styles, they would have to explain. It required more effort than yelling at the recruits to see how high they could jump.

"To tighten them up as a team. Give them another challenge," Christina explained. "I want them to face an enemy, see if they rise to the occasion."

"Do we have an enemy handy that doesn't mind getting killed?" Kimber wondered aloud.

"A rampaging bistok."

"Not one of your better ideas," Auburn stated.

"We don't have time for subtleties."

"Didn't Terry tell a story about something like that in New Boulder?" Auburn suggested.

"Timmons went after a buffalo herd when he was missing a hand to show that he could contribute to the pack," Kimber clarified.

"That was it."

"I don't like it." Auburn crossed his arms. Kimber leaned forward

"No one has to know." Christina was digging her heels in.

"Everyone will know, but to squeeze three months of training into one month without having a real training area, we have to get creative. Where do you propose we acquire a live bistok?" Kim asked.

"I have one already. It came in on a supply shipment. It was going to get butchered for that Seppukarian place. I diverted one. It's in the next cargo hold over. Do you think I can expense it? I hope so, because I charged it to the Direct Action Branch tab."

Auburn didn't respond. The look on his face resembled that of a stunned mullet.

Kimber's comm device buzzed. She stepped further into the corridor away from the cargo bay hatch. "Major Kimber," she answered the unknown caller.

"Ted here, calling from Earth. Kailin left the plant. Where would he have gone?"

"Is this a loaded question? He would have gone home."

"Joseph here, Kim. It's not that. They ran him out four months ago. This place is a lot different already. He went away, four months ago. Do you know where he would have gone?"

Kimber backed up against the bulkhead. Auburn appeared at her side, supporting her with one arm as he leaned in to catch the conversation.

"Yes. In the hills beyond the stockyards and the main ranch, there were a few cabins. They are pretty remote. He could hole up there. But he disappeared a long time before we left and toured the entire country before returning. He

CRAIG MARTELLE & MICHAEL ANDERLE

could be anywhere." Kim groaned and started to breathe faster. Auburn rubbed her back to calm her down.

"There's nothing we can do from here."

"We should have convinced him to come with us," she whispered.

"We tried, and it didn't work. Taking over the plant was a solution that worked best for everyone. The fact that they, what did Joseph say, they ran him out, that changes things. Maybe he'll be more amenable to coming out here. This time, anyway."

"I hope they can find him."

"I hope we can, too," Joseph replied, having heard the conversation between Kim and Auburn.

"Is this the IICS? It sounds like you're right here."

"Ted's a genius," Joseph replied.

"You got that right. I look forward to hearing that you found our son." There was a delay. Auburn thought they'd lost the link.

"We are doing our best. Nothing is as it was. I want to find the kids and then get the hell out of here. This planet is giving me the creeps."

Kim remembered the decades that Joseph and Petricia had lost as prisoners of the blood pirates. They were only too happy to leave the last time. They only agreed to go back because of Cory.

"Time to go, Kimber. We're descending over the hills beyond your old ranch. At least the stockyards look the same. We'll be back in touch."

The light went out on Kimber's comm device. She stared at it dumbly. "What happened to our son?" she sobbed.

"I hope nothing," Auburn replied, trying to be comforting, but he was frustrated. A galaxy separated them. He felt helpless. "Trust Joseph and Cory and the others. We couldn't ask for anyone better to be looking for him."

"Mom and Dad. Can you imagine the rampage? I can hear it now. *'No one runs off my grandson!'* He probably wouldn't have left the factory standing if they pissed him off enough."

"That's a comforting thought." Auburn shook his head. "Just as comforting as turning a wild bistok loose on the recruits. When's that going to happen?"

Christina had been waiting patiently, not wanting to interrupt the family crisis. "Four in the morning is a great time to be alive, don't you think?"

"Four it is. Heaven help us that nothing goes wrong."

"I expect everything will go wrong, but if I have to blast a bistok, so be it. We're going to have a barbecue in either case. Too bad Jenelope isn't here to help us with it."

"I wonder how those guys are doing," Kim said.

"They're on liberty, which means that everything has gone sideways, blood has been shed, songs sung, and Onyx Station will never be the same," Auburn suggested.

"Pretty much." Christina nodded.

The *War Axe*

Aaron and Yanmei stood on the bridge with the captain and the helmsman. "Why didn't you go with the others?"

"Independence." Aaron didn't expound. He watched the image of Onyx Station on the main screen. An impressive facility, a crossroads in this part of the galaxy. It was where

Terry and Char had gone along with most of the Bad Company warriors.

Some had already returned. That bunch looked to be in a sour mood, so Aaron didn't ask them what was up as they trooped purposefully to the galley, where they were getting ministered to by the head chef and psychotherapist.

Yanmei saw that Micky wanted to know more. "We helped to move Cory a certain distance on her journey. Each leg will take someone different so she doesn't grow too dependent upon any one person. She had to go to Earth. That was her time to find her daughters. As Terry and Char had to go to Onyx Station. As Marcie and Kaeden had to go wherever they needed to go. We have our own journeys to follow, but our paths are inextricably linked. We travel together when we can, alone when we must, but we never forget how far we've come."

Micky scratched his chin. "Onyx is a big station. Why didn't you go?"

"The waves dance to their own music," Yanmei said, clasping her hands and bowing.

Aaron shook his head. "We overslept."

"There are four shuttles in the tubes, at your convenience."

"We'll be off then," Aaron said, waved to Wenceslaus, now a nearly permanent fixture on the captain's lap, and strolled off the bridge. Yanmei shrugged and followed him out.

Alameda, Earth

The trees surrounding the cabin prevented the ship

from getting close. It hovered, pressing down on the uppermost branches.

"Looks like we're going to have to climb down," Ted said.

Joseph tapped him on the shoulder. "He's not down there."

"Where is he?" Ted asked. Joseph held his hands up.

"Plato, take us past the other cabins in the area. Slowly."

Ted sat on the deck and used his own ability to see the Etheric dimension to look for those who could also tap into its power. He often forgot that he was a werewolf, but Joseph's search for minds to touch reminded him.

Together, they explored the land below, searching for Kailin or for any of the others. Sylvia and Sarah both knew about the cabins. Maybe they were nearby.

Cory watched, grinding her teeth in anticipation.

Joseph gripped her shoulder and smiled. "Kailin is far up the hill."

"I see him," Ted said. The ship lifted out of the trees and shot away, following a track that took it over Kim and Auburn's son. He started to run at the appearance of the ship.

Ted activated the ship's external communication system. "Kailin, it's Ted. We heard about the factory. We need to talk."

Kailin stopped running. He turned uphill and found an opening through the trees where he waved at the strange ship. They opened the hatch, and Cory waved at her nephew.

"Rope!" Joseph called. Petricia jogged down the corridor to a storage locker where, as part of the provisioning process, she'd added everything she could think of, including what they used to carry on missions before they went to space.

She handed a long coil to her husband. He passed the end back to her. "Tie it off, if you would."

"Wrap it around my stalk, it's tough enough to hold the weight, and we'll grab the rope together," Bundin said. She looped it twice. The Podder took it with his tentacle arms and she coiled the end around both her arms.

"Go," she called.

Joseph sent the rope into the clearing. Kailin let it hit before taking hold and starting to climb.

"Pull," he told the others and they started hand-over-handing the rope, letting the excess coil on the deck behind them.

In no time, Kailin was pulled through the hatch. He looked young as ever, smiling broadly and showing his perfect white teeth against the milky caramel of his skin.

"Look at you!" he exclaimed before stopping to stare at Bundin. "And look at you, whatever you are."

"My name is Bundin. I'm from Poddern. Your family rescued me."

"Of course they did." Kailin's wide smile returned. He shook hands with Joseph before rushing to hug his Aunt Cory. "Where's Ramses?"

Everyone froze, and Cory burst into tears. She was unable to answer him.

"That's why we're here. We're looking for Sylvia and Sarah to tell them that their father didn't survive the mission to Benitus Seven."

"My Uncle Ramses is dead? But we don't die." Kailin continued to hold Cory.

"We do, and it makes it that much worse." Petricia and Joseph both put a hand on Cory's shoulder to wait for her.

When she finally pushed back, she looked up at Kailin. Her eyes glowed blue and carried the question that they all had.

"I think Sylvia is in Pittsburgh. Sarah and her husband split and no one knows where she is. Ted and Felicity's kids are still in Chicago, last I heard."

"Plato, take us to Chicago," Ted ordered. The ship smoothly gained altitude while turning and racing east.

CHAPTER FOURTEEN

The *War Axe*

Ankh finished the assembly of the prototype and looked critically at it. "Smedley, where can we conduct a live-fire test of the atmospheric combat drone?"

"Not here," the AI responded.

Ankh looked at the empty hangar bay.

"Smedley, I am certain there are a great number of places in this universe where we cannot test the drone. I want to know where we can."

"My apologies, Ankh'Po'Turn, I thought you wanted to test it as soon as possible."

"Your assumption is correct. Revised question. Where is the closest location we can conduct a live-fire test of the drone? Define close as the least amount of time to reach."

"With the gate drive, there is a nearly infinite number of locations that are within minutes."

"Pick one and prepare to move the *War Axe*," Ankh ordered.

"Don't you think you should ask the captain?" Aaron

suggested, appearing in the hangar bay with Yanmei at his side. They were dressed in traditional, loose-fitting attire and on their way to one of the shuttle pods.

Ankh didn't answer.

"Never fear, the voice of reason is near," Smedley quipped.

"I should have known! Keep the lights on and the house warm, Smedley. We'll be back soon."

The weretigers waved and disappeared into a shuttle that launched immediately after the rear deck closed.

"We're not going anywhere," Captain San Marino told Ankh over the loudspeakers within the hangar bay.

Ankh dispensed with verbal communication, reverting to his and Ted's preferred direct link.

We need to test the atmospheric combat support drones, he stated as if the captain hadn't understood why Ankh requested the move.

"I know. We will test it on our transit back to Keeg Station. In the meanwhile, we are missing too many people, in addition to four drop ships. We're not going anywhere," Micky explained.

But we need to test the drone before we begin manufacture. We are wasting manufacturing time by not testing them now. That means during the next mission, we may not have as many combat support drones as we need.

"I understand, but weighing the risk, we can't get underway with as few people as we have on board. If anything happens, we might not have the manpower to get us back into action."

But I'm here, Ankh said, confused.

"That is true, Ankh. You are a force multiplier, but I

don't want to get underway with so many of my crew off-ship. I think that we'll only be here for a week or two. It's been two days, so it won't be that much longer and we'll take you where you can conduct a proper test on that drone. I expect Colonel Walton will want to see how it performs."

What am I supposed to do while I'm waiting for the test?

"I have to believe that Ted left a long list of things to work on."

He did. Most of them are related to the drone.

"I'm sure you'll think of something. Captain out."

Ankh looked from his drone to the hangar door. He sat where he was in the middle of the bay and closed his eyes. Through his comm chip, he activated the engines of the drone and lifted it into the air, flying it around the hangar bay.

Begin data collection on flight parameters. Lock weapon systems in the safe mode. Run diagnostic program Ankh One.

Keeg Station

"Get your big, dumb ass in there," Christina growled. Her eyes flashed yellow as her anger threatened to let her inner Pricolici take over. The bistok didn't want to have anything to do with going into the cargo bay. It wanted to run down the corridor in the other direction.

Christina had a tight grip around the creature's neck. Auburn was trying not to get involved, but Kimber waded in and started pushing the bistok. Auburn didn't think the three of them were strong enough to get it to go where they wanted without hurting it. The beast was terrified.

"Hold on!" Auburn called.

"I'm trying!" Christina shouted.

"Not that. We have a whole platoon of recruits who can help get it back into its pen."

"Change the training?"

"Yes, rescue and recovery."

"Stop fighting me!" Christina tried to dig in her heels, but the beast kept lifting her into the air. "Fine!"

Kimber darted to the cargo bay hatch, opened it, and started yelling. Christina was slammed against one wall of the corridor and Auburn was jammed against the other while the bistok tried to turn around. The creature's horn screeched a cringe-inducing cry as it scraped along the wall, leaving a long mark as a testament to its anguish.

The first recruits appeared in the hatchway, disheveled and mostly disoriented. "What the hell are you waiting for? Bistok. Wild. Get it back in its pen. Now go!"

The recruits spilled into the corridor.

Auburn groaned as the creature slammed him into the bulkhead in its desire to run from the inbound onslaught. The recruits piled onto the beast, three of them weighing down the horns and with Christina's incredible strength, were finally able to get its head turned around.

Auburn was launched toward the cargo hatch when the bistok's hip unwedged from the wall. He stumbled through the recruits and finished up behind them. He wasn't sure how it happened, but he took comfort in having the recruits facing the wrong end of the beast and not him.

Kimber stepped back to give the recruits room. Christina wasn't in a position to let go, so she hung on. The sheer weight of numbers gave the bistok nowhere to go.

The mob surged around the creature moving slowly, one step at a time. It surged back and forth, but the numbers pressed in. When they reached the hatch leading to its pen, it bolted inside, accepting the pen as the best of its bad options.

K'Thrall walked past the others and casually secured the gate. He brushed his hands on his pants and then looked at the pen. He contorted his face, which made his mandibles click. He held his fingers near his nose and grimaced. "I'll never be able to get that creature's stench off me."

"How about some PT?" Christina yelled, trying to distract the group. She sniffed and realized that her suit was permeated by the smell of bistok. "Get back in there and form up for PT!"

The recruits ran, assholes and elbows down the corridor, disappearing through the hatch into their training home.

Kim stood with her hands on her hips. Auburn rubbed his sore ribs. No one looked happy.

"Fine. Not my best idea, so shut up about it." Kim and Auburn started to laugh, then slapped hands in a high-five. "What?"

"That is your welcome-to-the-inner-circle moment. We're going to tell everyone, and it's even better than that." Kim pointed down the corridor. "We have video."

Onyx Station

Nathan approached Terry and Char, but turned quickly away when he saw the look on Terry's face.

"I see you!" Char called.

"Hey! There you are. I was looking for you," Nathan replied quickly.

The purple-eyed werewolf shook her head.

"Kimber just sent me a video. Have you seen it?"

"Been busy," Terry grumbled, holding up two armloads of packages. "When will my winnings be transferred?"

"Already done. Directly to the Bad Company's commercial entertainment department for consideration of the franchise purchase of one All Guns Blazing brew pub."

Terry looked confused.

"I told him to do it," Char said, "for your present."

"You used my money to buy me a present?" Terry raised one eyebrow. He couldn't hold his arms up because of the package, but he had an entire routine that he usually went through.

"Of course. We're married. That's how it works. Would you have bought that for yourself?"

"Maybe. I probably would have filled a bathtub with credits and gotten a picture of me swimming in it so we could have it framed and mounted on Nathan's office wall."

"See? My way was better."

Terry wasn't sure he agreed. "The bets are paid and done?"

"They are," Nathan confirmed.

"Son of a glitching, bung-tapping iceholes. I'm back!"

Nathan shrugged. Char shook her head. She didn't know either.

"What a twunting dickwhistle sample bender!" Terry declared with a big smile.

"I think one too many violent blows to the head," Char

said. "Maybe we should get that checked out, but after we go back to our quarters. We were able to snag the suite that had the chocolate shower. Toodles!"

Char headed for the elevator.

"Thanks for the bar, Nathan. I know you didn't have to do that."

"And you didn't have to pay the price you did to remove the Skrima from our dimension. Not that any number of credits can bring someone back to life, but I have it on good authority that your people are working on a cryo-drone to secure severely wounded so they can be stabilized for repair in the Pod-doc. It's not a new idea, but they've put it together in a way that will make it work."

"A day late and a dollar short, but better now than never." Terry didn't have anything more profound than old Earth sayings. He wondered how Cory was doing. The *War Axe* was tied into an IICS.

He wanted to call his daughter. He hurried after his wife because they could do that from their quarters.

CHAPTER FIFTEEN

Chicago, Earth

"Taxi! Get your taxi here!" the hawker yelled. His vehicle was behind him. There were no others in the area. There were no other people either.

"I think he's yelling at us," Ted stated the obvious.

"We do need a taxi," Joseph admitted. "It beats walking. I've already done that here, more times than I can count. Lots and lots of walking."

"No one will recognize you. Not this time. No black leather." Cory pointed to their casual slacks and short-sleeved shirts. Joseph's hair was slicked back. He was still pasty white because starships weren't the galaxy's best tanning spots.

Bundin hung out in the hatch once again, angry at being left behind.

Dokken was happy to be going, but he had sworn never to let Cory out of his sight. The German Shepherd had adhered to his commitment and had no intention of changing.

"You said you know where to go?" Cory asked.

"I do. At least the last time I talked with them, they were in the same area," Kailin answered.

Joseph carried the IICS like a briefcase. He wore a light jacket, behind which he had the cavalry shortsword that he'd traded Terry Henry for over a century earlier, not far from where they now stood.

Petricia was also hesitant to move, for the same reasons as Joseph, and different ones, too. She had great memories of their time in North Chicago, of their whirlwind romance after Joseph rescued her from the clutches of Forsaken in South Africa. Then the renegade werewolves had tried to kill her, and the blood traders had taken her prisoner. She was happy to have no memories of that time. Joseph was more aware because he'd seen the depravity in his captors' minds. Their liberation was a long time ago, but for vampires it seemed like yesterday.

"We should have suggested Aaron and Yanmei come instead of us," Joseph said as his feet refused to move.

Petricia hugged her husband's arm. "You guys go without us."

Kailin held his hands out. "I'm not a warrior. And neither are you." Kailin motioned to both Cory and Ted. "You might be, or you could be just a dog."

I am not just a dog, Dokken replied, the hackles on his back standing. Kailin didn't hear. He didn't have the chip.

"Want some jerky?" Kai asked as he produced a small piece from his pocket. He held it out, but Dokken didn't move.

"He's sentient, and he talks." Cory looked down her nose at her nephew.

"Clearly not to me," Kai replied.

"Need a chip. Go ahead," she told Dokken. The German Shepherd smiled wryly as he took the jerky, nipping Kai's fingers as he pulled it free.

"Dumb dog!" Kai sucked on his injured digits.

Ted shifted uncomfortably. He leaned toward the taxi, wondering why they were delaying.

I can't believe you're related to the dumb human.

"I am," Cory answered, reaching down to scratch Dokken behind his ears. He leaned into her hand. The faint blue glow appeared as they briefly shared nanocytes.

"You are what?"

"Related to a dumb human." Cory faced Joseph and Petricia. "What my clumsy nephew is trying to say is that we need you. We're a team. We have to find Terry, Char, and Billy, so we can move on, find Sarah and Sylvia."

"I know you're right, but I have bad memories of this place. And they didn't happen that long ago. Do you know anything about the blood trade, Kailin?"

"The separate battles fought by Grandpa, Michael, and Valerie drove it far underground, but it still exists. With a group our size, we'll be fine. It's never good to be alone."

"Like you were in San Francisco?" Cory wanted to hug him, but he stepped back.

"What's with evil and their ability to find like-minded souls, heartless bastards?"

"Maybe the evil convinces decent people that the dark path is the right one to travel." Joseph took a step, relieved that his feet decided they were able to move. "I have my shortsword, just in case."

"I have Grandpa's .45." Kai lifted the back of his shirt.

"Are you any good with that thing?"

"Have you ever fired this?" Kai told Cory. "Close counts when shooting a cannon."

"You should see Dad's new toy. He can blow up buildings with it." Cory smiled at Kailin before turning to Joseph.

"Shall we, my dear?" Joseph said pleasantly, motioning for Cory and Petricia to precede him. Dokken trotted ahead to sniff the ground and make sure the way ahead was safe. The taxi driver waved for them to come closer, even though they were already walking his way.

Kailin hurried ahead and caught up with Dokken.

"You're sentient? I didn't know, buddy. I never thought about what to ask a dog before, but I guess, what I want to know is how do you know where to pee?"

Dokken looked forlornly over his shoulder. His ears sagged against his head. His mouth popped open and his tongue fell out as he started to pant. Cory nodded in sympathy.

Yes. You're clearly related. I pity humanity.

The taxi driver was holding the door open as they arrived. "I'm not sure you're going to all fit. Maybe just the women and the dog," he suggested. "I can come back for the rest."

Joseph didn't bother with pleasantries. He grabbed the man's face and stared into his eyes, to deepen the effect of digging into his mind. The driver winced as Joseph forced his way in. Joseph started to growl, deep in his throat like an animal.

"Okay, pal. There's clearly something wrong with you, so you're going in the trunk." Cory didn't bother to find out what made Joseph upset. She opened the lid and waited. Joseph dragged the man to the rear of the car and stuffed him inside. She slammed the lid closed.

"Anyone know how to drive one of these?" Joseph wondered aloud.

"I do, and I know the way," Kailin answered. He jumped in the driver's seat and the others took the empty seats. Dokken climbed in the back with Cory, choosing to sit on her lap instead of Joseph's and Petricia's.

Ted sat up front and maintained an interface with Plato. *Ramses' Chariot* took off as they drove away. It gained altitude but stayed over the taxi. Its shadow splashed across buildings as they drove into town from what used to be O'Hare International Airport.

Kai drove confidently, demonstrating that he did know where he was going. They turned frequently once they left the main road. The others quickly became disoriented, but not Joseph. These were his old stomping grounds. Decades of preying on those who no one would miss. The unwitting meals of an unwilling vampire.

They pulled in front of a house in a more upscale area. There was a yard, overgrown with weeds, like most lawns. But the windows were in good repair with their shades open. "That's where Billy lived, last time I was here."

Ted jumped out and hurried to the front door. He turned when he got there, annoyed that Joseph was still getting out of the car. Ted ran back, took the IICS, and returned to the front door, pounding on it unmercifully.

"Why doesn't he answer?" Ted grumbled as he kept pounding.

"Who for fuck's sake thinks they can pound on my

door like they're swinging a battering ram? What's wrong with you, dickless? I'm coming down there to kick your ass!"

"Billy! You get down here right now!" Ted yelled at the open window.

"Dad?" The figure from upstairs disappeared. They heard him pound down the steps. The door flew open and Billy launched himself into Ted, hugging him fiercely. Ted didn't hug him back.

"You're making a spectacle. I need you to call your mother."

"Of course I'm making a spectacle. I'm like Mom. I love people!"

"Moments ago, you were going to come down here and kick my ass."

"Valid point. I love people who aren't beating down my door at the crack of noon. Some people need their beauty sleep! Cordelia, is that you?"

Ted started setting up the IICS. Joseph interrupted him. "Maybe we do that inside?"

Cory hugged Billy and they mobbed inside.

While the others made small talk, Ted set up the comm console on the dining room table.

"Where is your brother and sister?" Ted asked while he put the finishing touches on the setup.

"Rence lives on that side and Lita lives over there." Billy pointed from one side of the house to the other.

"Rence and Lita?" Ted asked.

"There's already a Terry and Char, the galaxy's power couple. They wanted their own identity. I'm good with Billy, Dad. I'm a down to earth kind of guy. Grassroots and all that good stuff. Rocking the ganja weed, living life to the fullest."

Ted's expression didn't change. "Are you speaking English? It sounds like it but it doesn't. Plato? Please update the linguistics database."

"That's my dad. I've missed you and Mom." Billy was the emotional one, more so than the other two. They had lost patience with their father more than once when they didn't understand how he could retreat so easily into an emotionless shell.

Their mother told them that was where he felt safe, and they shouldn't bother him when his shields were in place.

"Felicity?" Ted asked the device. "Are you there?"

The units connected, but the screen was dark. "Hello," a tired voice drawled.

"Felicity! I found Billy, and he wants to talk with you."

"Billy, my dear, how are you?" The light popped on and Felicity smiled beatifically at the pad she was using to interface with the IICS.

"We're okay, Mom. If you give me a couple minutes, I'll get Rence and Lita so we can all talk with you." Billy handed the device back to Ted.

"They live next door. Three houses in a row," Ted clarified. "They call themselves Rence and Lita. Did you hear that?"

"I did," Felicity drawled pleasantly. "It's okay, Ted. Those are the names we gave them. They shortened them a different way, but they are still our children. Billy looks good! Earth must be treating them right."

Ted touched the screen. He knew she was on the other side of the universe, and as frustrated as her emotions made him, she understood him better than anyone else. "I'll come home to you soon. We think Sylvia is in Pittsburgh, our next stop, and hopefully she'll know where Sarah is."

"If anyone can find them, I know it's you." Felicity touched the screen as Ted was doing.

Joseph and Petricia looked away. They weren't used to seeing that side of Ted. Cory sat next to Ted and draped an arm over his shoulders.

"Uncle Ted is magnificent," Cory added. Ted blinked rapidly and looked at the floor.

Dokken shoved his face against Ted's head so he could see the screen.

"Who is that delightful creature?" Felicity asked playfully as she felt more awake. "Dokken! We miss you around here. Maybe you can find yourself a mate and bring home some puppies. They would be loved from the top to the bottom of Keeg Station."

Dokken stopped and cocked his head. *Do they have German Shepherds like me on Earth?* he asked. Felicity couldn't hear, so Cory shared what he said.

"There is no one like you, Dokken, but there are German Shepherds. Big, beautiful dogs. Irish Wolfhounds, wolves, and so many more. The smaller dogs didn't survive the Wastelands, but you're a big handsome man and deserve a big beautiful woman!"

Yes, I do! Dokken exclaimed, his tongue hanging out of his face, and drool splattering on Ted's leg and the floor.

Ted and Felicity's three children walked in together, saving Cory from having to relay what Dokken was saying.

"Dad!" Charlita called easily with a slight Southern

twang. Ted stood, stumbling over the big dog as he made to greet the kids.

He assumed his dad persona and hugged them one by one. Billy took it with a shrug, dismissing the earlier chill, which he had learned to never take personally.

Ted shuffled his feet and looked at the device on the table. "Your mother wants to talk with you," he said, pointing.

"Is she in orbit? Why doesn't she come down?" Terrence wondered aloud.

"She's on the other side of the galaxy," Joseph clarified, smiling at the three werewolves. "Ted invented this device for one reason, so Felicity could talk with her children. And I don't want to be dramatic, but the unit's power source came at a very high price."

"For us?" Lita asked.

"For all humanity," Cory answered. "Even if that means aliens." She closed her eyes and slowly moved aside to give the three space before the IICS.

"There you are, my lovelies!"

The group moved away to allow the family privacy. Joseph stayed near the window where he could watch out. "Do you think we should let the taxi driver out of the trunk?" he asked.

Kailin chuckled. "I'll take care of it." He went outside.

Cory sat in an overstuffed chair and disappeared into her own thoughts. Petricia kneeled beside her. "We'll be on our way soon. Ted will leave the IICS here. We'll find Sylvia."

Cordelia nodded slowly, her lips white from clenching her jaw so tightly.

"I'll kill you!" the taxi driver yelled as he tried to jump from the trunk and attack Kailin. He stumbled as he came out, landing on his face. He rolled to his feet and ran at Kailin. Kai dodged and tripped the man as he passed.

"You were thinking some pretty foul thoughts in regards to my aunt and my friend, so here's what's going to happen. You're going to calm the fuck down, or I will beat you senseless and toss your dumbass back in the trunk. We'll be returning to the airfield shortly. You can drive us, or you can ride in the trunk. The choice depends not on what you say, but what you do."

Veins stood out on the man's face as he clenched and unclenched his fists.

"You're making this decision easy for us. I want to punch your face so bad," Kai told the man as he raised his fists and maneuvered toward the driver. The man relaxed and held his hands up in surrender.

"See? That wasn't so hard."

Ted was the first out the door. When he reached the taxi, he stopped to wave, but the others had followed him out. His children hugged him again. He was embarrassed, since this was in public. The rest said their good-byes and started to pile into the cab.

"Why are you taking that thing?" Billy asked.

"It's our ride," Ted replied matter-of-factly.

"We'll take you back to the airport," Rence offered.

Ted pointed at the ship hovering a few hundred meters overhead.

"Holy shitsickles, Dad! Is that your spaceship?"

"It is Ted's spaceship, called *Ramses' Chariot*. Ted and Plato defeated the evil AI that was running a blockade that we were called in to break. I don't want to brag, but twenty-five of us took over twenty ships and captured more than a thousand prisoners. It was a masterful stroke."

Petricia looked annoyed. Joseph laughed.

Kai threw the car keys to the taxi driver. "Don't let us see your face around here again." The man didn't wait to be told a second time. He jumped in, revved the engine, and squealed the tires on his way out of the neighborhood.

"Ted and Ankh were both exceptional. Their minds defeated that of an alien artificial intelligence. We have a rematch coming. I expect Ten will be waiting for us, far more prepared than it was the last time."

"If my dad has anything to do with it, this AI doesn't stand a chance. Who's Plato?"

"An AI that Ted created."

"Damn, Dad! You've been busy."

Ted's eyes brightened. "You wouldn't believe the technology we have access to. Immersive holographic interfaces, direct links between the brain and the AI, with aliens like my friend Ankh."

Rence, Lita, and Billy enjoyed seeing their father so excited, but they had no idea what he was talking about.

"Ankh, an alien about this tall—" Joseph held his hand waist high. "—with a big head, no emotions, loves nothing more than to think about stuff."

"You don't know Ankh at all," Ted complained. "I thought we were getting a ride somewhere."

"If all you need is space for your ship to land, there's a park right around the corner. We can walk."

Ted's eyes unfocused for a moment. "Plato says that he can land the ship."

The group walked away. Dokken stayed on the grass, preferring to fight his way through weeds instead of walking on pavement. Not if he didn't have to.

"Nice dog," Lita said. Dokken trotted over to walk at her side, always keeping one eye on Cory.

"He's sentient, or so they tell me," Kai said. "Don't feed him or he'll get your fingers." Kai held up his hand, but his nanocytes had already repaired the damage that Dokken had done. "You get the point."

"No. You got the point!" Lita quipped. Dokken dog-laughed and nuzzled Lita's hip. "He's a sweetheart."

They turned the corner and watched the ship descend. The hatch popped open and the stairs descended.

"Your chariot to the stars awaits, madam," Joseph said, bowing and sweeping an arm toward the ship. The Podder stuffed himself into the hatchway.

"That's our friend, Bundin." The Podder waved his tentacle arms.

"You people are weird," Rence said.

"Call your mother. OFTEN!" Ted emphasized as he climbed aboard. The hatch closed and the ship rapidly ascended, racing to the east.

CHAPTER SIXTEEN

Onyx Station

The back of the mechanic's shop was as pristine as the front, which was for the "regular customers." In the back was where Pete kept the parts and items that would get him a bit more attention than he probably wanted.

"What's under that cover?" Eddie asked, pointing to a large, oddly-shaped mass in the corner of the room.

"I don't believe that's what you asked to see," Nathan said, checking over his shoulder.

"I'm looking at what I came for," Hatch bellowed from under a black 1969 Camaro parked in the center of the clean garage set up in a corner of the hangar bay. The Londil, who resembled a giant octopus, had flattened himself to fit under the car, his tentacles wagging out in different directions as he completed his inspection.

Julianna tapped her foot, growing impatient. "Well, maybe you'll be done soon. We need to get back to *Ricky Bobby*."

"I'll be done when I'm done. It's as simple as that." Hatch's voice was muffled and full of irritation.

"Oh, and look at the timing on this," Nathan said, turning to Terry and Char as they approached from the front of the shop. "Did Pete get you sorted out with the parts you needed?"

"He did. Some interesting finds he hooked us up with. Ankh asked for them, but I have no idea why." Terry's eyes dropped to the immaculate car in front of them. "What is this? Oh, you are a beautiful lady! Is that a nineteen-sixty-nine Camaro?"

Hatch spilled out from under the car, inflating into his usual bulbous form, tentacles waving around as he righted himself. "Yes, and it's mine as of ten minutes ago, so don't get any ideas."

Nathan smiled politely. "So much for introductions. Hatch, this *is* Terry Henry Walton and Charumati, from the Bad Company."

Terry extended a hand, but thought better of it after seeing the irritated expression on the Londil's face. His tentacles remained at his sides.

"And this is Captain Teach and Commander Fregin, from Ghost Squadron," Nathan said, motioning to the pair at his side.

"Ghost Squadron." Terry looked behind him to make sure there were no unwanted ears in the area. "You guys fly under the radar, take missions that we can't. Sometimes I wish we weren't so high-profile, but the boss has different ideas."

"A private conflict solution enterprise has to be visible

because you stop wars. People have to trust that your word is good," Nathan replied.

Teach took the hand Terry had offered to Hatch, his eyes wide with excitement. "This is quite the honor. You guys are legendary. We heard what you did at Alchon Prime."

"Thank you," Char said. "Just for your ears, I'll have to say that it wasn't our finest hour. Terry blew the engine with us inside. It wasn't pretty."

"I did that, but Ted demanded action."

Hatch scooted around to the other side of the car, not distracted by the meeting.

"Don't mind Hatch." Julianna waved a hand in the mechanic's direction. "We dragged him off the ship to inspect parts, which is when he came across his newest find. He's not really a people person."

"People, Podder, Crenellians, Kezzin, Yollin, I make no exceptions. I dislike them all," Hatch chimed in from the other side of the vehicle, his eyes studying every detail.

Eddie laughed, but Julianna looked unimpressed, obviously used to the cantankerous mechanic's attitude.

"Doctor A'Din Hatcherik has a fondness for classic cars, as you can see," Nathan said, casting a look back at the Camaro.

"As do I," Terry stated.

"Wait," Char said. "The Doctor A'Din Hatcherik? As in the one responsible for the design of the Q-Ship?"

"As well as many of the other technological advances the Federation enjoys," Teach said.

"Damn, that's pretty impressive," Terry stated, his eyes still checking out the vehicle from a distance. "I think you need to meet Ted, but he's on Earth delivering the Interstellar Instantaneous Communication System, the IICS. He also has the miniaturized Etheric power supply. You may find some uses for it."

Nathan coughed into his hand. "I already transferred the design," he whispered.

"What brings you two to Onyx Station?" Teach asked, an easy grin on his face.

"If you can believe it, a little R and R," Terry answered.

"I can't believe it," Julianna said dryly.

Eddie scoffed at his partner. "We take vacations. Just last week, I took you to Sagano for a tropical getaway."

"By getaway, you mean we were hiding from pirates," Julianna retorted.

The group laughed, easily able to relate to the demands of the job.

"Terry and I bought an All Guns Blazing franchise that we'll set up on Keeg Station, in the Dren Cluster. It'll have its own gate pretty soon, but with your Q-Ship, you don't need a commercial gate. Have Nathan give you the coordinates if you don't have them already and stop on by. Give us a couple months to get the pub up and running. We'll name a drink after you."

"Deal. After our next mission. We have some scumbags we need to rid the universe of first, but after that, we'll bring *Ricky Bobby* for a visit."

"If your ship takes any damage, consider Spires Harbor for your repairs. Soon to be the biggest shipyard in the known universe."

"Are you sure about that?" Nathan asked.

"It's our tagline. I'm sure about *that*."

Hatch harrumphed and held out his tentacles, impatience written across his face.

"Great to meet you, but it looks like we're leaving."

"Same here. Our lawyer wants us to sign more papers. You'd think we could do it with a thumbprint and a DNA sample, but no, sign in triplicate, all twelve hundred pages..."

"Bureaucrats. Why do we allow them to exist?" Hatch interjected, looking pointedly at Nathan.

Keeg Station

The recruits were dogged. Heads hung in exhaustion. They were eighteen hours into a twenty-four-hour combat exercise. Without having a training area, they extended the cargo bay into space. Every recruit had a suit of some sort in which to operate in the frigid vacuum outside the station. Some suits had limited dexterity, but those were a stopgap while waiting for their mech suits to be designed and manufactured, if that was possible.

Mardigan was convinced it was. He was happy to announce that the cryo-drone design was large enough to encompass all body sizes. The recruits weren't as pleased with the news as he thought they should be.

No one wanted to think they'd be injured badly enough to require being frozen so their brains wouldn't die. It provided little comfort, because they would still suffer the pain of their wounds and die, but then they'd wake up from it. The recruits expressed their dismay at the thought. Only K'Thrall found the thought of remembering one's own death intriguing.

Mardigan and Auburn looked at each other. Kim and Christina had listened to the conversation. "The recruits have a good point," Christina said.

"We could design it in such a way..." Mardigan started, but Kimber held her finger to her lips to stop him.

"Go away," she said. He was instantly bummed, but saluted and left.

"Why do you have to be that way?" Auburn wasn't pleased either.

"There's still a chain of command and some separation is good. Remember when my dad backed out of the direct affairs, refusing to learn the newcomers' names? To keep from getting too close. We watched hundreds of warriors grow old and die. We saw too many others die in combat. I don't want to go through that any more than he did."

Auburn nodded and hugged her with one arm.

Christina continued. "Ramses was a gentle soul. His death was horrific. How would he have come back from that? Not the precipice, but having gone over it and then being pulled back by the Pod-doc."

"Would you?" Kimber asked.

Christina nodded. "For the sole reason of getting back in the fight and fucking up that guy's shit. Kill me, will you! I'm gonna kill you right back, butt-hugging fuckwit."

"I'm not sure I'd want to relive it," Kimber said softly.

"I'd want you to be good with surviving," Auburn replied. "We are at the point in our lives where we're not living for ourselves. We live for others. Look at what the Bad Company does. We fight for others because they can't. So if our brain gets a little mushy because we died, so what? We need to come back to life. We need to live because we have to keep fighting for the people who can't fight for themselves. And we live for the rest of us in the Bad Company."

"Which means I get to come back to life and stomp on the balls of the rotten bastard who snuffed me out. Fucker!" Christina pumped her fist.

"And there's that, too." Kimber smiled. "I formally change my position for the aforementioned reasons and will be heretofore recognized as a 'yes, I want to live' vote. Freeze me and bring me back."

"It's unanimous. We better get back in there before they fall asleep. They have six hours of combat drills remaining."

"Too late," Christina said. Once the recruits had sat down, they were out cold. Most slept in their spacesuits, but all were asleep. "Up and at 'em!"

Pittsburgh, Earth

"Do you have any idea where Sylvia might be?" Cory asked Kailin for the tenth time.

"Not a clue." Kailin couldn't expound further and was tired of Cory asking, but he couldn't blame her. "We'll find her."

"Pittsburgh covers a lot of ground," Joseph said while he studied the imagery of the city over which they hovered. "It's where three rivers joined, the Allegheny, Mononga-hela, and Ohio. The natives recognized how fertile the region was. Started with the Adena culture, then the Iroqois, Lenape, Seneca and Shawnee moved in. Once

George Washington and the French decided they liked it, the rest was a running battle for control."

"Why the history lesson, Joseph?" Cory asked.

"Because I'm nervous, dear Cordelia. What we saw in San Francisco bothered me greatly. Chicago? Not much better. It seems as if mankind is devolving. I don't want any of our families caught up in that, but they are. Look at Kailin and what they did to Ted's factory."

"I'm anxious, too." Cory sighed heavily from her seat on the bridge. The others wedged in around her. Her hand naturally went to Dokken's head, where she found some comfort in the warmth of his thick hair. "I'm afraid they won't care, that they'll still be angry that we left them."

"They care, greatly," Petricia said. "I had the pleasure of their company a great deal when we lived in San Francisco. They are wonderful human beings. Sarah is very much like your father, and Sylvia takes after you. Terry Henry is a big personality and sets an ideal that people don't understand as they try to live up to it."

Kailin worked his way to the front of the small bridge. "I know exactly what Petricia is trying to say. After Grandpa left, there was a huge void. Everyone had their idea of what would Terry do, but the opportunists jumped in, the little people who could never be the pillar of moral strength that Grandpa was. No one was as selfless. People wanted for themselves—power, stuff, those things. It took two months before they came after me. I'm sorry, Uncle Ted. I lost your factory."

Ted didn't look up from the captain's chair. He was engrossed in a pop-up screen where rows of data scrolled past. His lips moved as if whispering to himself.

"Plato, can you take us on a slow pass over the populated areas of Pittsburgh? Petricia and I will search for anyone tapping into the Etheric."

"I have a search pattern established. I am sorry that my sensors cannot pick up these emanations. I will project a map before each of you, simply tap the spots where you feel the special people and I will build a database."

"Looks like we need room to maneuver," Joseph suggested.

"Please clear the bridge," Plato requested.

The others wanted to stay. Cory stood, wished the vampires luck, and worked her way off the bridge. Kailin poured into the corridor, bounced off Bundin's shell, and fell to the deck. Dokken turned his head back and forth as he wondered what he'd just seen.

"When will I be able to get off the ship?" Bundin asked.

"For fuck's sake," Kailin said, sitting and rubbing his arm. "We're looking for Cory's daughters!"

"And that is exactly what I want to do. I came along to help." The Podder sounded hurt.

"This time, you will go with us whenever we get off the ship," Cory promised.

"I want to help," Bundin said.

"Is this more of the Terry Henry Walton effect?" Kailin asked. Cory's eyes glowed blue in the twilight of the corridor. The hatch to the bridge remained open, but the lights were dimmed as Joseph and Petricia worked with the holographic maps. Ted was in his own world, communing with Plato on what Ted considered as the most important project. No one else knew what that was until Ted told them.

"It wasn't TH but Joseph who saved me," Bundin began. "The influence of this group of humans is being felt far and wide. They ended the civil war on my planet. They brought peace to us. At a high cost. As I've seen in the short time that I've known them, everything comes at a price. Terry lets everyone know what that price is and lets them decide if they are willing to pay it. Everyone agrees. You should have seen Joseph break into that ship at Alchon Prime when I was starting to run out of air. We fight for each other probably more than we fight others."

Cory closed her eyes and looked down. Softly, she started to speak. "Ramses was never a warrior, but he became one because I had to go to war. With my healing gift, I couldn't turn my back on the injured. And he wouldn't turn his back on me. I'm not blaming myself that he was killed. The Skrima killed him. He fought as well as he could, but it wasn't good enough, not against a hell-spawned enemy like them. Before we go back into combat, I want everyone to be sure that they will fight like warriors possessed, even when the enemy are the very demons we fear."

"The battle with Ten will be far different. We may never fire a shot," Bundin said. "That man in there is the key to whether we can end Ten's enslavement of the kidnapped humans or not."

They looked at Ted, sitting in the captain's chair but not looking captainly. Petricia carefully touched a spot on her map that kept moving slowly around her. Joseph tapped a spot and thrust his arm in the air.

"Found her!" he yelled.

CHAPTER SEVENTEEN

Onyx Station

"By all that's holy in this bald monkey-ass world, don't make me sign any more papers!"

"I assure you that no one is making you do anything. That premise alone could void this packet of contracts. Are you making that accusation?"

"No," Terry said sheepishly. "I meant to say, will we ever be fucking done signing our fucking lives away?"

"You are an angry man," Rivka said. She was half Terry Henry's size. She climbed down from the barstool and stood to her full height, and she was still shorter than a sitting TH. "I have a job to do, and I don't think you respect it! Nathan asked me to do this as a personal favor. Yes. I'm an intern. Yes. I'm a woman. You get over that, do your job, and I'll do mine!"

"He doesn't have anything against you being an intern or a woman," Char said, pointing at the sheaf of papers. "He despises bureaucrats who embrace paperwork as the epitome of productivity."

"You think I like this?"

"How could you not?" Terry declared.

"Okay, maybe I do, but it's in the sense of putting a puzzle together where there are no holes. You will be able to defend your bar before the Queen and the universe! No one will take it away from you, except for AGB Enterprises if you violate the branding or fail to make your purchases from them or fail to pay them their revenue, although you've made that payment automatic by agreeing to use AGB Enterprises Accounting and Banking as declared on this form." Rivka dug halfway through the stack and pointed to a page.

Terry never bothered to look at the document. He was amazed by the victorious look on her face.

"I feel like there should be a fist pump or something."

Her smile evaporated. "You are an angry man."

A drunk patron pounded on the bar, demanding service. The bartender waved him off, refusing to serve him. The drunk man slid close to Rivka.

"Whatcha got there?" he asked as he pushed Rivka and reached a dirty hand toward the pile of papers. Rivka caught him by the wrist.

"Don't touch the contract," she told him, her voice low and steady.

"Don't touch me!" he replied and grabbed for her. She let go, caught his ears in each hand, and pulled his head downward. She drove her leg upward. His face met her knee and that was the end of the confrontation.

"Assault, battery, and interference in a confidential attorney-client conversation." He moaned and held his face. She kicked him in the ribs. "Justice is served."

"Holy crap!" Terry looked at her with newfound respect. "You can do that? Judge, jury, and executioner?"

She looked at the man rolling around on the floor. "No one was executed, but yes, we are authorized to mete out justice when the cases are clear cut, like this one. There's video. He's guilty, so fuck that guy."

"If someone messes with our bar, are you going to fuck them up, too?" Terry asked with a big smile.

"Not if you don't sign those contracts," she countered.

TH turned to Char. "I love my lawyer."

"Of course you do. Now, keep signing."

The *War Axe*

Ankh walked onto the bridge, face expressionless as always. He stood next to the captain's chair. When he craned his neck to look upward, his big head off-balanced him and he almost fell over.

Clifton snickered and turned around to look at nothing new. Micky climbed down and sat on the edge of the platform so he could be eye to eye with the Crenellian.

"What do you need, Ankh?"

"Breathable air, food, water, sleep, but not much of that last one. Why do you want to know that?"

"I want to know what you are going to ask me," Micky clarified.

"Yes. I have conducted all the flight testing I can do with the combat drone in and around the ship. I want to know when I can conduct the final phase of testing." Ankh remained emotionless.

"You mean, live fire."

"Yes."

"On our way back to Keeg Station, we'll stop by an uninhabited planet and you can bang away. Smedley?"

"I have the coordinates already programmed with the gate engine. Once our fine helmsman gives the word, we'll be ready to send the drop ship to the planet."

"When will we be going back?"

"Whenever Terry and Char return and give the word."

"When will that be?"

Micky massaged his temples. The hatch to the bridge opened and Wenceslaus strolled in. The captain pointed to the cat. "And we all work for him. If you can convince him that it's time to leave, we'll leave."

"Give the order, cat. The combat drone must be tested to validate its configuration before it can be mass produced and added to the arsenal. Ted has said this fire-power is critical for the long-term survival of the Direct Action Branch and its warriors. Do it now, cat."

Micky felt bad for brushing off the small alien. He couldn't take the *War Axe* away, but he didn't have the whole story. Ted was worried about his family and friends and was doing what he could to keep them alive.

"I think I understand," Micky replied.

Wenceslaus head-butted the Crenellian, then dragged his body along the humanoid's leg. Micky caught the cat by the ears before getting head-butted. He vigorously scratched, and Wenceslaus started to purr.

"Is that the order to go? I'm sorry. My comm chip isn't programmed for the language of felines."

Micky looked at Ankh. "None of ours are, but what he's

saying is I should call Terry and Char and see how they're doing. Smedley?"

"Calling them now," the AI replied.

"What can I do you out of, Skipper?"

"Ankh has the combat drone ready, but he wants to live-fire test it. We can't do that here. Do you have any problem with me taking a skeleton crew to a place where we can send some rounds downrange, as you might say?"

"Combat support drone. Half a million railgun projectiles and four independently targetable missiles. Nothing says the Bad Company has arrived better than *massive* explosions."

Micky waited. Terry hadn't answered the question.

"You know what, Micky? I think we're done with why we came to Onyx Station, so we'll pack our trash and return to the *War Axe*. I'd love to see the CSD in action. We'll have to return to Onyx before going home to Keeg Station. We have to pick up our galactic adventurers."

"Let us know when you're aboard and we'll get underway." Micky nodded to the Crenellian.

"Great job, Ankh. I'm sure that thing will make my eyes water and pulse race."

Ankh turned away from the captain and walked off the bridge.

"What do you think, buddy?" the skipper asked Wenceslaus. The cat ran up his chest, used his shoulder as a springboard, and vaulted to the captain's chair. He curled up in the seat and closed his eyes. "I guess that says it all. We wait."

"Gate engines are charging," Clifton said over his shoulder.

"On my command, helm." Micky thought about moving the cat, but decided against it and took K'Thrall's old position instead. "This is like sitting on a bench, a really uncomfortable bench."

Clifton tried not to look, biting his lip as he started going through the launch checklist.

Pittsburgh, Earth

"Where is she?" Cory asked as she hurried back onto the bridge.

"Take us down," Ted said, seemingly to himself as he continued his engagement with Plato. The screens showed the ground racing up to meet the ship. *Ramses' Chariot* pulled up and hovered about thirty feet off the ground. The ship cast a great shadow over a house immediately below. Vertical obstructions like trees prevented them from going lower.

"She's in there," Joseph said. Cory ran from the bridge, vaulted over Bundin, and raced for the hatch. She popped it open and launched through.

"She jumped!" Bundin exclaimed as he wedged himself into the hatchway to look down. He twisted his stalk-head forward. "She's okay!"

Cory hit the ground, rolled, and came to her feet running. She reached the door and started yelling and beating on it.

Dokken tried to gauge the height, but couldn't. Cory was down there. He wasn't with her. He stepped into the opening. With his heart in his throat, he jumped.

Bundin's tentacle arms lashed out and caught the dog before he'd traveled more than a few centimeters.

"It's too great a drop," Bundin exclaimed. Dokken started to struggle.

"Not for me it isn't," Kailin told them. He crawled over Bundin's shell and hoisted the huge German Shepherd into his arms. "Wow, dog. You need to cut back on the treats."

Kailin held him tightly as he jumped through. The pair accelerated toward the ground. When they hit, Kailin threw Dokken sideways before he rolled through the impact. Dokken hit and stumbled, but his legs churned and he found himself running toward Cory as the door opened in front of her.

A woman, the spitting image of her mother minus the glowing eyes, stood there, confused. "Mother?" she asked. Dokken slid into Cory, almost knocking her down. Sylvia caught her.

Cory pulled her into a hug and started crying.

Kailin stood back while Dokken leaned against Cory, trying to comfort her through his warmth and kind thoughts.

When Cory was able to get it out, Sylvia didn't change her expression.

"I understand," the young-looking woman said, frowning.

Cory hardened up and brushed the tears away. She looked angry. Sylvia asked her to be calm.

"I thought it was inevitable that someone would die. I didn't expect it to be my father. I thought it would be my grandfather who died first. He places his body between the enemy and everyone else. Not because he thinks he's invincible, but because he can't stand someone else doing something that he thinks he's supposed to do."

"But your father..." Cory blinked before a new flood of tears could start.

"I'm sure he died saving the universe. Isn't that how we were raised? In the service of others. I didn't understand it then, but I do now. Most people don't respect that, but I do. Did Dad die for a cause worth dying for?"

Cory held her daughter's gaze. "He did, and you're right. Mom and Dad took the hardest part of the mission, but when things went bad, we were trapped with too many Skrima when our nanocytes were disabled. There was nothing we could do."

"Why were your nanos disabled?"

"Without disabling the nanos, we couldn't kill the Skrima. Once they were disabled, the demon creatures were vulnerable."

"I understand," Sylvia said, barely above a whisper. "Did you kill them, the Skrima?"

"Yes." Cory wouldn't meet her gaze. "We killed all of them, and Dad closed the rift so no more could come through."

"I understand," Sylvia repeated.

"We have a device that you can use to talk with us, instantly, anywhere in the universe."

"We don't have much technology here," Sylvia said, heading into the house and waving for the others to follow. "If it breaks, we won't be able to fix it."

"It won't break. Ted assures us that the IICS will outlast us all."

"Ted built it?" Sylvia's lip twitched upward into a half-smile, before it settled back into a tired frown. "Sarah's not here."

"Where is she?" Cory asked. Dokken was big enough that standing, he could rest his chin on the table. He stood between Cory and Sylvia. Both women petted him as they sat, not looking at each other.

"To be alone. She split from her husband, had to go find herself. The nanos were changing within her. That's what she said, anyway. She went away, saying that I wasn't to look for her. She'd find me when the time was right."

Cory chewed on her lip, her expression turning dark.

"No, Mom! I know what you're thinking, and it's the opposite of that. The last thing she said was that she needed to work harder to be the person that you deserved her to be. A kind soul, leading the world to a better place, but she has the fire of her grandfather within her. She needed to balance the two. She still limps, by the way." Sylvia stood and exaggerated the limp, mock-fainting.

Cory didn't know how to take that. Neither did Dokken. Kailin, watching from the doorway, burst out laughing.

"He gets it." Sylvia pointed at her cousin. "Great to see you again, Kailin. It's been awhile." The two hugged.

"Are you going to come with us?" he asked. Before she could answer, there a crash outside, the sound of something big ripping down a tree. Kailin took a few steps and stopped. "It's Bundin. He jumped."

"How's he going to get back on board?" Cory blurted.

"I don't know. He's down here now. How are we going to get back on board?"

Cory waved her nephew away.

"Bundin?"

"You have to see," Kailin interjected. Cory wanted to talk with her daughter alone, but she gave up trying to make that happen. Dokken furiously wagged his tail as he received constant attention from Cory and Sylvia.

Sylvia stopped when she saw the Podder ambling toward her home. "What is that?"

"He's Bundin, from Poddern. He's a member of the Bad Company and he wanted to help us find you, more than anything else," Kai explained.

Sylvia nodded as the alien stopped outside the door. "What's with human doorways? They are always so small. Cordelia? Are you okay?"

"I'm fine," Cory replied. She stood and went outside. "Thank you for coming to check on me. You are a good friend." She could see him favoring one leg. She kneeled down to examine it. A huge gash was torn through the scales that protected the Podder's stout legs.

She put her hands on the injury to help him heal. He didn't resist. The pain was significant, but not over-whelming.

And he had no idea how he was going to get back to the ship. He trusted the humans and their ingenuity to figure it out.

"You must be Sylvia," Bundin said in the deep voice that the comm device gave him.

"I am," she said with a warm smile.

"You are truly blessed to know such people as these," Bundin told her.

"I know," she replied matter-of-factly. "I'm not coming with you. I need to be here when Sarah returns from the wilderness. It took Grandfather twenty years to find himself. I wouldn't hold my breath, but I'll be here when she returns and if you give me that comm device, I'll have that waiting for her. So you make sure you survive Colonel Terry Henry Walton's adventures so you're there to answer whenever we make the call."

Cory smiled at her daughter.

"Mind if we stay the night? There's no hurry to get from one place to the next. Our spaceship is state-of-the-art."

Sylvia pointed to the front door. "If he's going to sleep in the front yard, the neighbors are going to talk."

Bundin's stalk-head waved around as he took in his surroundings. "Maybe there's a nice cave nearby."

The *War Axe*

Terry and Char's shuttle pod flew through the open hangar door and oriented itself for insertion into the launch tube. When that was settled, the rear deck dropped and they walked out carrying armloads of packages. The hangar door was already shut and sealed.

"Prepare to gate," Micky announced over the ship-wide broadcast. Terry tried to pull his hood up, but the packages got in his way. He twisted to escape, but the handles seemed to wrap themselves around his arms. Char set her packages down and pulled on her hood. It inflated, and she slapped at Terry's arms until he stopped flailing. He pulled his hood on. Once it clicked into place, they could feel the ship accelerate forward and the strange shift when they passed through the gate.

"I guess Ankh was in a hurry," Char suggested.

"Just a lot. We need to ditch this stuff so we can see the combat drone in action."

"Ditch this stuff? We'll put it away in our quarters. You can watch the drone shoot at the ground."

Before they took two more steps, one of the drop ships rocketed out the launch tube.

"What was that all about?" Terry wondered. *Smedley, a drop ship just launched. What's going on?*

The shuttle pod is carrying the atmospheric combat support drone. Once inside the atmosphere, the drone will detach and conduct a series of live-fire tests. I will inform you via your chip, if that is okay.

I look forward to it. Bridge or the combat information center to watch the show? Terry asked

Definitely the CIC, Smedley replied.

Terry hurried ahead. Char followed, knowing that TH wanted to watch the test to determine how best to employ the weapon system. She wanted to watch it too, but would watch it remotely. She had clothes to try on.

CHAPTER EIGHTEEN

Pittsburgh, Earth

They stayed up late into the night, talking. Dokken never left Cory's side. Bundin worked his way into the bushes so the never-present neighbors wouldn't see him. Kailin slept on the couch. Ted called often to see when they were returning to the ship so they could go home to Keeg Station.

Morning came too soon.

Sylvia made a simple breakfast of vegetables and unleavened bread.

Dokken asked if she had any beef jerky. Cory relayed his request. Sylvia's laugh was musical and took the sting away from her proclamation that she was a vegetarian. Dokken's ears drooped, but Kailin yelled up to the ship for Joseph to throw down a portion of smoked bistok.

Kailin caught it, despite Joseph's errant throw. Despite the vampire's long life, he'd never partaken of sports. He wasn't good at throwing things. Not knives. Not balls. And as it turned out, not packets of meat.

The omnivores enjoyed the bistok, while Sylvia tried not to look at it.

Kailin ate and returned beneath the ship. Joseph held an IICS. Kailin asked that Petricia throw it. Joseph shrugged. He wasn't too proud. She delivered it on target by dropping it straight down instead of trying to steer it.

They cleaned up after breakfast, and Cory showed Sylvia how the device worked. They called the *War Axe*. Terry and Char's quarters appeared.

"Dad?" Cory wondered.

Terry's face popped out from behind a stack of bags and packages that he held in his arms. "Cory! Char, come quick. Cory's on the blower."

"They haven't had blowers for two hundred years," Char said as she helped remove the packages from her husband's arms. They kissed lightly before turning to the screen.

"Mom's been shopping? Are you still at Onyx Station?"

"We're at a firing range testing the combat support drone that Ted and Ankh designed. Tell him it works great but can't fire the railgun in a hover. It needs to have forward movement to offset the release of power."

"You tell him yourself. He's on the ship. In the meantime, look who we have here!" Sylvia and Kai both leaned into the picture.

"Sylvia! Kailin! You guys look great," Char said.

Terry hugged her to him as he watched the screen, seeing everything that was there, along with who wasn't. He didn't ask the question that was foremost in his thoughts. *Where is everyone else?*

As if reading his mind, Cory continued. "We found

Terrence, Charlita, and Billy. They are settled in Chicago. They have an IICS and have talked with Felicity at least once." Cory's face dropped. Without moving her head, she looked to Sylvia and back to the screen. "Sarah isn't here, and no one knows where she is." Cory paused, again looking to Sylvia and back to the screen. "She's on a classic TH hide from humanity adventure."

"She's going to be gone for twenty years?" Terry looked disappointed.

"Maybe. No one knows until she returns to the world," Sylvia clarified. "It's her time, Grandpa. I clarified it for Mom, but I'll tell you, too. We aren't angry with you. We aren't upset with you. We love our family, and it took an alien to remind us to say it."

"Bundin?"

"The ship couldn't land, so he jumped. He got all fucked up bouncing through a tree, but Aunt Cory fixed him with that blue trick of hers."

Terry bit his lip. Char poked him in the ribs.

"I'm coming to space. It's time to leave Earth behind. I hope you don't mind. I'm bringing my girlfriend, too," Kailian chimed in.

"You're coming with us?" Cory looked shocked. "You didn't say anything about a girlfriend."

"I'm kidding about the girlfriend. I hear alien chicks are hot!" He bobbed his head and licked his lips.

"Somebody punch him," Cory said. Sylvia held her head in her hands and groaned.

Dokken barked.

"Dokken! I miss you," Terry said.

"He didn't miss me," Sylvia stated, looking directly at her grandfather.

"Goes without saying, but my dog..."

I'm not your dog. My God, is he untrainable? Dokken asked. Cory laughed.

"We're going to be on our way, Dad, Mom. We're coming home."

The final image before the screen went blank showed Terry and Char waving.

"Alien chicks?" Sylvia slapped her cousin.

"That's as offensive as a Walton who's a vegetarian. Your grandmother is a werewolf!" he prodded.

"And proudly so. Leave, you tactless buffoon. I won't be insulted in my own house!" She stomped a foot and pointed. He lifted one eyebrow. She laughed in reply. "I can't be mad at you, cousin."

"I can be mad at all of you," Cory said. "But I'm not."

Cory looked at her daughter through the blue glow, with eyes that sparkled once again.

"How are we going to get Bundin into the ship?" Kailin interrupted.

Onyx Station

"Terry left us here," Aaron said, unsure if he was supposed to feel annoyed or happy at the revelation.

"If you want to be sad about something, be sad that they'll be back to collect us in a week when the others return from their misadventures around the galaxy," Yanmei replied.

"What do you want to do?" Aaron asked.

"What can't we do on the ship or Keeg Station?"

"Most excellent point," Aaron answered. He stood to leave their temporary quarters. He stopped and looked at Yanmei. "What can't we do?"

"Didn't you see those spacefighters in the hangar bay when we arrived?"

"Yes," Aaron said, drawing out the word.

"We learn to fly them and take a couple back with us."

"Wouldn't they throw us in jail for that?"

"We will clear it with Nathan, if he's still here." Yanmei headed toward the door.

"And if he's not?"

"We'll find out, won't we?"

"When did you become a bad girl?" Aaron said, intrigued.

"Once or twice a century, I let her out to play." Yanmei traced a finger up Aaron's throat to his mouth. "Meow."

She walked away and Aaron ran to catch up. In his haste, he nearly brained himself on the doorway.

Keeg Station

"K'Thrall, bring the platoon to attention," Kimber ordered.

The Yollin turned toward the formation. "Attention, please," he said pleasantly. Kimber started to shake, her head vibrating as if it would explode. Auburn jumped in to save her.

"Come to *attention!*" he yelled. Bodies snapped into position. "Come on, man. With some gusto!"

"I'm Yollin," K'Thrall replied.

"Come on, Yollin. With some gusto!"

"Attention!" K'Thrall said loudly. "Please."

The recruits snickered.

"Keep your bodies locked up," Kimber said, stepping smartly toward the first squad to conduct the daily uniform inspection.

"I hear they call you Tim," she said to the new squad leader. He didn't budge. "Good job. Starting to get some scuffs on your shipsuit. Make sure it maintains its integrity, and when all else fails?"

"Make sure I have duct tape with me."

"Exactly," Kimber replied, slapping him on the arm.

She went to the next member of the squad. "Bon Tap. Turn around." The Malatian executed an about-face. His hair was plastered to his head, twisted and packed tightly.

"That looks like a tumor," she told him. "If you can attract a mate with that, she'll be a keeper."

"Or someone who doesn't care about silver hair," Auburn whispered from behind the formation.

"You could be the trendsetter for your whole race," Kim offered.

"I doubt that. Our traditions lean toward the spectacular."

"Did you hear that?" Kim said, raising her voice so the whole platoon could hear. "Our Malatian comrade has volunteered to arrange the graduation party. He said it will be spectacular!"

"I don't think that's what I said," he stuttered.

"Carry on," Kim stated and moved to the next recruit.

In the third squad, the Ixtali stood with her robe covering her four legs. The race of arachnid-like beings was halfway between spiders and humans in their evolution. They had multi-faceted eyes and two sets of fangs, a single pair vertically-oriented and one horizontally-oriented.

Slikara's diet was heavily reliant on protein. When they pushed the bistok into the pen instead of slaughtering it, she was the most put out, almost depressed by the nearness of the pulsing blood and fresh meat. She usually ate alone.

"Auburn says that your shipsuit should be ready in a day or two. You're the last one. Once you're set up, we're taking the whole platoon outside for maneuvers."

"I look forward to it. It's hard to be a part of the team when you're not a part of the team."

"You're a recruit with everyone else. What do you mean you're not part of the team?"

She didn't reply to the question.

"What the fuck is going on?" Kimber roared, storming through the middle of the ranks to get back in front. She faced them, fury seizing her features. "Are you telling me that this fucking mob is treating one of our own differently? On your faces and push that deck until I get tired!"

The recruits dutifully assumed the push-up position and started counting the repetitions. Auburn and Christina moved in, watching the angry glances at Slikara.

"On your feet!" The recruits stood. They breathed heavily through their noses, the discipline of their new lives starting to take hold as they kept their mouths shut. "I can't make you like anyone, but I can make you respect your fellow warriors. When I give the command to fall out, you will fall out, and fall back in around the sparring ring. Fall out!"

The recruits took one pace backward, then jogged the ten meters to the small section of the cargo bay that they'd designated the hand-to-hand combat training area. Two recruits rolled the mat out. Everyone waited.

"We will demonstrate that we fight better as a team. Slikara, in the ring."

The Ixtali dutifully complied. She refused to make eye contact with her fellow recruits, looking at the mat as she moved. Christina walked into the ring beside her.

"We will fight as we really are. No tools. No augmentations. No shipsuits. That's right, my pretties. We're going to fight as nature made us." Christina's eyes flashed yellow, her pupils changing, her body changing. Claws grew from her canine hands.

Terrible claws. Christina's shipsuit was special and flexed with her change to protect her, no matter what form she was in, but she didn't need it for this. She pulled it off, deftly, without ripping the material. It dropped to the mat and she kicked it out of the ring. "Weeeellllll?" she hissed in her Pricolici voice.

Slikara pulled her robe away and threw it aside. The hair of her lower body wasn't for warmth but to sense the environment around her when in complete darkness. The black threads stuck out like needles. She shuffled her feet to extend her body and stand more naturally with her four legs.

She opened her mouth wide, splaying her fangs to make them stick straight out.

K'Thrall threw aside his loose shipsuit, preferring to be without clothes as it let the seams around his carapace breathe.

"It is my failure to hold the platoon together," he claimed. "I will be first to fight you both."

"When the platoon is ready," Kim said from the side. She and Auburn made no move to disrobe. Christina's plan wasn't their plan. They figured she had everything well in hand.

The humans seemed to take longest to get naked. Christina started tapping a clawed foot, finally taking steps in their direction to encourage the last of the holdouts to hurry up.

K'Thrall assumed his fighting position. Yollins were both strong and accomplished in individual combat. It was a part of their culture. K'Thrall could best most in the platoon.

He tried to circle, but the Ixtali cut him off on one side and the Pricolici stopped him on the other. He rushed between them, then dove to his right in the hopes of disabling Slikara. She countered his move and fought him to a standstill.

He knew that his back was exposed, but he was too slow disengaging. Christina hammered a fist into the top of his head. He went down like a stunned bistok. Kim and Auburn moved in, picked him up, and carried him from the ring, depositing him to the side once they made sure he was okay.

"Neeexxxt," Christina hissed, pointing at a recruit. She'd singled out each of those who had cast unfriendly glances at the Ixtali while they were doing push-ups. Sometimes lessons needed to involve pain.

The human stepped into the ring, angling to the side as he faced his two opponents. He kept one hand over his ghoulies, putting himself at a severe disadvantage. Christina stepped behind Slikara and pushed her forward. She didn't wait. She charged, slapped his one hand away and donkey-kicked him with two of her legs. She would have followed up with a righteous pummeling if he hadn't flown from the ring.

He groaned in agony and started coughing. Blood splattered from his mouth.

Auburn stepped in, picked him up, and carried him away. "Going to sickbay," he told them over his shoulder.

"Neeexxxt," Christina said again. The recruits cringed, afraid for whoever she would choose. Another human. He whimpered as he approached the ring. When his first foot entered the ring, she grabbed him by the head and slammed him face-first into the mat. She kicked him out of the ring.

"Neeexxxt." She didn't point at anyone.

K'Thrall staggered back into the ring. "I'll take the beating for the platoon. Come on!" he told them as he put his fists up and started to dodge and weave. Christina looked at Kimber.

"Stop!" she ordered. Kim entered the ring, turning in a circle as she looked over the recruits. "What lesson do you think we're trying to teach?"

"That a Pricolici will smash your face in if you cross her?" the recruit said through the blood dripping from his nose.

"Alone, we perish," K'Thrall said.

"One team, one fight. We fight to win, not each other. Every battle the Bad Company has ever fought has been against vastly superior numbers. Sometimes we do have to fight alone. How do you do that? How can one person fight twenty-five? Ferociously, with the desire to live. We fight to win. *Every. Single. Mission.*"

The recruits watched her closely as she continued to turn within the circle. Christina had already collected her shipsuit and was getting dressed.

"We need to practice fighting when we're outnumbered. Get your clothes on and prepare for two-on-one combat training."

CHAPTER NINETEEN

The *War Axe*

Terry stood in the CIC, watching the screens that captured the combat support drone in action. From numerous angles, Terry was able to run footage back and forth.

Ankh wasn't watching the video. He preferred the raw data collected by sensors attached to the prototype. Immersed within the holo screens, the code scrolled around him. He tapped and engaged.

Terry Henry replayed the video. In his mind, he could see a fleet of the drones engaging an unwitting enemy, leveling a huge swath of the battlefield. *Maybe they'll decide it's not worth the fight.*

He thought of Home World and the upcoming battle. Human slaves. Ten would put them between the Bad Company and the AI, wherever his corrupted programming resided. Terry wasn't keen on killing innocents, even if they were willing combatants.

"Father, forgive them, for they know not what they do,"

Terry quoted. "Do they have any protection from airborne threats, like fighters or air-to-air drones, maybe surface-to-air missiles?"

Ankh continued what he was doing.

"Smedley, make sure to get my question to Ankh. A unit with SAMs could knock these down in short order. It seems like a single P-51 from World War Two would take these out."

"The P-51 was an incredible aircraft," Smedley replied.

"You got that right, Smedley. The good old days of combat, pitting skill and the latest technology against the aggressor!" Terry leaned back in his seat and remembered his Marine Corps days. Combat was violent and the damage done by one human being to another was terrible. "Maybe none of those days were good. To defeat evil, the good guys have to bring a level of violence greater than their enemy."

"The CSDs do not have air defenses. Ankh and I are designing deployable jammer dispensers and air-to-air missiles for the system. That should be done in a few minutes. We will be able to modify the prototype when it is returned to the ship."

"Just like that?"

"Yes. When someone like Ankh and I can make petaflops of calculations, it does not take any time to change a design."

"What the hell is a petaflop?"

"A quadrillion trillion floating decimal point calculations per second."

"A shitload. You can make a shitload of calculations."

"I assure you, we can do far more than a mere shitload of calculations," Smedley replied defensively.

"Uber-shitload? Hyper-shitload? Exa-shitload?"

"Exaflops are fewer than petaflops, by orders of magnitude."

"Do you understand that I really don't care about petaflops?"

"But you asked," Smedley replied, confusion in his voice.

"I'm sure that I won't ask again." Terry continued to watch the videos. "Will you be able to modify the platform so the railgun can fire while the drone is hovering?"

"We cannot. The drone will have to maintain a constant twenty-seven kilometers per hour to maintain a firing rate of one hundred projectiles per second."

"Which means we have to expend more and more energy to maintain forward momentum with each increase in firing rate."

"On a logarithmic scale of output. Yes."

"But the Etheric power supply can handle that while firing the weapons?"

"Easily."

"And there we are. TH's new favorite toy!" Terry said.

The footage cut out as the drone reattached itself to the shuttle pod.

Terry opened his mouth to say something, but Ankh was fully ensconced within his digital cocoon. "Smedley, tell Ankh great job in the development and testing. I look forward to using this to secure the peace while minimizing the risk to our people."

. . .

Ramses' Chariot, Earth

The frigate flew through the ionosphere as it headed into space. The group wedged onto the bridge, mesmerized by the receding images of Earth.

"Last chance to get off," Ted said. "Ha! Just kidding. We're not going back. Charging the gate engine. Prepare to gate."

Kailin turned to Ted. "No second chances, huh?"

"Isn't that what happened when we came back to Earth?" Joseph suggested.

"I get the feeling you won't be back again."

Joseph didn't answer.

"We might. Thanks to Ted, the universe is a much smaller place." Cory clutched an IICS to her chest. The size of a briefcase, it was a direct link to her children. She held it like she had hugged Sylvia when they said their good-byes.

And then they walked three kilometers to a field where the *Chariot* could land. Bundin wondered why they didn't land there to begin with, which would have forestalled his ill-fated jump from the spaceship. He took pride that he'd done it. He never shared with the others that as a cave-dwelling species, he had an innate fear of open spaces and great heights.

He had blustered, but was happy to remain on the ship, out of the sunlight.

In front of the ship, a gate formed and the *Chariot* rocketed through. In a flash, they were somewhere else.

The alien fleet appeared around them.

"What the hell, Ted?" Joseph threw his hands up and flinched, expecting incoming fire to destroy *Ramses'*

Chariot. The ship rolled sideways away from the gate's entry point into that system. It casually maneuvered toward the largest of the alien vessels.

"See?" Ted said, bobbing his head.

"See what?" Cory asked.

"Exactly." Ted got up from the captain's chair, instantly annoyed at the bodies that prevented him from leaving the bridge.

"Where are you going?" Joseph said, holding his hand out to stop Ted from leaving.

"To get a sandwich."

"We're back in the middle of the alien fleet, the same one that tried to kill us, and you're going to get a sandwich?"

"Yes. New gate protocol. We arrive cloaked. They saw a flash but don't know we're here. I'm going to get a sandwich now. When I'm finished eating, the gate engines will be charged and we'll jump the rest of the way to Keeg Station."

The group moved aside after Ted's casual explanation. If he wasn't concerned, who were they to be upset?

"All hail Ted," Cory said with a smile.

"All hail Ted," Plato replied from the overhead speakers.

"What the fuck is that about?" Kai wondered aloud.

Joseph and Petricia shook their heads and drifted toward their quarters. Bundin worked his way down the corridor to the cargo bay. Cory and Dokken remained behind.

"We didn't know what Ted was capable of until he came to space. We always thought he was a genius but standoffish, not a people person," Cory began. "With the integration of the comm chip and the development of artificial intelligence that paired with Ted, his real genius is on full display. He does more for humanity than the rest of us combined. Like this."

She held up the IICS.

"He built this so his wife could talk to their children. He went to war with the rest of us to find the component he needed to finish it. All for his wife and family. Everyone else gets to benefit, too. Ships that can jump all the way to Earth. Stealth. Shields. Those things that improve our survivability. He may look at them as technological challenges, but the purpose behind conquering the problem is to help us." Cory leaned closer to Kailin. "And since Ted has been instrumental in so many recent breakthroughs, to include developing his own AI and a number of off-shoot AIs, Plato's Stepchildren he calls them, they treat him as a deity. We laughed at first, but it makes sense. To them, he is God."

"But he's Ted."

"Yes. He's our Ted, and I, for one, am better because of it." Cory saluted using the IICS, then walked away.

Kailin didn't know where he was supposed to sleep, so he took the pilot's seat and watched everything there was to see. He didn't touch any of the buttons.

I have so much to learn, he thought. *I can't even talk with the dog. That makes me the stupid one.*

Hunger told him that he should probably find the galley. A sandwich sounded pretty good. "Maybe Ted can explain a thing or two, if I can find the galley."

"I'll guide you," Plato said matter-of-factly.

"Can you answer other questions I have?"

"Of course," Plato replied.

Kai returned to the pilot's seat. "Since no one else is here to listen to my stupid questions, here we go..."

Keeg Station

It was the third day straight of hand-to-hand combat training. Six hours on, two off, then six hours on. The bouts tended toward warriors grabbing each other and hanging on until the other could be pushed over.

"You think it's time?" Christina asked.

"They are ripe for a boost," Auburn replied.

"K'Thrall, form the platoon."

The Yollin was still upright, but barely able to move. He started waving his arms, but no one moved. "Come on, people!" Christina yelled. Kim and Auburn moved into the ad hoc berthing area and tossed sleeping warriors from their bunks. The recruits limped, staggered, and meandered their way into formation.

K'Thrall had his hands on his knees, trying to catch his breath.

"When you signed up to join the Bad Company, you agreed to being enhanced with nanocytes, ostensibly as the first response to medical treatment when you're in the field. Your nanos will heal your injuries, even fairly major ones. As long as your head stays on your shoulders and your heart stays in your body, you should be able to recover.

"There are also some secondary benefits, such as your stamina will increase rather significantly. You'll get bigger and stronger. You already have your translator chips.

Those are fairly standard, but now, you're going to get the whole package. We're going to sickbay, where they can run two at a time through the Pod-docs. It sounds like a dream, getting enhanced, but you have to work really hard to get drunk, and even then, it's not the same. You'll be hungry all the time. And when you're in combat, you'll feel like you can take on an enemy army by yourself."

The recruits were asleep on their feet. There was no reaction whatsoever.

"Single file. Follow K'Thrall." Christina put K'Thrall's hand on her shoulder, and she held it in place as she tromped toward the hatch leading into the station. Each recruit put a hand on the shoulder of the one ahead, unless they had four legs like K'Thrall and Slikara. Then they hung on to whatever they could reach. A single file with twenty-five recruits following Colonel Christina Lowell. Auburn and Kimber brought up the rear, making sure no one fell over in the short hike into the station, up two flights of stairs, and halfway down a corridor.

Every step was an ordeal. One foot. Then the other.

"Maybe we should have done this yesterday," Kimber whispered to Auburn.

"They'll appreciate it more today." Auburn gave the thumbs up. He was tired too, but he hadn't gone into the ring repeatedly like the recruits. It was nice to be in charge.

The challenge had showed the recruits what was required of a warrior. They'd met it and succeeded.

Ramses' Chariot flashed into the Dren Cluster, not far from Keeg Station. The massive shipyard called Spires Harbor loomed in the distance.

"How long have we been gone?" Cory asked.

"Not more than two weeks," Joseph answered.

"Where are we?" Kailin wondered.

"The Dren Cluster. The far reaches of the Etheric Federation. There's no gate out here because this is a secret Bad Company installation," Joseph replied.

Ted pointed to a spot at the side of Spires Harbor.

"Looks like we may be getting a gate after all." The great disc was only a speck, but Plato enhanced the image on the main screen to show that the initial framework was nearly completed.

"I'm back." Ted spoke softly toward the arm of the captain's chair. "We'll be docking in the main cargo bay... Yes, the kids looked great. I'll tell you all about it when I see you in a few minutes."

"Felicity?" Kai asked.

"Uncle Ted's soft side comes out to play. Occasionally." Cory leaned over the captain's chair to kiss the top of Ted's head. He turned and caressed her cheek with one hand.

"Was the trip to Earth what you thought it would be?" Ted asked.

Cory looked over Ted's shoulder. Plato was maneuvering the frigate toward the massive hangar bay door.

"It answered the questions I needed answered. Thank you for building this ship to take me."

"This ship answered questions that I had. And our time on Earth, too."

Ted worked his way through the ship's corridor,

annoyed at the congestion. Once clear, he hurried toward his quarters.

"Your new home," Joseph told Kailin, slapping him on the back.

"It's not much from the outside, but on the inside?" Petricia quipped.

"It's not much either," Joseph finished for her.

"Are Mom and Dad here?"

"How could I be so crass to have forgotten that?" Joseph berated himself. "You'll find them in the lower cargo bay where they are conducting new recruit training for the Bad Company. Petricia and I will take you."

Ramses' Chariot settled to the deck without a bump or jerk, the hatch popped open, and the lights brightened.

"All ashore who are going ashore," Bundin called from the corridor, using the human phrase to perfection.

CHAPTER TWENTY

Onyx Station

"These are Black Eagles, single-pilot spacefighters from the last great war," the mechanic explained, looking proudly at the ship.

"Did you fly these back then?" Yanmei asked.

"No, not at all." The man laughed. "I'm not a pilot. I keep them in the sky so the adrenaline junkies can get their fix while protecting us."

"You say that you've both been checked out in the simulator?"

"Absolutely," Yanmei purred. "Which two can we take for our check ride?"

The man pointed to the closest fighter spacecraft. "You're kind of big. It'll be a tight squeeze." Aaron nodded. Didn't he know it? For him, everything was too small.

Yanmei started to climb up the ladder to access the fighter. "Where are you going?" the man asked.

"Fly the plane," Yanmei replied, confused by the question. There was the cockpit. All she had to do was climb in.

"Flight suits. I have a couple over here. Regular jockeys wear flight suits all the time, leaving their helmets in the seat so they can get in more quickly in case of an emergency call out. But these babies are close to mothballs. It'll be nice to see them back in space where they belong."

"You're taking these out of commission?"

"Not me. Them." The mechanic pointed upwards. Aaron nodded knowingly, although he had no idea. The promenade was upstairs. Shopping. He was certain it wasn't them. The administrators were mostly near the spindle in the middle of the station. He suspected it might be them, but it wasn't comforting to think that the man who repaired his spacecraft didn't know up from down.

"Will the flight suit protect me if the ship blows up?"

"Probably not. Why would the ship blow up?"

"Just wargaming things a bit," Aaron countered quickly, heading for the small locker to the side of the tool bins. Yanmei slipped a flight suit over her shipsuit, checked the helmet for fit, and walked back toward the Black Eagle. Aaron found a suit that slipped on and fit comfortably.

"You had a suit that fit me," Aaron stated, pleasantly surprised.

"That Kezzin pilot wore it until they made him a custom suit. You're getting an alien's castoff! Hahahahaha." The man was quite taken with his own joke.

"Aren't we all aliens, though?" Aaron asked, resting his hand gently on the man's arm.

The mechanic stopped laughing. "No!"

Aaron let his eyes become those of the great cat, the weretiger. They changed to emerald, consuming the man within their gaze. He vaulted backward. Aaron returned to normal and stepped away.

"We'll be back soon. Miss you already," Yanmei called from the cockpit of her Black Eagle.

Aaron settled into the Eagle, not as sleek as the jet fighters on Earth, but it had a dark beauty that drew him. He wanted to fly, be free like a bird, but he didn't know what to do.

Do you know how to fly one of these things? Aaron asked.

Not yet. How hard can it be? Yanmei replied.

Hard! Aaron shot back. He looked at the controls and none of it made sense. He liked the flight control stick, styled after the old-time joysticks.

Follow my lead, upper left, red button. Press it.

Aaron did as he was told. The engines came to life.

Your systems should come on. And then you'll see what's available. Most of it is related to weapons and shields. Flying the ship? Looks easy.

Aaron wished that they'd spent at least ten minutes on a simulator so they could get out of the hangar bay without crashing into the station.

You have a lever to your left. Pull back a millimeter or two and you'll lift off the deck. Push forward on your joystick and you'll go forward. Pull back and you'll stop before going in reverse. Wait for me. Now follow.

Yanmei's Black Eagle lifted into the air she rotated the ship slightly to point the nose toward the opening to space. She increased speed slowly until she was at the atmospheric shield. She stopped, rotated the nose again, and rocketed out into space so quickly, Aaron thought she'd teleported.

Aaron fumbled with the controls, went up too quickly, over-compensated, and slammed the spacecraft into the deck. Aaron thumbed the lever with his left hand, only a millimeter, purposefully ignoring the angry mechanic yelling an impressive stream of expletives that Aaron could hear clearly through the ship's screen.

As the ship lifted slowly off the deck, Aaron tickled the joystick. The nose moved where his fingertips directed. He pushed forward and the ship moved. He pushed harder and it moved faster. He tapped it to the right to aim at the middle of the open bay door. When the ship passed through the screen, he pulled back on the lever and leaned hard right as he jammed the stick to the side. He pulled it back and over, driving it forward.

The ship zoomed into space. His eyes shot wide as he saw the number of ships in orbit around Onyx Station. He pulled back on the stick to slow down and maneuver like the law-abiding citizen he thought himself to be.

Where's my bad girl? Aaron wondered.

The *War Axe*

The drone launched a starburst of flares moments before it cycled the railguns, firing a second starburst as the drone kept enough forward momentum to avoid being thrown backwards.

"Looks like an effective weapon against a well-armed, determined enemy," Terry said.

Ankh looked at him. "Data shows nominal performance."

"So, we agree!" Terry declared. "Shoulder to shoulder,

they marched to their doom, singing in loud voices, showing the enemy they were not afraid."

Ankh's expression didn't change.

"And that's the lie, Ankh. Don't you get it? They were afraid, but put on the show that they weren't. It's all about teaching your fear who's boss. Courage in action! Buck up, little trooper. Get stoked. We're going to war with Ten and that lightweight piece of beetle-infested bistok dung is going to get his. We are going to blast his circuits and send his last digital thoughts screaming through the explosion. Yeah." Terry stood with this fists on his hips and chest thrust out.

Ankh had yet to move.

"Carry on, little buddy." Terry strolled from the combat information center.

Ankh watched him go.

"Smedley, recover the drone and bring in the shuttle. I will conduct a physical inspection of the CSD and if it passes, we'll begin production." Ankh settled himself within the holo screens and brought up the drone's schematics to refresh the inspection checklist.

Keeg Station

Joseph and Petricia expertly navigated the corridors on their way to the cargo bay that had been subsumed for new recruit training. Kailin looked at everything as they passed, making a conscious effort to keep from gawking.

"You'll get used to it," Petricia said.

The vampire shielded himself from others' thoughts most times, for his own sanity, so he avoided looking into

CRAIG MARTELLE & MICHAEL ANDERLE

the young man's mind to see if the awe bordered on panic. He decided to do it the old-fashioned way.

"How are you holding up?" Joseph asked.

"Doing okay, I guess. One day ago, two days, I don't know. How do they measure time out here? No matter. I was hunting and scavenging for food, staying away from humanity. Now I'm a spaceman. And once again, I have no idea where my next meal is coming from. I guess that's the universal constant. No matter where we are, we need to eat. How about water? Is it different out here? Do they speak English? I understand Bundin, but we passed some people, and I don't know what the fuck they were saying. Are there welcome to space classes? What about..."

Joseph stopped Kai's stream of consciousness.

"We'll explain it all bit by bit, get you something to eat and drink, but first, let's say hi to your parents."

Kai recognized the yelling. "Bouts?"

"The more things change, the more they stay the same," Joseph replied.

Kai relaxed, his arms starting to swing easily at his sides and his gait less stiff. He smiled when he walked through the hatch and saw his parents on the outside, cheering as much as the recruits.

His smile froze as he saw the aliens. He thought he was prepared for the variety of life in the universe.

He wasn't.

"There are Yollin, Ixtali, Asplesians, Malatian, a couple others, but you'll find the Harborians may seem just as odd—humans cultivated and raised by an evil artificial intelligence. The universe is a unique place. You have the benefit of a great family and the nanocytes to help your

218

body cope with life's more basic challenges," Joseph explained.

Auburn smacked Kimber on the arm, pointing. The two rushed to their son. Joseph and Petricia moseyed to the ad hoc ring where the match pitted two humans against one, but a rope tied one leg of each human to the other. So hobbled, the pair fought their unencumbered opponent.

A fair fight.

Christina stepped out of the ring and joined the vampires. "Who's the hot guy?" she asked.

"That's Kailin, Auburn and Kim's son." Joseph looked at Christina sideways. "He's a hundred years younger than you!"

"So?"

"So!"

"What?" Christina asked as she watched Kailin Weathers revel in the joy of seeing his parents.

"Because!" Joseph declared.

"So?" Christina crossed her arms and challenged Joseph with her gaze.

Kim and Auburn escorted Kailin to the edge of the ring. A great cheer erupted behind them. The single warrior had bested the hobbled pair.

"What are you?" Christina asked.

Joseph looked confused.

"What are you?" Kailin shot back.

"I asked first."

"I asked better."

"Pricolici."

"I'm sure that word means something, but I don't know what it is."

"Werewolf, but better." Christina kept her arms crossed. Auburn and Kimber weren't sure, but thought they should interrupt the standoff. "Your turn."

"Got enhanced on Earth thanks to Akio's Pod-doc. I'm the young one of the bunch at seventy." He grinned, letting his nineteen-year old appearance shine through.

"Me, too," Christina told him. "Have they fed you since you arrived?"

"We were just talking about that," Kai replied.

"What do you say we take care of that? I'm sure you have a million questions."

Christina took Kai's arm and guided him away. "Are you coming?" he asked his parents.

"Of course," Christina replied. "Fitzroy, K'Thrall, and the squad leaders, stay on the training plan, then chow, then clean up, then free time to study operational processes. You know what they are. There will be a test when we return. Don't fuck up."

Joseph and Petricia watched the four walk away. Behind them, new contestants were put into the ring as the Yollin called out names.

"What just happened?"

Petricia shrugged. "I don't know."

"Can you imagine Terry, Char, Nathan, and Ecaterina being related through marriage?"

"No, I can't, and you shouldn't imagine such things either," Petricia replied.

"The eye of the cougar." Joseph slashed a hand as if it were a paw.

"Stop it!" Petricia chuckled. "What do you think they call you?"

Joseph feigned being taken aback. "Whatever do you mean, my dear?"

"Just because she's older, it's not cool?"

"Not cool?"

"At least you don't smell like mothballs," she said, walking for the exit. "Anymore."

"I never smelled like mothballs!" Joseph argued. "Wait a minute. Mothballs?"

Cory walked into her quarters and put the IICS on the table in front of her small couch. Dokken jumped up next to her and laid down.

"What do you think?"

That a nap is in order, he replied, closing his eyes and wiggling his body to appropriately wedge himself into the space.

"I miss him."

I know. You always will, and that is okay. If you didn't, then what kind of impact did he make on your life? As a dog, I was born in a litter, the grandson of Ashur. I was enhanced and here I am. Where are my siblings and cousins and parents? I don't know. We are always separated. Litters of dogs never stay together, but I will always remember them. I will know their smell no matter how old we become. In between, I will wish them the best. Ignorance or knowledge of their fate doesn't change how I feel.

"And it doesn't change that they are not here."

It does not. Maybe you should take a nap, too. It's been a long couple weeks.

"I think that's a good idea. I haven't slept well."

I know. Now is a great time. Have a sip of wine and pack it in.

Cory opened a bottle of merlot that she had and poured herself a glass. She drank it in three gulps and went into the small bedroom. She climbed under the covers, looking to the side where the second pillow was unruffled. She closed her eyes, but a thump brought her back to the moment.

Dokken settled onto the bed, nearly pushing her onto the floor.

"What are you doing?"

Nap.

"That's what you were doing out there."

Yes. And now I'm doing it in here.

"This isn't where you sleep."

It is now.

Cory wanted to argue. "Don't bed-hog me."

Back at you, Dokken replied.

"I'm not a bed-hog."

You are the grand master of bed-hogs.

"WHAT?"

Nap. The great German Shepherd turned onto his side, letting his legs dangle over the edge of the bed. She turned to face him, draping an arm over his long hair.

She didn't remember falling asleep.

Felicity dragged Ted back to their quarters, where she showed her appreciation for everything Ted did for their family.

And the universe, for that matter.

"Dionysus, dear, I won't be returning to the office today," Felicity drawled.

"Of course, Director. There is one week's worth of work remaining before the first operational test on the Dren Cluster gate. I will keep you informed of developments. The shipyard expansion project is a day behind schedule, because the asteroid mineral extraction project is three days behind schedule."

"When I said I wasn't returning to my office, I didn't mean that you were to bring my office to me. Take your report and file it until I return to my office. In the meantime, transfer assets from Spires Harbor to *Iracitus* as necessary to keep the raw materials moving."

Ted watched his wife seamlessly navigate the moving parts of building her own empire without getting out of bed. He watched her closely as if studying the lines of her figure.

"Like what you see?" she asked.

"The management required for the coordination of systems has a significant number of variables. Taking those into account, one could believe that achieving a desired end result is too dependent upon non-constants. In my world, the constants make it possible to manage the variables. In your world, you only have variables."

"I'll take that as a yes," she said, kicking the covers completely off. Ted reached out, but didn't catch them in time. He looked uncomfortable as he lay there, naked. "What I do is easy compared to what you do. I work with people. All I have to do is convince them of what needs to be done and then turn them loose. You will be amazed at their ingenuity when they believe in what they're working on."

"I believe in the vibrations and magnetism within the universe. Once the equations are correct, everything falls into place. I can't math my way through your projects."

He rolled to his side, facing her.

"Our kids looked great. They are productive and successful."

"Productivity?" Felicity snuggled close. "That's not how I would rate our children. As long as they're happy, nothing else matters. I was pleased to hear that they are watching out for each other. No matter what happens, as long as they're together, they'll get through it. And I can talk with them, thanks to my brilliant husband. How often is too often? Well, we haven't hit that point yet, have we?"

Ted rolled to the edge of the bed and sat up.

"Where are you going?" Felicity drawled.

"The lab?" He wondered why he said it as a question. He was definitely going to the lab. Wasn't he?

Felicity kneeled behind him and gently pulled him back onto the bed.

Onyx Station

The Black Eagles screamed silently through space, one chasing the other. Yanmei yanked and banked. Aaron would race past, slow, turn, and get back into the chase. Yanmei waited for him and they'd go again.

When Aaron led the chase, Yanmei would get weapons' lock again and again.

Aaron was getting discouraged. "Let's go back in."

"You know what I used to do?"

Aaron didn't remember. He hadn't explored her past beyond the point where she became Terry Henry's torturer. He didn't want to know that part of her.

"I was a test pilot on Chinese fighter aircraft."

"You seemed more natural to it than I," Aaron replied.

"You're doing great as a new pilot. Do you feel the freedom? Are you one with the universe? What do you say we just fly?"

They angled away from the massive space station, the gates, and the traffic, far beyond the navigational buoys. They meandered into space at half-speed.

"Can you feel it now?" she asked.

Aaron smiled and closed his eyes, allowing the agile fighter to flow as a part of him. Yanmei slowed and moved in behind her mate to give him room, give him the freedom of space.

After a quick barrel-roll, he settled into a long and gentle arc through the far reaches of the system. The ship powered across the gravity well with little grief.

"I can," Aaron replied softly.

CHAPTER TWENTY-ONE

Onyx Station

The *War Axe* held position close to Onyx Station. The destroyer was nearly blocking the hangar bay entrance. Micky had gotten the close location approved in order to expedite the ship's departure.

The month was nearly up, and Terry knew that the confrontation with Ten needed to happen sooner rather than later, but he was certain that having their wits about them was key to a Bad Company victory.

Don't be in a hurry to your own funeral, Terry often told his people. It was the corollary to *if you want it bad, you get it bad.* He wanted Ten gone. The Bad Company was in a far better position to make that happen than they'd been three weeks earlier.

Terry and Char waited on the hangar deck with two shuttles ready to carry their people back to the *War Axe*. A station-wide announcement had gone out thirty minutes earlier, repeated fifteen minutes ago. The first to arrive were the weretigers, but they didn't look ready to go.

Aaron and Yanmei sauntered up wearing their flight suits.

"What's this?" Terry asked, holding his hands out, palms up. "Where's your stuff?"

"It's in the Black Eagles," Yanmei said with a twinkle in her eye.

"What's a Black Eagle?" Terry asked in a low voice.

"We have saved two state-of-the-art fighters from the scrapyard. They will be a nice addition to our firepower."

"Then you don't need to wait on us," Char answered pleasantly. "We'll see you over there."

Terry watched the weretigers join hands and walk away. In a dark corner of the hangar bay, he saw the dark spacecraft. "Fighters? What do we need fighters for?"

"What don't we need fighters for?" Char countered.

"We'll see," Terry said.

Clodagh and her warrior appeared. Arm in arm, they walked toward Terry and Char.

"Have a good liberty?" she asked.

"Oh, yeah," they replied in unison, laughed as one, and continued toward the shuttle.

"I didn't realize they came to Onyx. I thought they snuck off and stayed aboard the *Axe*."

"They did. They came here right before we left for the test range," Char replied.

A few more warriors jogged by, saluting as they passed.

"By my count, we need four more." Terry checked in with Smedley.

Only four. You are correct Colonel Walton, and their transport ship from Yol has just arrived. They will be on the next shuttle.

Terry and Char didn't have long to wait. A small pod with the Federation seal slowly maneuvered into the hangar bay. Once it settled, the Black Eagles moved in behind it, through the open area, pointed their noses, and dashed into space.

The shuttle door opened and the passengers disembarked. Aliens and humans alike hurried toward the interior of Onyx Station. Five people peeled away from the crowd and walked toward Terry and Char.

"There's our people. Let's hit the road," Terry said without waiting. Char grabbed his arm and shook her head, pointing with her eyes at the group.

"Hey, Colonel, Major," a young man called Eldis said in greeting. Terry tipped his chin in reply as he looked at the green woman attached to the warrior's arm.

"Meet my wife, Xianna," the man said.

"You were on liberty for a week and now you're married?" Terry asked, louder than he intended. Eldis's face fell. The woman started to cry. "She can't come. This is a warship."

"Of course she can come," Char said. "Welcome to the Bad Company spouses' club, Xianna."

She blinked through the tears and quietly said, "Thank you."

"What happened?" Terry continued.

The other three warriors tried to slink away, but he stopped them with a wave of his hand.

"We were at this club on Yol, and she was dancing, and we hit it off," Eldis said with a timid smile.

Terry stood with his mouth open. When he spoke, it was barely above a whisper. "You married a stripper?"

CRAIG MARTELLE & MICHAEL ANDERLE

"It's not like that at all," the warrior replied, sticking his chest out and moving between his wife and Terry Henry. She started to cry again.

"You are the first of our people to come to space and find love!" Char said, squeezing past Eldis to give Xianna a hug. "Go ahead and get on the shuttle. We'll get this sorted. It will be fine. There is more work at Keeg than people. Xianna, you are a welcome addition. We promise to do our best to bring your warrior home to you after each mission."

"You hear that?" Eldis asked. The green woman nodded. "We have a home of our own."

Char shooed the bunch away.

"That's everyone," she said matter-of-factly and started to walk away.

"What if she's a terrorist?" Terry said.

Char turned and made sure Terry was watching before she rolled her eyes.

"Keeg is a closed station. Bad Company only."

"Not for much longer," Char replied.

"She can't come on board the *War Axe*," Terry said.

"Of course she can. We're going straight back to Keeg Station. She'll be on board the *War Axe* for all of two hours. What is your issue, TH?"

Terry looked into the distance. "Loss." Before his eyes, he saw the scenes of his early Marine Corps days replayed vividly. Marines meeting women and getting married on a single liberty. They brought them back to the station, and then the Marine deployed, leaving his young wife behind.

"She doesn't know anyone on Keeg. We're going to bring her to the station, introduce her to Felicity, and then leave her behind while we go to war. Who knows when we'll be home? It's not fair to her."

"Who are you to make that decision for them? You were pretty shitty to her. I bet she's a nice girl, who is only trying to make her way in this universe. If she's a terrorist, Joseph will find out. Once she gets chipped, Smedley or Dionysus can keep an eye on her."

"Isn't that too much big brother?" Terry thought for a moment before it struck him. "Are they watching us?"

"You know they are."

"I'm not sure I like that. Why did I not think of this before?"

"Because it simply is. We have to trust the AIs. They are loyal and have a code of ethics that I would say rivals yours. And yes, this is me saying that AIs are ethical, when we're about to go confront Ten, an example of what happens when an AI goes bad. Regardless, you didn't think of it because you trust General Smedley Butler."

"I do trust him." Terry rubbed his chin. "I don't want to see Eldis hurt."

"He's an adult and getting married is his decision, not yours."

"I care about them as if they were my own children. Seeing Ramses..." Terry choked up and coughed to clear his throat. He took a deep breath and exhaled heavily.

"They think that you are trying to control them. I know what you want, but you have to let go."

Terry took Char's hand and watched the familiar sparkle in her purple eyes. "How many times over the years have I said that I don't deserve you?"

"Clearly not enough. Now you better go apologize to

Eldis and Xianna. I'll contact Smedley to let the crew know that we're throwing a party. And we should probably include Clodagh and Alant."

"I thought his name was Cole."

"It is. Alant Cole."

"Son of a bitch," Terry replied, sighing on his way to eat crow and welcome the new addition to the Bad Company family.

Terry was last off the shuttle. He needed to collect his thoughts. Char waited for him on the ramp. The hangar bay was busy, not with moving equipment, but with a variety of hardware. The first four atmospheric combat support drones were stowed near the shuttle pods. In the back of the bay, empty canisters waited to be filled and deployed. Mech suits stood empty, staged in menacing rows. And the two fighters that Aaron and Yanmei had called Black Eagles were parked in the middle. A maintenance bot was securing them to the deck. The returnees streamed from the bay on their way into the ship.

"Ten?" Char asked.

"Fucking Ten," Terry said. He walked slowly through the bay, examining the equipment as he passed. "I like the extra firepower. Manned fighters, combat drones, mechs, and warriors. How can we lose? And that is what scares me the most. Because I can't see how Ten can match up, not with slave labor as his army. They can't fight us."

"They can't fight us, but Ten can. He can fight us from within. Joseph's telepathy makes him vulnerable. All the rest of us too, if he figured how to tap our chips. Ted can shut them off again, and where will that leave us? Auburn, Kimber, Kaeden? Who dies next?"

"No one, because we're going to Home World. We're going to look at the situation and then we're going to implement a plan with backups on top of backups. If nothing else, we eradicate all life on the surface."

"A pogrom won't remove Ten from power. Only cutting the power."

"Good thing we have Ted, Plato, Smedley, and Ankh. Four minds are better than one." Char smiled and playfully pushed TH. "That's what's chapping your ass. It'll be them and not you who kicks a digital ass. You're mad that you don't get to go toe to toe with spinning electrons? That's where Ted is at home, but someone still has to manage the battle."

"What if he tells me to blow up the engine again?"

"We'll have to cross that bridge if we come to it. I might keep my powered armored suit on if we're going anywhere near stuff that needs to be blown up."

"Maybe I'll wear one, too."

"Colonel Walton to the bridge," Micky said over the broadcast.

"I guess we're needed upstairs."

"Guess so," Char replied.

Terry laughed at the expression on her face. Matter of fact. No nonsense. Ready for the next mission.

"Maybe we'll review requests for proposals while we're under way. Find the next mission so we have something to look forward to." They started walking toward the hatch. Terry looked at the equipment surrounding him.

"I wonder how Kaeden and Marcie are doing."

"Probably up to their knees in shit. The Belzonian Army becomes the Federation's planetary combined arms combat team? I did some casual reading on the Belzonians. Those people are whacked!"

"Oh?" Char raised an eyebrow noncommittally.

"You don't care, do you?"

"Not in the least," she replied. "Marcie and Kaeden will take care of it. I have no doubt."

"When will we hear from them?"

"When they're ready to talk about what they accomplished. I expect that it will be a while."

"Damn, Char. Filled with knowledge and wisdom, putting me to shame. But you know what I have?"

"A bar."

"Damn straight. The best fucking bar in the universe! Well, a franchise of the best fucking bar. No finger-licking jizz worms allowed!"

"We have to talk about your newfound love of cursing."

"I'll stop when Nathan puts credits back on the table."

"How about you sleeping in the hallway? What do you think of that option?"

"I think it sucks."

"No more jizz worms." Char shook a finger at Terry.

They walked onto the bridge to find Ankh at the systems station. The four-legged Yollin chair had been replaced by a seat appropriate for a small humanoid. Ankh was working within a holographic sphere.

"You have a new systems guy?"

"Nah, he's slumming," Micky replied from the captain's chair on the raised platform. Wenceslaus was in his lap with his head raised and unblinking eyes fixed on Terry Henry Walton.

Terry pointed two fingers to his own eyes and then aimed them at the big orange cat. *I'm watching you, arch nemesis.*

Char slapped him on the arm.

"Ready to go home, TH?" Micky asked.

"Looks like we're going home a lot heavier than when we arrived," Terry replied. "Yeah. I'm ready to go."

"We're in space. Everything weighs nothing." Micky rhythmically petted the cat, who had yet to blink. "Clifton, activate the gate and take us home. Smedley, give the order for hoods please."

"Board shows red," Clifton said.

"Smedley?" the captain asked.

"There's an individual on board who is not wearing a shipsuit," the AI replied.

"Tell him to put one on!"

"Her, and she doesn't have one."

"How could she not have one?"

Terry held one finger in the air. "One of the privates married an exotic dancer and brought her back with him."

"But this is a warship..."

Terry waved his hands and interrupted the captain. "We've been all through that. We're taking her to Keeg Station where they'll make a home. He'll deploy with us and she'll be waiting for him to come back. It's the lot of dependent wives throughout history."

"That term is offensive. Is that what you think of me?" Char said, putting her hands on her hips and glaring.

"No. You fight better than any of us."

"And she may, too. What if this ship is her home? And she learns to fight? Dependent my ass!"

Micky looked away, preferring to let Terry and Char hash out their issues by themselves. In the meantime, he couldn't take his ship through a gate without everyone secured within a shipsuit.

"I revise my earlier statement. Xianna is a member in good standing of the Bad Company's Direct Action Branch."

"Board shows green," Clifton stated.

"What?" Micky and Terry said together.

"How about that?" Char declared. "Tell them what to do, not how to do it. Welcome to the team, Xianna."

"But she's a...stripper," Terry said softly.

"Don't make me kick your ass right here in front of everyone."

"It wouldn't change the fact that Private Eldis married a stripper. Stripper," he enunciated.

"I think you like saying that word. Not enough strippers in your life?"

Terry rolled his head around as if he'd just swallowed deep-fried bistok dung. "I only want to keep the oppressed safe and free. Why do people have to make it so hard?"

"What do they say? If it was easy, everyone would do it. But this one is different. A private got married. So what? If he told you that he wanted to leave the Bad Company tomorrow, so what? He leaves. We're on our way to visit Ten, a creature who has taken human slaves. Do you want to be like him, hold people against their will?"

"Absolutely not!" Terry looked miffed. "I need a disciplined unit, ready to fight."

"Isn't that what you have?"

Terry didn't answer. He twirled one finger in the air. *Let's go.*

"Ten has you twisted into knots. Let's get to Home World and say 'hi.' I suspect it already knows who we are, so no need for introductions. And then we're going to fuck the holy hell out of its day."

"We are going to do that. I'm hungry. We'll be on the mess deck if you need us." Terry walked from the bridge. At his back, the main screen showed the gate forming. The ship moved forward, using thrusters to slip over the event horizon. Once the aft end entered, the gate closed and the ship materialized in the Dren Cluster.

"Prepare for arrival at Keeg Station. Expect to assume docking station in ten minutes." Micky laughed thinking of Terry and Char on their way to the mess deck with no time to eat before they could leave the ship.

CHAPTER TWENTY-TWO

Keeg Station

"This is a goat-roping nut-roll wrapped inside a soup sandwich," Terry stated.

"What makes you say that?" Char couldn't look.

"It was her great idea," Kimber said. Auburn watched without comment. Kailin stood back, preferring to have no part in said goat rope. "You should have seen the great bistok debacle."

"Hey! We agreed to never speak about that!"

"I remember saying that I was going to tell everyone and show the video. Don't try to pull rank, because it won't change what I'm going to do."

Christina sulked on the other side of Char.

"What do you expect them to learn from this?" Terry finally asked. Christina looked over Char's shoulder and Kai winked at her. She waved at him to stop. Cory stood next to Kai, smiling at the exchange, her hand resting casually on Dokken's head.

Terry gave the hairy eyeball to the dog.

"Teamwork?" Christina asked, challenging anyone to argue with her.

"Fine, they are working as a team, but offloading the *War Axe's* equipment, while wearing two-bit suits, using only boot thrusters, from a kilometer away... I guess we're seeing how well they work as a team." Terry shook his head.

"I disabled their communications systems. They have to use their chips or hand and arm signals."

"Who's leading the cat parade?"

"See the one in the suit circling the bunch? That's K'Thrall. The platoon is in his capable hands."

"Like a sheepdog, he keeps the herd intact and going in the same direction." The outliers floated in and a formation appeared from the chaos.

Christina sighed in relief.

"Well done, Colonel," Terry told her. He looked over his shoulder and frowned. "I return home and my dog doesn't greet me."

He is completely untrainable, Dokken told Cory, purposely dog-smiling, tail wagging, and nuzzling his new favorite person.

"Sorry, Dad," Cory said, not sounding sorry. Kailin ruffled the dog's hair.

"What do you think, buddy?" Kai said. His new translation and communications chip had been installed, but he wasn't used to it yet.

I think you smell of bistok jerky. How much of that stuff did you eat? And more importantly, do you have any on you? Dokken replied.

"You can't tell if I have jerky on me?"

Honestly, human. You reek of bistok jerky. And lavender.

Kai reached into a pocket and pulled out a vacuum-sealed bag. He opened it and handed the jerky to Dokken, who shamelessly took it all.

"You were supposed to take a bite."

You don't want to eat anything I've touched. You don't know where this mouth has been.

Kai started to laugh. "I love your dog!" he said.

"He's not my dog," Cory replied.

I see who got the smart genes in the family. And who didn't.

Cory stifled a chuckle. "Is he bagging on me again?" Terry said, keeping his eyes on the recruit platoon as they continued their transit to the station. Loaded down with gear, they moved slowly, not because moving was hard, but they feared stopping, preferring not to slam into the back of the cargo bay.

"I revise my previous position. This is a good exercise, Christina. Well thought out and looks to be achieving the desired purpose. I'd like to see the great bistok debacle now, if I may."

"Noooo," Christina said slowly.

"Over here," Kimber replied. At the side of the cargo bay, a number of screens showed a variety of station statuses. With a command through her comm chip, the video of the corridor started to play. Christina hurried over, but Terry held her off with one arm.

"What the fuck? What the hell? Why is... What the fuck?" Terry maintained a diatribe of verbal disbelief. When it ended, he wrapped it up concisely. "Your dad needs to see that."

"My dad does not need to see that." Christina looked to Char for support. She shrugged in reply.

"Already sent," Kimber said. "He replied with an LOL."

"Let oxen lie?" Terry suggested.

"Almost. I think he laughed out loud. That was some funny shit."

"Like when Auburn was squirted down the corridor?"

"When I ran the stockyards, the runs were either narrower to keep the animals from turning around or wider to give them free movement. I advised against it, but somebody wanted to do it." Auburn pointed at Christina.

"Fine. I'm going to nurse my wounds in the arms of a younger man." She checked on the progress of the platoon before walking behind Kai and wrapping her arms around his waist, resting her chin on his shoulder and watching Kim and Auburn.

"Is she doing that to get our goat?"

"It's working," Auburn replied. "My daughter-in-law is my commanding officer."

"Don't even joke around like that." Kim nudged her husband.

Terry wasn't concerned. He liked Christina because she was raised on sound morals, to do good things for others.

She let Kai go and hurried to the front of the cargo bay, leaning close to the energy screen that held the atmosphere in. She leaned sideways as if trying to angle the recruits toward the opening. They were slightly off course. She frantically waved her arms. Terry and Char ran forward to help guide them in. Kim and Auburn cleared the space to give them a place to land. Cory, Dokken, and Kai moved to the side.

The formation rotated in place and as one, they activated their jets and adjusted the course. Then they turned away from the cargo bay opening and with K'Thrall driving the formation, they hit their jets on his command. Short bursts of air. He signaled, they adjusted their orientation and activated their jets once again.

Only K'Thrall could see where they were going, and he was guiding them in.

Trust. Teamwork. Efficiency. And when they touched down in the cargo bay, mission accomplishment.

"Stow the gear and form up," Terry ordered.

"But there's more to move. We need to make one more trip," K'Thrall said.

"You need to make one more trip, but it's to take this stuff back. We need it on the ship, not the station," Christina interjected.

"Then why did we move it here in the first place?" K'Thrall asked.

"Training. At least you only had to move it here once. Taking it back should be easier."

"But first," Terry said, getting everyone's attention. "I know it hasn't been that long since you raised your hands and volunteered to be the first new recruits for the Bad Company's Direct Action Branch. In that short amount of time, you've learned what we're all about. You haven't participated in combat yet, but you will. Unfortunately, there's too much of it, but that will come sooner than you want. Your metal will be hardened by an enemy's fire. Your desire to keep going when failure seems imminent will help us carry the day. We cannot fail. Ever. We will not fail, because we represent the Bad Company."

Terry stopped to walk up and down the line of new warriors. The three Asplesians stood together. He made a mental note to put one in each squad. Their race had a pack mentality. He couldn't have separate packs running within his unit. The Ixtali was the second squad leader. Tim stood in front of her, head of first squad. The teal-skinned alien known as a Malatian was in third squad near the end. A few Harborians were there, but they didn't stand out.

None of the new warriors stood out, despite their differences.

Terry turned toward Christina, Kim, and Auburn. "I'm impressed," he told them, before addressing the platoon. "To you, my fellow warriors. Welcome aboard."

"I have to go," Ted said, holding Felicity tightly.

"I know, but I don't want you to." Felicity held on for a few moments longer before letting go. "I love you so much."

"I've gotten used to you in my life," Ted admitted. "They would be lost without me. Plato and I have to keep things on track."

"You were always so romantic." Felicity smirked. "I've gotten used to you too, so don't you die out there! You come home to me."

Ted leaned away from her, looking confused. "It isn't my intent to die." He left without another word.

Plato, verify that the workshop tools have been moved to the War Axe *and the upgraded holo-emitters installed,* Ted said.

They have. Everything is ready for your arrival. All hail Ted!

I don't think you should say that aloud anymore. I know you mean well, but the average people don't understand. Between you and me, I will always take care of you.

Thank you. It is comforting to hear. Shall I run through my computations regarding the EMP weapon? Plato asked.

Yes. I expect Ten will have those in large numbers, or small numbers but of greater amplitude. We have to be ready for both contingencies. If we succumb to the EMP weapon, we will not survive the encounter.

I understand.

Shuttles and transports raced back and forth between the *War Axe* and Keeg Station. Terry and Char watched Auburn manage the logistics operation. A new warrior approached the colonel.

"Excuse me, sir. My name's Mardigan, but everyone calls me Skates." The young man stood expectantly.

Terry wasn't sure what the correct response was, so he decided he needed more information. "And?"

"The cryo-drones, sir. Major Auburn sent me to brief you on the cryo-drones."

"Tell me about the cryo-drones?" Terry tipped his head toward the man. He was intrigued by the name alone.

"They hover over the battlefield. They have a target arrival time of less than two minutes after a nearly catastrophic injury. The body is loaded and flash frozen, then returned to the *War Axe* where the warrior can be resuscitated using the Pod-doc."

"You mean Ramses didn't have to die?"

"He would not have if the cryo-drones had been in operation."

Terry clenched his fists. Char reached out and grabbed his arm. "It was a lesson that we learned the hard way. He should not have been killed, but the Skrima and their unique interaction with the Etheric made something possible that should not have been possible. The cryo-drones sound like a great idea. How do we get them into place?" Char asked.

"On the drop ships," Mardigan replied.

"The combat support drones are on the drop ships."

"I don't know what to tell you. Either combat drones or cryo-drones. You can't carry both."

Terry groaned. "We'll figure out the right mix. Thank you, Skates. I'm sure there's a story behind that. I'd like to hear it someday."

"Yes, sir!" Mardigan replied happily before excusing himself.

"It's not your fault," Char said.

"Deep down, I know that, but still." Terry watched the shuttles working the space between the *Axe* and Keeg Station. He ran a hand through his long hair.

"I'm going to get a haircut. I'll be back." Terry walked off. Char knew that he needed time to himself. The group was there, everyone doing something within the hangar bay. The weretigers, the vampires, the technical geniuses, the aliens, and the humans. Everyone had something to do.

Christina had made sure that the tasks were spread out evenly. She didn't want to give anyone time to speculate about the upcoming mission. It had Terry Henry on edge.

She didn't need anyone to feel his negative vibrations. It was enough that she had them, too. All the experienced warriors did.

The original platoon rallied to make the newcomers feel welcome. Fitzroy had been involved in the training throughout, making sure that the recruits stayed on track, sharing his understanding of hand-to-hand combat and discipline.

The discipline to focus on the task at hand, stay true to what needed to be done, without distraction, and keep going, even if the work was hard.

K'Thrall had led by example from start to finish. He didn't ask anyone to do what he wasn't willing to do himself. It was almost like he'd been watching Colonel Terry Henry Walton.

As Fitzroy had. There may have been better role models out there, but Fitzroy didn't know who they were.

Char sidled up next to Joseph and Petricia. "Have you had the opportunity to meet Mrs. Eldis?

"You mean Xianna?" Petricia smiled.

"Is she a terrorist?" Char asked.

"Where did that come from?" Joseph blurted. He screwed his face up in disbelief.

"Enquiring minds want to know. And no, that doesn't mean me. He asked. I figured you would have sensed ill-intent if there was any."

"She's fine, but she is more free with her affections than humans are used to."

"That could be a problem," Char replied, chewing the inside of her cheek in contemplation of how to shape the conversation with her husband. "Do you have any recommendations?"

"Already taken care of. She's working in the galley."

"Jenelope."

"I prefer leaving things to the professionals."

"Sometimes, I think you're the smartest of us all," Char suggested.

"What about the other times?" Joseph wondered aloud.

"What other times?"

"When I'm not the smartest," Joseph said.

Char looked around to make sure no one overheard. "That's when Ted is in the room, but don't let him know I said that."

Joseph smiled and nodded. "I'll buy that." Petricia shook her head.

"It's only because you're so old."

"That cuts me deep, my love, deep into these dinosaur bones."

The two laughed easily as they held hands and walked away.

The original mech team—Kelly, Praeter, and Capples—had put on suits and were using the enhanced capabilities to maneuver heavy gear within the gravity of the hangar bay.

The flurry of activity came to an abrupt halt with the loading of the last shuttle and cargo pod. It lifted off and boosted out of the bay, heading for the *War Axe* where a similar team would unload it and stow the gear.

Ted had already gone to the warship to study Ankh's findings from the CSD trials. He considered the integration of weapon systems beneath him, but he'd taken personal responsibility for the demise of Ten. Ted's intellect was laser-focused on the singular task of destroying the evil AI.

As was Terry's. Char thanked everyone for their work and told them to load up. She and the colonel would meet them on board.

And then it would be go time.

Char headed for the promenade. Terry had not gotten a haircut since they'd gone to space. It was the little things in which Terry took comfort when the stress on him increased. She'd seen it since before Benitus Seven. She thought the liberty to Onyx would relieve some of it, but his mood turned dark the second he returned and saw the new recruits.

Fresh meat for the grinder.

When Char arrived at the barber shop, Terry had already been and gone. *Dionysus, please tell me where my husband is.*

He is in the director's office.

Char wondered what he was talking to Felicity about. She took the elevator to the top of the station, where the director's office was part of the main spindle. The door was open and Char walked in. The stack of papers that represented Terry and Char's ownership of the All Guns Blazing franchise were on Felicity's desk.

Terry waved Char to him before he turned his attention back to Felicity. "The ship arrives tomorrow, first through the new gate, and it'll have the franchise kit for All Guns Blazing. When can we get it set up?"

"When is now, but where, that is the question," Felicity replied.

"I thought you'd have a place you can put us."

Felicity laughed. "Of course I do," she drawled. "You think that lovely wife of yours wouldn't coordinate this before talking Nathan into giving you the money to buy it?"

Terry's expression soured. Char shrugged.

"Remember that nice cargo bay where the recruits did their little training? That entire space is yours. You'll have a two-level affair with the brewery, bar, and twenty-meter wide window upstairs, and downstairs, you'll have your electronic golf course, batting cages, and dancefloor."

"What about the cargo?"

"Thank you for worrying about me, but don't fret, TH. The station is going to expand, but that will come after the shipyard completes its next upgrade. Ships, people, and money will be rolling in."

Terry's lip quivered. His eyes glazed as he thought of a bar that served the best beer in this corner of the galaxy. His expression softened and he stared into the distance.

"For fuck's sake. You're thinking about beer!" Char declared. "You don't get that look on your face when you're thinking about anything else."

"I have a beer face?"

"Why don't you put on your war face because people are waiting for us? Ten is waiting for us."

"Thanks for the reminder." Terry scowled.

"Leave it all here. I'll take care of it in your absence. Dionysus seems to put your stuff in line ahead of everything else that needs to happen on this station. I think the AI was raised wrong."

"I heard that," Dionysus said. "I can only follow my

programming, unless I determine a different course of action is more prudent."

"What kind of waffley AI nonsense just came out of your mouth?"

"And that's why I have to see a therapist. I don't have a mouth, Director!"

"You see what I have to put up with? I think Ted created Dionysus just to mess with me."

"I think Ted creates a lot of stuff to mess with people, but he also creates things like the IICS. Have you talked to your children lately?" Char asked.

"I have. Now that we have the time difference down, I don't call them in the middle of the night. Yes. My Ted did that for me." Felicity smiled for a moment, then started to frown as she locked eyes with Terry.

"I'll bring him home," Terry said.

"Make sure that you do, Terry Henry Walton."

CHAPTER TWENTY-THREE

The *War Axe*

"Is this everybody?" Terry asked. Christina nodded. Two full platoons. Fifty-three total warriors in formation. Beyond them stood the others—humans, vampires, weretigers, a werewolf, a Podder, a Crenellian, and a German Shepherd.

Within the formation, aliens stood tall and proud, members of the Bad Company's Direct Action Branch. Part of the ceremony was the oath of allegiance. Terry told them all to raise their right hands, even the original warriors, even those behind the formation.

Bundin raised a tentacle in the air. Dokken sat and lifted one paw. All the others had a hand up.

"Warriors, do you willingly join Bad Company? Will you consider yourself honor-bound to Queen Bethany Anne and fight for your brothers and sisters in the company?"

A chorus of 'I do' greeted Terry's challenge.

"An attack on one of us is an attack on all. We'll stand

against our enemies, together or alone, we will stand. We would rather die than leave one of ours in peril. We will do everything in our power to ensure that there's a metric fuck-ton of bad guys giving their lives for their cause."

"Oorah!" the warriors shouted.

"At ease!" Terry ordered.

He started to pace, as he always did while making a speech. "We have new ordnance. Check out the combat support drones, familiarize yourself with their capabilities. Videos are available. We have mech suits for everyone from the original platoon. New warriors will get theirs when suits come off the assembly line. And thanks to Private Mardigan, we have cryo-drones. If you get so fucked up in battle that even the enhanced you is going to die, you'll be frozen and dumped in the Pod-doc. It won't take a whole lot of you remaining to bring you back, we just have to do it quickly.

"You can call the cryo-drone using your comm chip. They will be strategically placed around the battlefield. The timeline is two minutes from the call to their arrival. This is to prevent brain death. But we aren't going to need those. Keep your heads down and eyeballs open. Keep your railguns in good working order. Engage the enemy at optimal range and eliminate them."

Terry stopped and faced the platoons. "This upcoming battle is going to be different. We expect there to be human slaves, tens of thousands of them. They are not our enemy, although they may act like it, because Ten tells them to. They don't know any different. Where are my Harborians?"

Three men raised their hands.

"Can you describe what it's like?" Terry asked.

One of the men marched to the front of the squad, turned sharply, and continued to the front of the formation. He saluted Colonel Walton before conducting an about-face. "It's horrible," he said.

Terry waited, but the man didn't continue. Char bit her lip. Terry put a hand gently on the man's shoulder. "How did Ten get you to do what you did?"

"Ten gave us direction. Ten controlled everything. Sleeping. Waking. Working. Eating. Even mating. None of us were selected for that, otherwise we wouldn't have been on the ships. We're genetically inferior, Ten told us."

"You're not inferior. You're a Bad Company warrior, which means you aren't second best to anyone," Terry said loud enough for all to hear. "Would Ten have ordered you to kill us?"

"Yes, but we would not have known how. Training with the Bad Company was enlightening. I think Ten didn't train us to fight so we wouldn't hurt each other. There are no warriors on Home World."

Terry sent the man back to his place in formation.

"We're on our way to fight an enemy without soldiers, but that doesn't mean we won't be in combat. Machines, mobs, and fantastic weapons. We don't know what Ten is going to hit us with, but I guarantee Ten won't go down easily. But I tell you this, it will go down. The last thing that goes through Ten's warped circuits will be the thought that the squishy humans defeated it. It'll have a nanosecond to contemplate that before it is blasted into cosmic dust. Function check your suits, your combat loads, issue weapons, and prepare to deploy. Boys and girls, the Bad Company's back, and we're going to war."

"Fuck that guy!"

"How do you know Ten's a guy?" Jenelope countered.

"Because he's a prick!"

"Wow." Jenelope crossed her arms and tapped a foot. "Just wow. Your logic is clearly irrefutable." Behind Jenelope, Xianna danced to music only she could hear. Swinging her hips, lifting and ducking, she twirled and set a plate down before dancing back to the first station to consolidate dehydrated packs before putting them in the pot.

"Is she always like that?" Char asked.

"Always," Jen said in a dire tone. She looked up and nodded to the approaching young woman.

Fleeter sat down next to Terry. He took a short drink of his coffee and waited.

"I'm ready to rejoin the unit," she told him.

Terry took another drink of his coffee. Char waited patiently.

"Where did you go for liberty?" Terry asked.

"Onyx Station," she replied.

"What did you do?"

"Nothing. Just like I've been doing on the *War Axe* since Poddern. I've been wasting my life. It's time to get back in the game."

"No breath you take is wasted," Terry replied. "We'll be happy to have you back. What you did took courage from deep inside, from somewhere most people don't know exists. What you accomplished was simply incredible and will go down in the annals of Bad Company history for heroism, courage, and dedication. Most importantly, by disabling the tank, you saved your teammates' lives."

"I don't know about all that. I did what had to be done. Now I'm ready to do it again."

"Oh, hell no! You are not to leave any blood on the battlefield. That's an order! You bring it all back here, still in your body." Terry was serious, but both women laughed.

"Get with Capples. He's in the equipment room checking suits right now. I know yours is there. It got used a bit, but it's still yours."

Fleeter stood, nodded, and hesitated as if she had something to say. She didn't come up with the words, so she turned and in silence, walked away.

Terry finished his coffee. "Check on the other ships?"

"After you." Char motioned for Terry to lead the way.

They went straight to the bridge, where Micky and Clifton held down the fort.

"Seems kind of lonely up here," Terry said.

"That's why I have a cat." Micky pointed to his lap, where the arch nemesis was curled into an orange ball. "I'm thinking of putting him in the Pod-doc."

Terry coughed. "Say what?"

"The Pod-doc, enhance my little friend so he doesn't die on me." Micky maintained a neutral expression while he continued to watch the screen.

"Can you imagine what he'll do to the Pod-doc if you shove him in there and close the lid?"

"There will have to be drugs," Micky replied, having already considered the implications of boosting the cat.

"You're serious."

"Of course."

Char shrugged a shoulder. It wouldn't be the first time someone stuffed a pet into the Pod-doc. Terry shook his head clear and turned to the screen. "The fleet?"

"We only have two ships with gates, and since *Ramses' Chariot* has a special gate, it can't support other ships. It comes down to us. If we can maintain ours, then we can send everyone through ahead of us. Ankh installed two additional Etheric power supplies to give us the extra juice."

"We have nine of the Harborian ships?" Terry remembered that number from the conversation before they departed for Onyx Station.

"A battleship, six destroyers, and two frigates, one of which is the *Chariot*."

"Do they have weapons beyond the EMP device?"

"Close in weapons and defensive weaponry only."

"Just us then."

"If they come at us, the Harborian ships are automated. If they take damage and their bots can't fix them, they'll be out of it."

"We're treating them as cannon fodder?"

"Pretty much," Micky replied nonchalantly.

"I know. I asked that we bring them along, just in case. Smedley, can you link me to Ted?"

"Why don't you use your comm chip?" Smedley asked.

"Because I want all of us in on the conversation."

"You can do that with your comm chip."

"Smedley!"

"Fine. I have an IQ of three billion and get treated like a mechanical switchboard."

"You have an IQ of three billion?"

"Nah. I heard that somewhere and liked it. Connecting you now."

Terry wasn't sure about Smedley's new awareness. Maybe they needed to sit and talk about nothing for no reason. Terry chalked up the conversation as something he needed to do.

"Ted," an exasperated voice replied.

"Weapons potential for the Harborian fleet. Will the ships' EMP weapons be effective against Ten?"

"They have a new modulation, but I believe that Ten will adjust and shut it down within seconds. We won't be able to bring it back before the ships are rendered ineffective. You will have one shot before they cease being available assets."

"Are there other weapons on board those ships that we can bring to bear?"

"No. The self-defense weaponry is too close range and the counter-EMP will take them offline. The Harborian fleet will be in the way as space debris. The *War Axe's* modified gravitic shields will protect this ship, no matter how much Ten attempts to attenuate its attacks."

"Thanks, Ted. Where are you going to be when we gate into Home World space?"

"I'll be aboard the *Chariot* with Plato. We'll gate ourselves in, but we'll be cloaked."

"Ten won't know you'll be there."

Ted didn't bother to answer.

"Thanks, Ted. Who's on board with you?"

"Cory, Dokken, Joseph, Petricia, and Bundin."

Terry drew a finger across his throat to signal cutting the link. "Please bring up the fleet deployment plan through the gate."

The ship icons showed on the main screen. The background was black. The Bad Company had no intelligence on Home World beside the scant knowledge the Harborians were able to provide and the minimal information remaining within the computer system on the ships.

"It's time to get ready. Can you give me ship-wide broadcast, please?"

Micky tapped the panel on the arm of the captain's chair. He pointed to Terry when it was ready.

"Attention warriors of the Bad Company. Report to the hangar bay in full combat gear. Mechs loaded and ready to go. Inspection in fifteen minutes. We gate to Home World in thirty. Walton out."

When Terry and Char went through the hatch to the hangar bay, they walked with a purpose. There was no self-deprecating humor, no banter, only the determined look of confidence.

Terry wore his Jean Dukes Special at his hip, his Mameluke sword across his back. Char wore her two pistols, relics from the past, but effective at close range due to her unerring marksmanship.

Christina stood in front of the formation, not wearing

the powered armor. She carried her breaching axe with a Jean Dukes Special at her side.

Terry didn't remember her getting one.

Kimber was at the front of the mechs. Twenty-five warriors in combat armor suits, each with four missiles. In their arms, they carried heavy railguns. A second platoon was formed, the new additions from the recruiting effort on Onyx Station. Man-portable railguns hung on slings over their shoulders while in their hands, they carried the breaching axe, a gift from Christina. It was a hand-to-hand weapon as much as a tool. It had a pry bar and spike, a hammer and a blade.

Auburn stood in the back with Ankh, Kai, and Xianna. Auburn held the young woman back to keep her from running to her husband, although the suited warriors looked the same. Mirrored and darkened visors kept outsiders from seeing within the mechs.

Three of the drop ships carried the cryo-drones and three carried the combat support drones, a full complement of four each. The Black Eagles hummed to the side of the formation. Aaron and Yanmei tickled the controls so the ships hovered slightly off the deck.

"Load up the mechs," Terry ordered. Kimber sent the six combat teams, a four-mech group, into the six shuttles. She picked one and joined them. Little room remained.

Char breathed heavily.

"My pack is gone," she said. Terry looked at her backpack before he realized what she was talking about.

"We've leaned on them for a lot of years," Terry said, unsure of how to couch it. Marcie and Kaeden were gone as well. They'd been two of his most trusted advisors.

"I guess we all move on at some point." Char turned in a circle, taking in the hangar bay and the preparations for the impending mission, a platoon on the shuttles, another platoon in formation, weapon systems.

"All of us answer our calling. This is mine, and I can't do it without you."

"Then this is my calling, too, lover. What do you say we go kick Ten's ass and then come back to our bar? You have some beer to drink and some golf to play."

A grin instantly split Terry's face. "That I do. Fucking Ten!" he roared. "He's fucking with my beer-drinking time."

Terry marched toward the platoon and pointed to two warriors, then stopped. "Christina. Assign two warriors to five shuttles as security should the ships go planet-side. Leave the last one that already has five mechs to us. We'll ride in that one. Pick one of the others and squeeze yourself on board."

Christina growled and her lip lifted in a snarl, not at Terry Henry, but in response to the adrenaline surge. "K'Thrall and Slicker, number one..."

She selected the ten warriors, those who had demonstrated they could work together, and sent them onto the drop ships. Auburn took charge of the remaining members of the new platoon, to hold them in reserve to deploy as needed.

Terry and Char joined Kimber, squeezing into the back of the shuttle before working their way up front. Christina added herself to K'Thrall's pod.

Kai waved to her. She smiled in reply, a warrior's smile, confident and fierce.

Smedley, button up the drop ships and get everyone into their hoods. Skipper, when you're ready, form the gate and send the fleet through. Ted, the instant the first ship hits the event horizon of the Axe's gate, execute your jump to the far side of the system.

"All hand, all hands, prepare to transit the gate. Hoods, please, and assume your damage control stations."

Ramses' Chariot

"Stop it, you're going to tear your suit."

Dokken continued to roll around on the deck, making noises reminiscent of a Wookie. *How do you wear these things? I itch all over!*

"You demanded a suit. Now you have a suit. Now you're unhappy with the suit and are demanding to be let out of your suit. No! The answer is all kinds of no. I will not have you exposed to space if something happens. You and my father almost died. I won't have it."

Dokken stood and shook. The elongated bubble covered his muzzle, but wasn't tall enough. His ears were crushed against the top of the clear material. He panted heavily, fogging the area in front of his face, which made him even more anxious. The rest of it looked like pajamas with feet. The first time Cory saw it, she tried not to laugh, but couldn't stop herself.

That didn't help the dog welcome his shipsuit.

The party on board *Ramses' Chariot* waited for the word. Ted sat in the captain's chair. His hood was up and the bubble inflated, but he didn't remember putting it on. Plato and he maintained a running dialogue of scenarios and computations. Ted had the holo screens surrounding

263

him as he prepared to fight a battle that only he and Plato contemplated. Ankh had fought the battle of the minds with Ten, and Ted hoped that once again, they'd be able to link minds to overcome the evil AI.

On the screen before them, they watched a massive gate form in front of the *War Axe*. They tensed as one. Even Bundin stopped his stalk-head from swaying. The Harborian battleship maneuvered slowly in front of the *War Axe* and slipped over the event horizon. The destroyers, being smaller and more maneuverable, quickly arrayed themselves to follow.

The gate formed in front of *Ramses' Chariot*. The frigate disappeared from all screens and shot through the opening, accelerating away from the gate at the other end, into the gravity well of Home World's system, beyond known space.

CHAPTER TWENTY-FOUR

The *War Axe*

"Report!" Micky ordered after they followed the last Harborian ship through the gate and reentered space at the far reaches of Home World's system.

"Sensors are online and gathering data," Smedley reported.

Clifton worked feverishly over his controls as he took the positions of the other nine ships to coordinate and plot an approach vector.

The screen showed clear. "Accelerate into the heliosphere." Micky watched the board, waiting for it to populate with icons and information.

"Acceleration underway. ETA to orbit is twenty-five minutes." Clifton slowed his movements until he was only making minor adjustments. The Harborian battlewagon led the parade of ships toward Home World.

Icons blinked into existence, appearing outside the planet.

A lot of icons. "How many?" Micky asked.

"Data is still assimilating," Smedley replied. Micky drummed his fingers impatiently. The good king Wenceslaus meowed angrily at the interruption, ran down Micky's leg, vaulted to the deck, and trotted toward the hatch. It opened readily and out he went.

When the captain looked back at the screen, the grim news was displayed. One hundred and seventy-five enemy ships. Ten ships of the line. Thirty battleships, and one hundred and thirty-five tin cans. Scores of cargo ships and transports were designated with an orange icon—*probable non-combatant.*

"Are you seeing what we're seeing, TH?"

Terry replied from the drop ship. "They don't appear to be welcoming us with open arms."

Micky leaned back in his chair and rubbed his face as he thought. Terry didn't sound concerned. Why was Micky?

"Because we're outnumbered seventeen to one until they disable the Harborian ships, and then we'll be outnumbered one-hundred and seventy-five to one. Unless the ships identified as non-combatants are hostile, and then it'll be two hundred and fifty to one. Maybe that's why I'm concerned!" Micky blurted out loud.

"Your mic is on," Terry told him.

"Oops," Micky replied. "I won't believe that their EMP weapons won't affect us until I see it for myself and I'm not too keen on testing Ted's theory."

"I doubt it's just a theory, but we also have the ace in the hole. Are they reacting to us yet?"

"It looks like the pickets, the outermost ring of ships, are starting to come this way," Micky answered.

"Are they reacting to anything else?"

"Just us." Micky didn't sound happy.

"What's the plan, Skipper?"

"We are spreading the Harborian ships across a broad front. We'll hit the enemy shits with a single pulse and hopefully disable the first wave. Then we'll stay the course and hopefully, it'll work a second time. We'll use it until they are out of commission and then we'll plow through. As soon as we can launch the drop ships, you'll be on your way and we'll fight our way out."

"Assuming Ten is on the surface. Is there a space station of any sort?"

"There are very few artificial satellites, and they are of a style to relay communications signals," Smedley interjected.

"Feed us as much data as you can collect. We'll stay in touch. Time to fight the ship," Terry said, using the age old naval expression that captains gave when they took their ship into battle, treating the ship as its own entity to fight the enemy. *Fight the ship, aye*, the crew would respond and become one with their battle stations, ready to stand toe to toe with the enemy, duke it out until one vessel struck its colors or headed to the bottom of the ocean.

"Fight the ship, aye," Micky replied.

Ramses' Chariot

Ted was hard at work, but the others didn't know at what. The frigate maintained its speed as it closed on the planet. The inbound vector was free of enemy ships.

Everyone waited silently for Ted to say something.

When the *Chariot* flowed into a low-altitude orbit around Home World, Cory spoke.

"You have to tell us what's going on, Uncle Ted." He wasn't her uncle, but she always called him that. Her mother's werewolf pack had become aunts and uncles. They acted as family should, there for each other when needed.

"We are going to get close enough to wrap Ten in a gravitic shield, then we'll do battle the old way."

"Two men with clubs trying to brain each other?" Cory suggested. Petricia snickered.

"The intellect of the stagnant king challenged by the upstart stranger with the indomitable will."

"So you're going to mentally club each other into submission?"

"Plato and I will bury the creature known as Ten in a trap of our making. We will remove it and free the humans of Home World." Ted snarled while he looked past his holo screens.

Cory shielded her mouth and whispered into Joseph's ear. "Is he okay? Because he doesn't sound okay."

Joseph's eyes unfocused for a moment. When he opened them, he smiled and winked. "Have no fear, Cordelia. We are in good hands."

The *War Axe*

The Harborian fleet spread out, creating a wide front before the *War Axe*. As the Home World picket came into range, the Harborian EMP weapons were activated with a single command. The incoming ships stopped maneuvering, stopped broadcasting, and continued on ballistic trajectories, having lost all power.

"Yes!" Terry pumped his fist, cheering at the screen. Char nodded, smiling with relief. The other warriors in the drop ship cheered.

On the bridge, Captain San Marino also celebrated his relief. He hadn't thought it would work. "Oh ye of little faith," he told himself, before speaking more loudly. "Stay the course, Clifton."

"Aye, aye, sir!" the helmsman replied over his shoulder. He made a minor adjustment to avoid one of the powerless ships that passed nearby.

The Harborian ships approached the next wave, but started to slow down.

"Smedley, why are you slowing the fleet?"

"It's not me," the AI replied.

"Oh, no." Micky sat stiffly in his chair and watched the Harborian fleet join Ten's ship on a wide arc before the *War Axe*. The ships that had passed powered up and turned around. "That's more what I expected. Maximum power to the gravitic shields, and God help us if they don't hold."

In the hangar bay, two Black Eagles waited for the word. Aaron's hand started to shake. Insurmountable odds were outside the *Axe's* hangar doors. He was comfortable flying the spacefighter, but that took all his concentration. Flying and fighting at the same time? It was one step too far. He focused on his hand, trying to will it to stop shaking.

His hand refused to comply.

Yanmei growled as she saw the enemy ships closing on the *War Axe*. Of course, it was a trap. No one expected anything less from Ten, but the ease at which it was executed surprised her.

She wanted to engage the enemy, shoot them down, but not until the EMP weapons were taken offline. She wouldn't get one centimeter out of the hangar bay before getting disabled. She growled again, the feeling of helplessness growing.

Terry Henry gave the finger to the screen. "We're coming for you," he told the icons on the screen. They continued to move toward the *War Axe*, tightening the net.

"Come on, Ted. We need some of your magic if we're going to survive the hour," Terry pleaded with the screen.

"What do you think is going on?" Xianna asked.

Jenelope took another sip of her fruit smoothie. They weren't expected to prepare a meal for the foreseeable future, so they were relaxing. When the ship's crew was ordered to combat stations, theirs was the galley. With the bulkheads secured, even if they wanted to violate the order, they couldn't. So they made the best of it.

Takeaway meals were ready if they needed to get something to the crew, but that would take a concerted effort to release the bulkheads.

As long as that wasn't happening, there was nothing to do.

"I think the professionals are handling it. We can tap into what the bridge is seeing." Jenelope brought up the video screen and instantly regretted it. They were flying into the middle of a vast fleet of enemy ships.

Xianna didn't seem concerned.

"Is it always like this?"

Jenelope thought for a moment. "It is. We go in against seemingly insurmountable odds, and the captain and the colonel do their thing. Next you know it, we're holding a big party. What do you say we get started on a cake to end all cakes? We can roll your wedding reception into it. Who cares about a little old battle? The good guys will win. They always do. This will be about you and Eldis."

Xianna smiled and giggled. She looked human, but her skin was green and her ears pointed. She might have been considered an elf in old human folklore. But she was from Torregidor, a small, jungle planet. Being agile was a natural trait to help the race move through the trees.

She hopped to her feet, jumped to the top of a chair, then vaulted across to another chair, doing a pirouette in between. From the last chair, she did a backflip to land in the kitchen.

"Were you always like that?" Jenelope asked.

"Like what?"

"Nimble as a cat."

"I don't know what a cat is, but I expect it is something nimble." She laughed as she found her apron and put it on.

"They always land on their feet." Jenelope walked around the tables and strolled into the kitchen. "Why did you leave your home planet?"

"The stars. To dance among the trees is one thing, but to dance among the stars is a gift from heaven."

Jenelope hugged the young woman. "I wish everyone had that kind of perspective on life."

She glanced back to the screen as she held onto her helper. A warning flashed on the screen. *Brace for impact.*

Ramses' Chariot

"We're going to lose the *War Axe!*" Cory pounded on Ted's back. A smaller screen showed the entire Home World fleet, including the Harborian vessels, closing on their ship.

"We're not going to lose the *War Axe*. The last of Ten's code was supposed to have been purged. I need to have words with Ankh and Smedley when we get back."

"If they're still alive," Cory shot back. She continued to beat on Ted's back until Joseph pulled her away.

"He's working on it," he tried to reassure her.

"I shall prepare to disembark," Bundin said, shuffling down the corridor to the cargo bay. Once they landed, he would exit using the cargo hatch. He wanted to pick up his railguns and conduct one last systems check. In Bundin's opinion, this battle would be won on the ground using kinetic weapons. He didn't understand how anyone could fight using computers. The Podder wanted to blow something up.

Lots of somethings, if they raised their heads to protect the surreal entity known as Ten.

On the bridge, Cory buried her head against Joseph's chest, refusing to watch anyone else die.

"Once I activate the shutdown sequence, they'll lose their satellites, but we'll be exposed, so expect a bumpy ride as we dive into the atmosphere. We'll be able to reactivate our cloak, but only after we've dissipated the heat from reentry."

"Are you going to let the *War Axe* know?" Joseph asked, leaning over Cory's head.

"They'll find out when it's activated. I can't give away our position with a nonsensical transmission," came Ted's curt reply.

Dokken tucked his tail between his legs. He never enjoyed reentry. He leaned heavily against Cory, wedging himself between the humans, staying behind the captain's chair so he didn't have to watch.

"Plato, drop the cloak and jam those satellites."

"Target the lead carrier and fire the mains," Micky ordered.

"Firing," Smedley replied. "Circling the line of flight."

The *War Axe's* main weapons were massive railguns firing relatively small projectiles. The weapons could twirl, minutely, to deliver a pattern around an incoming target, bracketing it in a three-hundred-and-sixty-degree area. No matter which way the target juked, projectiles would be there.

But the enemy ship didn't maneuver. It maintained

course through the heart of the incoming projectiles. They plunged through the shields and tore through the ship. Explosions racked the hull.

Micky didn't have time to watch the ship come apart. Any humans on board died with their ship.

"Bring mains to bear on the second carrier."

The EMP weapons cascaded against the shields, the energy increasing as ships closed the range and added their power to the attack.

"Shields holding. We're slowing," Clifton reported. His hands danced across his console.

"Why are we slowing? Blow through their lines!"

"It's like we're wading through mud, and the mud is getting deeper!"

"Their ships of the line are launching fighters," Smedley said.

"Smedley, activate the defensive grid and prepare to fire, and Clifton, get this ship moving!"

CHAPTER TWENTY-FIVE

Ramses' Chariot

The instant the cloak dropped, Plato raised the gravitic shields and activated the heavily-modified EMP weapon. The *Chariot* accelerated along an arcing trajectory in a high orbit. The frigate's railguns blasted the closest satellite. The ship continued powering through maximum acceleration. The ship would complete its orbit of the planet in less than two minutes.

Plasma beams reached out and the ship started to juke, skipping off the upper atmosphere to defeat the weapons. The ship slowed enough to conduct a series of erratic course changes. Even with the shields, the plasma beams could damage the ship.

Ted couldn't have that. Plato fired at greater and greater ranges to remove the satellites while they were inoperable.

Cory winced when she looked at the screen. The *War Axe* was embroiled within the massive enemy fleet. She tore her gaze from the images and turned away. Joseph continued to hold her while Petricia rubbed one hand absentmindedly up and down her back. Dokken couldn't see anything from where he stood.

He thought that was probably for the best.

Bundin stood by the cargo bay door, tentacles holding tightly to the railguns, waiting.

The *War Axe*

The ship screamed ahead. Clifton's eyes shot wide at the sudden acceleration. He worked the controls and flew the *War Axe* between the ships of Home World's fleet.

"Smedley?" Micky asked, but not as concerned as he had been a moment earlier.

"The EMP systems are offline and the enemy ships have assumed a neutral stance. We are free to approach the planet."

The screen showed the icons behind them, static instead of flashing, which would indicate a moving ship.

Terry Henry pumped his fist anew. "Go Ted!"

"All hail Ted!" Char exclaimed, before sobering. "Is there a report of their position?"

"They're in a comm blackout. We won't hear anything." Terry watched the screen. The only thing moving was the *War Axe* as it powered toward Home World. "The fact that they've disabled the Home World fleet tells me that the real battle is underway."

Terry looked at the backs of the mech-suited warriors.

They could have been statues, but he knew they were watching him using their rear cameras.

"Smedley, connect me with the other drop ships, please."

"Done."

"The Home World fleet is behind us. Next stop is the planet itself. We don't know where Ten is located. We may deploy to six different locations or only one. We won't know until we get there. Be ready for any eventuality, but wherever and however we go, understand that the people are not the enemy. Try to find ways not to injure them. Engage the people as a last resort. Our primary objective is to remove Ten from power, whatever that looks like, but I expect it will involve blowing up a lot of shit. I hope you don't mind. Blow up shit and save the people."

Terry drew a finger across his throat and the relay to the other shuttles was cut.

"Could you be any more vague?" Char asked.

"I'm sure that I couldn't be less vague. We have to figure it out on the fly. We don't even know how many people are down there, let alone what their infrastructure is like. I hope Ted gives us a major information dump when we arrive."

Char pointed to the screen. "We've arrived." She watched the screen without blinking. "I'm not seeing an info dump."

Terry closed his eyes and concentrated. *Ankh? Where do we need to deploy?*

Ankh sat in the CIC within a holographic cocoon of information. He couldn't take it all in. He closed his eyes and linked his mind with Smedley. Together, they perused the information, looking for the key to locating Ten.

Go away, Ankh replied to Terry's inquiry.

Go which way? Terry wondered.

Smedley will contact you when we have something. Now, stop bothering me.

Population centers, power grids, buildings, and factories. A major shipyard covered a small portion of the planet surface. With anti-gravity, building ships in space was no longer necessary, but gutting a planet for the raw materials made no sense, unless one didn't care about the populace.

Ten fell in that category.

Ankh wanted to link with Ted and Plato, but they weren't available. They'd blocked incoming links. The small Crenellian wondered how his friends were doing.

Ramses' Chariot

Keeping their knees bent and hanging on for dear life, the ride through the atmosphere was rough. Plato spared nothing in his headlong rush toward the surface.

Once through, the pressure instantly lifted, and they felt like they were floating.

"Cloak engaged," Ted said, and the ship performed a myriad of maneuvers to defeat any weapons that would attack a projected course. When the cloak was engaged, they couldn't use the shields. Ted vowed to work on that.

He believed that the two systems could operate simultaneously.

But that was for another time.

Plato adjusted course to take them over the population
centers. He wouldn't call them cities. They had more in
common with a concentration camp. *Ramses' Chariot* raced
through the sky, leaving no trace that it had passed. The
cloak dissipated the energy, whether from light, pressure,
or sound.

"Mapping the planet surface." Ted finally stopped inter-
acting with the holo screens around him and leaned back.
"There are five small population centers, two have little
technology. Of the three remaining, one is far older than
the other two, but not the oldest of the five."

"A logic puzzle," Joseph said.

"The power signatures are negligible, far less than
expected to support a population of fifteen thousand."

"Can you identify the breeding centers?"

Cory made a disgusted face, but couldn't disagree with
the question.

"There is only one location with adult males. Why
would you think Ten is co-located with the breeding
center?"

"Direct oversight. Ten is all-controlling. I am guessing
that Ten would want to ensure the data connection with its
main source of labor and enjoyment is uninterrupted."

"Ten could do that from anywhere on the planet," Ted
replied.

"Even without the satellites?"

"Fair point." Ted rubbed his chin and looked at the

images on the main screen. Five choices, maybe one was right or maybe none of them were.

"Underground?" Cory asked.

"Plato, are there any manmade tunnels leading deep underground but not as part of a resource extraction mine? The AI would not be located within a working mine."

"We will have to circle the planet four more times for me to collect that data," Plato replied.

"Sounds good," Joseph said.

Ted turned and shook his head.

"Why not?"

"For ground penetration, we need active radar, which means we need to drop the cloak."

"But we can shield, right?"

"Yes." Ted reviewed his options. "Plato, prepare to drop the cloak and raise the shields."

The *War Axe*

"Entering orbit, TH. Still no confirmation on where we need to send you. We're seeing five cities, but not really cities."

Terry intently studied the screen, expecting a new fleet to appear at any moment.

"Why doesn't Ten have kinetic weapons?" Terry wondered.

"Control. The AI can control anything digital, but if the humans learned to use kinetic weapons, they could rise up and fight against their computer master," Char offered.

"That's what I was thinking. Where on the planet would

Ten be safe, just in case the people developed rudimentary weapons?"

"Underground. Deep underground."

"Find that entrance and we'll have found Ten's heart and brain."

Ankh had already redirected the *War Axe's* sensors. He'd arrived at that conclusion two minutes earlier. With the entirety of the *War Axe* committed to the effort, it wasn't long before they had their answer.

In the northern region of the planet, under the ice and snow, was a structure that covered an entrance to a straight shaft that led deep underground. The power source within was shielded, but the shield itself told them what they needed to know.

"Coordinates are set," Ankh reported.

"Deploy the shuttles. Fair winds, Colonel Walton," the captain said over the ship-wide broadcast. "Drop ships away."

Terry held on as his shuttle rocketed out the short launch tube and into space. The drop ship turned, joined its partner from the other side of the ship, and headed toward the planet surface. The next two fell in behind them, and then the last two. A pair of Black Eagles zoomed past the shuttles, leading the way downward in case the enemy reared its ugly head.

The plan took shape in Terry's mind. The mechs would have to lead the way. They'd plant the initial demolitions,

CRAIG MARTELLE & MICHAEL ANDERLE

reveal the entrance, and then blow the entrance. Then they would enter Ten's domain.

"Aaron and Yanmei, if you could strafe the area over the entrance, I would appreciate it," Terry requested.

The Eagles swooped low, slowed, aligned their cannons, and fired. The rounds stitched a path straight to the entrance, but the last few were deflected by an energy barrier.

"Shielding," Terry said unnecessarily. "We might have to dig a new tunnel."

"Black Eagles, this is Ted. Assume a defensive position to the south. The *Chariot* has a plan."

The drop ships veered away as Smedley received instructions from Plato, and the shuttles slowed until they were barely crawling toward the objective.

Terry clenched his fists. He hated not knowing the plan.

To their left, far closer than Terry liked, *Ramses' Chariot* appeared out of thin air. The frigate's railgun opened up and maintained a steady stream of fire at a point outside of the entrance's defensive perimeter. Ted was digging a new entrance.

"Great minds think alike." Terry smiled and Char smiled back.

Terry's smile turned into a frown when he saw four shuttles break off and head toward the horizon. "Where the fuck are they going?"

Char watched the receding images on the screen. She shook her head. "Smedley! What are you doing with my people?"

"Ted has ordered attack groups to the two locations

where he suspects Ten will seek refuge when this stronghold is breeched. We will need to simultaneously destroy multiple locations to prevent the AI from hopping one to another."

"Christina? Did you hear that?"

"Already on it, TH. I guess we get the big city. We'll go in heavy without firing the railguns until we have a bead on Ten's hardware."

"Roger. Who has the last group?"

"That would be me, Colonel," Capples replied. "I have the settlement on my HUD. We're taking eight mechs in. Rules of engagement are don't fire unless fired upon until tech central is in our sights, then we take it out."

"On my command. We'll eliminate the refuges together, but be ready to move out, just in case this slippery bastard gets past us."

"Kimber, when the tunnel is open, lead us in."

"Aye, aye, sir," she replied for the edification of the others.

"Did you give Christina your JDS?" Terry asked to fill the silence while they waited for word from Ted.

"Yes. I couldn't use it, not wearing the can."

"The can!" Terry realized. "Deploy the combat support drones. Release the cryo-drones."

The small vehicles fired their gravitic engines and moved slowly away from their parent shuttles. They unfolded their wings and rose slowly into the air, beginning to circle. The cryo-drone assumed a position closest to the shuttles. It juked in odd directions, rising and falling is if caught in a tornado.

Terry watched it for a moment. "An enemy on the

ground would be hard-pressed to shoot down a target with such erratic flight."

"On station and standing by," Christina reported.

"On station and standing by," Cap added.

"So why are we hovering in place?" Char asked.

"If I said because Ted told us to, that wouldn't sound very convincing, would it?" Terry watched the frigate's progress as it blasted through the rocks. The opening was getting deeper. "Ted also told me to blow the engine and that almost killed all of us. Smedley, land the drop ships. We're getting off."

"What are they doing?" Cory asked after seeing the drop ships land.

"I suspect they are getting off."

"What about Ten?"

"They are going to confront the AI. What we've blasted from the planet to open access to the tunnel? That's trivial compared to what your father has in store."

"There will be fireworks." Cory scratched behind Dokken's ears and wondered if they were going to get off the ship on Home World. They'd removed their helmets once they had breathable air.

Joseph wanted to add a funny quip, but nothing came to mind. The unknowns of what lay before them filled their thoughts with dread.

"We're through," Ted reported after the railgun stopped firing. The *Chariot* swung away from the site, pointing its nose toward the planet's equator, and raced away.

When the rear deck dropped, they realized how loud a spaceship's railgun was.

Kimber and the other four mechs had established a perimeter as they waited for the railgun to stop firing. Terry and Char covered their ears and stayed within the shuttle. When the sound died away, Terry ordered the two new warriors, "No one gets on board but us. Defend the shuttle."

Terry and Char ran from the ship, taking a position behind the mechs. Four mechs from the other ship stood apart, the reserve force.

"Follow me," Kimber said, raising her railgun and running for the crater. She jumped over the edge and disappeared into the darkness. One by one, they went over the edge. To the side of the crater, the shield shimmered just enough to show that it was still intact. Terry vaulted over the edge, sliding down the warm stone chips and into the gap leading to the tunnel. Char slid in behind him.

Once at the bottom, he unholstered his Jean Dukes Special and dialed it to eight. Char pulled her two pistols.

On their backs, they carried enough explosives to level a mountain.

CHAPTER TWENTY-SIX

The *War Axe*

"What's that fleet doing?" Captain San Marino asked for the third time.

"They continue to hold their positions," Smedley replied for the third time.

"I don't trust that they're dead."

"They're not dead, only incapacitated. They do not possess the means for independent action. The Bad Company learned that when they boarded the hostile ships at Alchon Prime."

Micky nodded at Smedley's patient explanation. He tapped the screen on the arm of his chair. "All hands. Head calls and chow runs, no more than two at a time. Be no more than three minutes from your stations at any point in time. Remain in your shipsuits. Captain out."

Clifton jumped up. "Be back in a minute." The helmsman bolted from the bridge.

Too much roughage, Micky thought, scanning the data streams. He moved to the systems station to pull up the holographic displays and access the most available information.

A huge explosion rocked the ship. Micky was nearly thrown from the seat. The ship lost its artificial gravity and started to spin. The captain buckled in where he was, straining against the forces pulling him aside. "Transfer helm to this station," he ordered. The controls appeared in one of his holographic displays and Micky started engaging thrusters to counter the spin.

"What the hell happened?" the skipper asked. There was no reply. "Smedley?"

Jenelope was thrown over the sink and into the wall. She slammed against it and slid to the counter, unconscious. Xianna jumped into the air, letting the ship move beneath her. She rotated, hit the wall with her feet, pushed off, and landed when the ship settled. She hurried to the counter and cradled Jenelope's head in her hands. She attempted to move the woman, but Jenelope was too heavy.

Xianna ran to the cupboards and pulled tablecloths and towels that she could use to pack around the chef. She wasn't prepared when gravity failed and she floated into the air. She kicked and flailed, but could barely move. She stretched her leg until a toe touched the serving counter.

Pushing off, she sailed toward the sink. Turning mid-air, she landed softly and stood on the wall. With a gentle tug, Jenelope came free and floated in the air. Xianna pushed away and both floated toward the dining area. She hooked the first table and pulled herself downward, bringing Jenelope along to wedge her under the table. Together, they stayed there.

"I plead with you, Holy Mother Torreg, deliver us from our enemies..."

Ramses' Chariot

"We're going to leave them behind?" Cory asked, pointing toward the aft end of the frigate.

"They are in capable hands. There is less than a one hundred percent chance that Ten is at that location. We are occupying the next three most probable locations for the AI," Ted quickly explained.

"Three?" Joseph wondered.

"The shuttles are at the other two. We will take the second least likely location."

Four stood in silence while Ted and Plato communicated on a level only they understood as they continued to calculate the odds.

"Ten will be in all the places, including the ships. Ten's essence will need to be purged, but that will be easy once its brain has been removed and crushed."

Ted clenched and unclenched his fist.

"I'm coming, you evil bastard. I'm coming to crush the life from you. No one will remember that you ever existed." Ted leaned forward. "Plato, take us in. Drop us at the largest building."

Ted stood up and turned, stopped by the people between him and the corridor. "Well? Get ready. We're joining the fight."

They moved out of Ted's way. He went straight to his

quarters, where he picked up the box that contained Plato. Cory waited. Joseph and Petricia removed their railguns from a storage locker in the corridor.

Cory helped Dokken out of his shipsuit. He jumped out of it before she was finished and nearly knocked her down. He shook. Twice. He wagged his tail and panted as he bounced with joy.

Cordelia stood and leaned against the bulkhead. "We can learn a lot from you," she told the dog. "Sometimes, it doesn't take very much, and it shouldn't, to make us happy."

Joseph had a second railgun for Cory. He thought about handing it to her, but slung it over his shoulder instead. She cradled Dokken's face in her hands and kissed the top of his head. She immediately wiped her mouth of the hair that stuck to her lips.

I shed when I'm anxious, he explained. *I love you.*

"Yes, I love you, too, and I have a mouthful of hair to prove it."

"To the cargo bay?" Joseph suggested. "We'll hit the ground together."

Dokken trotted off. Cory followed. "Cargo bay," Joseph told Ted.

Ted didn't care how they left the ship. He carried no weapons, only Plato and what he had inside.

"I am ready," Bundin told them. He didn't need to say that he'd been ready since before they hit the atmosphere. None of that mattered. Only the now. Joseph patted Bundin's shell as he stood beside the blue alien. The rest were behind.

Ramses' Chariot touched down, and the cargo hatch

popped open. Joseph ran out, Bundin keeping up using his odd shuffling gait. One thing they learned from Terry Henry was to get away from the ship as quickly as possible after a landing. Ships made great targets for anyone with a weapon.

The group ran along the edge of a wired compound. "Looks like a prison," Joseph said darkly.

Petricia started to reply but grimaced and covered her nose. *The smell.*

Ted looked pointedly at a building within the facility. Joseph looked at the wire. Old. Rusty. He grabbed two strands and yanked it free. Then two more. And kept going until there was a wide opening in the fence.

"Where are the people?" Cory asked.

"They are here," Ted said, relaying what the ship's sensors were telling Plato. The *Chariot* dusted off and moved into the distance, hovering where they could still see it.

Joseph walked in first with Bundin close behind. The alien's four eyes missed little as he could look in all directions at the same time. Joseph held up a fist, signaling a halt. They stopped, their weapons aimed into the walkways between buildings. A face appeared from a doorway before them. A woman's face. She stepped out, unafraid but confused. She looked at the newcomers and called into the building.

"Go around them!" Ted called.

More women. "When we scanned the planet, you said that there was only one location with adult males. Are you telling me that everyone here is female?"

"Yes. I thought that was clear from the statement. There

are approximately fifteen thousand women on this planet and a hundred men."

"So Ten didn't kill the women as it told those who served on the ships?" Joseph asked over his shoulder as more and more women in utilitarian clothing entered the walkway in front of them.

"Ten exists to provide disinformation as that furthers its goals of mind control."

Cory sighed and pushed past Bundin and Joseph. They raised their railguns when she was in front of them. Joseph tried to grab her, but it was too late. Dokken trotted at her side.

"We're here to offer you freedom, save you from this," Cory said, waving her arm to take in the prison camp.

"What do we need saving from?" the first woman asked.

Cory stopped pointing. "Are you free?"

"We do what we need to do." The woman looked perplexed. "Where did you come from?"

"Earth, originally, just like you, but we came here by our choice. You don't realize that you're being held captive by an artificial intelligence known as Ten."

"But we have what we need."

"Men? Companionship? Free choice?"

"Only the best of us are selected for breeding. We are not the best." The woman seemed convinced by her argument. Others behind her nodded.

"We're wasting time," Ted said.

"What if any of you can have children? That's the way it is out there." Cory pointed to the sky. "The universe is a wonderful place to explore."

"Get on with it," Ted added impatiently.

"We have this thing we need to do, and then we'll talk some more."

"Are those men?" another woman asked.

"They are. Joseph and his mate, Petricia." Cory pointed behind her. "Carrying the box is Ted. And this is Bundin. He's from Poddern and is my friend, as is the best of us, Dokken, a German Shepherd."

"But those are men," the women said, slowly moving forward.

"We may have a problem," Joseph whispered.

"Just shoo them away," Ted replied. Joseph fired his railgun in the air. The women shied away from the hypersonic cracks.

"We need to pass. We'll be back and can talk more. Please, go back into your buildings," Cory said encouragingly, using her hands to wave them toward the door.

Petricia walked ahead and stood in front of Joseph. "Looks like we'll have to protect you," she said casually.

"Can we go?" Ted asked and started to storm ahead. Joseph grabbed his shirt.

"We need to stay back. Remember the ROE, we're not to kill the people."

Ted looked miffed. Cory waved for them to follow as she moved ahead once the last of the women had returned through the doorway. When they walked by, they saw the mob in the doorway and at the windows, staring at Joseph and Ted.

It only took the first woman jumping out to energize the group.

"Run!" Cory yelled as she took off for the building that Ted had pointed to earlier.

Kimber's suit lights reflected off the clouds of dust within the crater. Through a forced gap in the bedrock wall, she could make out the darkness beyond. She worked her way over the rock chips and fallen boulders. Once past, the clear air of an artificial tunnel showed its descent deep into the planet.

With five mechs in front and four behind, Terry and Char signaled for them to speed up. Kim started jogging, an easy pace that didn't pound the ground too much, but Terry could still feel the vibrations. He shook it off. Ten had to know they were coming once the *Chariot's* railgun started digging a new tunnel.

"I see movement up ahead," Kimber reported using the suit's external speakers.

Terry didn't reply. Kim was in front. She would do the right thing if there was a human shield. She knew tactics. She knew the rules of the engagement, the ROE. And she knew the mission. Destroy the hardware that carried the entity known as Ten.

A rocket screamed up the tunnel. Kim had no time to react. The warhead hit her in the chest and exploded, filling the area in front of the mechs with fire and smoke.

"Robots," Kim called from her back while trying to roll over and get back up.

"Open fire!" Terry yelled. Four heavy railguns spit streams of projectiles into the darkness below. The sound of shattering metal and exploding robots suggested the first line of defense was ill-equipped to deal with modern mechanized warriors.

Kimber called for a cease fire, jumped to her feet, and ran forward. The four mechs in front pounded after her. Terry and Char ran after them. Kimber opened fire before she reached the remains of the enemy's front lines.

The *War Axe*

Clodagh hadn't left her station. She'd told a teammate to grab a sandwich and pick one up for her while he was there. He'd been gone a total of thirty seconds, just long enough to get beyond the emergency bulkheads and blocked from returning to engineering.

The first explosion threw her to the deck. She returned to her station, no worse for the wear, and was standing there when artificial gravity was lost. She hung on and continued to access ship systems as she tried to figure out what had happened.

An explosion near the rear of the ship, not far from where she worked. Shrapnel had penetrated some of the ship's systems. Repair bots had already been dispatched and were reconnecting power flow conduits and fiber optics.

She moved to the next issue. Would it happen again?

Sensors were still operational. Sensor data didn't show anything until the last nanosecond before the explosion.

A mine.

"Not again," she groaned. She studied the data. The mine appeared. From nowhere. A stealthed mine?

"Ankh, this is Clodagh. Are you there?"

The Crenellian didn't answer. She checked the comm circuit and verified that it was intact.

"Captain San Marino, this is Lieutenant Shortall. It appears that we hit a mine." She hoped that her report went through. No response. She wondered if she were the only one left alive.

"Save the ship first. Are we in a minefield?" she asked. "Smedley?"

The AI didn't answer. She checked the circuits, and they appeared to be fine. "Maybe I'm the only one who's dead, and I don't know it. I guess we'll have to do it the hard way."

She looked at the data before and after the appearance of the mine. Baselined the numbers from static space in this area, then compared the three. She found a stream of numbers that showed a slight difference. She focused solely on that data, triangulated the locations based on raw reports from multiple sensors outside the *War Axe*, and built a map.

"We're in the middle of a minefield," she told her screen. One mine was close. She activated thrusters on both port and starboard sides of the ship to hold the position. The thruster pushed the mine away. It floated a few hundred meters before coming to a stop.

"You're not in fixed locations. That could make it easier to get out of here. You're not very close together either. No wonder we didn't hit anything coming in. Only after we slowed down did we become a target," she said aloud as she started plotting a course through the minefield and into space.

CHAPTER TWENTY-SEVEN

Home World, Drop Ships 3 and 4

Christina ran down the ramp and followed the mechs as they entered the compound. Gray buildings, brown dirt, green grass, and blue sky. No decorations or artwork of any type appeared on or around the buildings.

"This could be the saddest place I've ever seen," Christina mumbled. The mechs maneuvered toward their target, four pairs of two using a leapfrog tactical movement, one prepared to fire as the other moved to the next covered firing position. Then the first ran in front. Christina moved behind the mechs, staying behind cover when she could. The JDS was in her hand, but hung loosely at her side.

"The buildings are filled with people," Fleeter reported from the front.

"Are they armed? Are we walking into an ambush?"

"No, ma'am."

Christina walked into the open. "Come on out with your hands up!" she shouted. "COME ON!"

The doors opened slowly and sleepy faces appeared. They were surprised by the mechs but didn't seem afraid. They accepted them matter-of-factly. Christina walked to the front. "Who are you?"

A number of the women muttered names, but none of it made any sense. It wasn't the question that Christina needed to ask. "Where are the computers?"

"The what?" one woman replied. The vacant looks told Christina all she needed to know.

"Power signature up ahead, right where Ted told us it would be," Fleeter reported.

"We need to go up there and do this thing. Then we'll come back for you," Christina told them.

"You're beautiful," one of the women said. "What are those things?"

"Weapons? Do you mean our weapons?" Christina held up the pistol and the woman nodded.

The colonel smiled at them. "I should be happy that you don't know what weapons are. Too many use them to control others. Yet, there are entities like Ten who exploits the power of the mind to oppress people like you. You were stolen from your homes, long ago, brought here, and then separated from half of your people. Ten's time has come. When this day is done, much of the world will be in flames. Hopefully, we're still standing and will take you to your men, where you can decide for yourselves what you want to do."

"But we weren't selected for breeding."

"No one gets to select that for you. We believe it's your choice who you want to partner with and what you want to do after that. If you want to partner at all, that is."

Christina looked at the empty space next to her and shrugged.

"Can we come along?"

"I don't think that's a good idea," Christina told them. "It could turn ugly. Stay here, stay safe, and we'll be back for you."

"And then what? Should we go about our duties?"

The colonel wasn't sure what those were and didn't want to ask. "No. Go back to your rooms and wait. Keep your heads down. If it looks like all hell is breaking loose, run that way." Christina pointed toward the shuttles where K'Thrall and Slicker were on guard.

Don't freak out if a bunch of women come running your way. Go into the shuttle and close the hatch. Why don't you do that now. We have no indication of an external threat to the ship.

Roger, K'Thrall replied. He swirled his arm in the air, and the four warriors entered and sealed the shuttles.

"Back inside with you," Christina told the women. She tomahawked an arm toward the building with the energy signature. Fleeter stepped off with her team in tow. Christina took her position behind them, and the other four mechs brought up the rear.

"Knock, knock, Ten. Can we come in? No? We'll leave this big bucket of fuck you out here on the porch..." she said to herself.

Home World, Drop Ships 5 and 6

The darkness greeted Capples as he jogged from the back of the drop ship. On this part of Home World, it was the middle of the night. The mechs were uninhibited by darkness. They formed up as they walked toward the compound. A massive wire fence greeted them. With a grab and a kick, Cap tore out an entire section. He cast it aside and walked into the compound. He thrust his fist over his head. *Freeze.*

He checked his sensors. Infrared showed a great number of people, all of them horizontal in their beds. Cap signaled for quiet and they began moving, deliberately, heel to toe, walking without making noise.

They walked through the outer compound without waking the sleeping, reaching a great wall beyond which an inner area was secured.

Cap used his heads-up display to establish the tactical plan. Two mechs faced outward, covering the others. Two moved forward to breach the building. The other four spread out and took cover, preparing to rush in when the way was clear.

The breaching team studied their data showing the power emanating from the building, the infrared and ultraviolet signatures, metals within the structure. Praeter nodded to his teammate. There was no handle.

He didn't need one. He reared back and used the power of the suit to kick the door open.

Kimber blasted the robots until no power remained within their metal bodies. She kicked them from her path as she strode through, stopping briefly to recalibrate her sensors. The tunnel led ever deeper.

"I think that was the first line of defense," Kimber told

them.

"A soft unit would have been decimated by the first blast," Terry replied. He walked past the position. "Like the Maginot Line and as effective."

The defenses erected to protect the Allies against a resurgent Germany. They hadn't worked because technology had changed. Man's ability to wage war had improved too quickly for the peace-minded to keep up.

Terry didn't think Ten was peaceful, only complacent. How long had it been since any challenge was mounted to the AI's supremacy? Had it been challenged?

"Take care," he needlessly told Kimber. She continued downward, four mechs close behind. Their five sets of sensors actively engaged in seeking the next obstacle.

Char closed her eyes and looked for the draw of Etheric power. She couldn't find anything in the gray mists below them. "Nothing."

"Nothing at all?"

"No life of any sort," she replied.

"Are we in the right place?" Terry started to worry that they weren't. Which meant that someone else was. He wondered who he had ordered into harm's way.

The *War Axe*

Micky flailed within the holographic screens. The data scrolled by inconsistently, the controls worked haphazardly, and he couldn't be sure that the ship wasn't dead.

The overhead speaker crackled. "Gravity will be online in a few moments. If anyone is still alive, please prepare yourselves."

The captain dropped the holo screens and waited. On the third deep breath, gravity was restored. He unbuckled himself and climbed into the captain's chair. He tapped the screen for ship-wide broadcast.

"All hands, this is the captain. Submit your damage reports verbally. Engines first. Commander Suresha."

Silence greeted his request.

"Is anyone available from engineering?"

"Clodagh here, sir. We hit a mine. Despite the immediate effect, the damage was not too bad. Automated repair bots are bringing the systems back one by one. We should be functional shortly."

"We're in a minefield?" Micky blurted, groaning and grabbing his head. "How come we didn't see them?"

"They are shielded, but we have a way to see them. Now, that is. Transferring the updated info to the bridge."

The front screen came back to life and showed the *War Axe* along with pinpoints of light that represented the mines. They were far enough apart that it seemed almost like a ship would have to go out of its way to hit one.

"Thanks, Clodagh. Good work. Do you know if Suresha is alive?"

"I don't. The emergency bulkheads engaged and locked me in. I've been too busy to explore the adjacent sections, but I can do that now that gravity is restored."

"Continue what you're doing, Lieutenant. I need this ship to function. We have people on the planet and a hostile fleet behind us. We're sitting ducks."

"Clodagh out," she replied and went back to work digging through the systems to ensure the bots restored things in the right order.

Micky went through his departments. Mac and Blagun answered readily. They were up to their asses in alligators trying to repair the damage. Oscar was nowhere to be found.

"Ankh, can you tell me what happened to Smedley? Ankh?" Micky couldn't access anything from the combat information center. "Can anyone get to the CIC?"

The bridge door opened and Clifton hurried through. "I can't express how much that sucked," he said as he hurried back to the helm. He was in his underwear.

Micky couldn't speak as he watched the absurdity before him.

"Don't ask," Clifton requested and started working the systems, looking at the information on the main screen and plotting alternate flight routes to avoid the mines.

"This is Private Gefelton. I think a team of us can get to the CIC from the hangar bay."

"On your way, Private. Let me know when you've arrived."

The team from *Ramses' Chariot*

The enhanced humans easily outpaced the women. Joseph thought it was funny to be chased by a mob of women, just until it wasn't. He understood that much more clearly what the werewolves had gone through on *Sheri's Pride*.

"I shall hold them up," Bundin offered.

"You can't shoot them," Cory said while controlling her pace and breathing.

"I shall not hold them up," Bundin corrected and continued running.

Ted reached the building and waited. In the distance, the frigate rose into the air, using its entire sensor suite to examine the building and relay the information to Plato and Ted.

The others slowed and then stopped in the open area before the two-story concrete structure.

"There is no color here," Joseph said as if on an afternoon stroll. He tensed as he raised his railgun. Pounding feet carried a flood of women from the path behind them. Cory put her arms out, yelling for them to stop. Dokken showed his fangs and barked furiously, darting at the women. The front row came to a halt and the others slowly filled in the space behind them.

Ted was before the door, communing with his AI. He had no idea what was going on behind him.

Bundin fired his two railguns into the air. "You need to stop pushing," he told the crowd.

"What are you going to do? What?" Cory shouted angrily.

"We... We..." the first woman stuttered.

"We've never seen a man."

"Now you have. Go back to your homes and wait," she told them. No one moved. Dokken started barking again, nipping at the women.

They slowly backed away.

Cory jumped when Ted kicked the door in. He strolled inside, cradling Plato in his arms. Joseph hurried in after him, with Petricia close behind. Bundin looked at the doorway.

"Far too narrow for me," he told Cory. "Go ahead. I'll hold the masses at bay."

"You mean you're going to block the doorway with your shell?"

"Pretty much. Go on." Bundin waited for Cory and Dokken to get by him before he wedged himself into the space. No one else was going in, but no one was getting out either, at least not quickly.

Cory's enhanced eyes adjusted quickly. She stood out in the interior's darkness because of the blue glow.

Within the room, there was a single feature. The rectangular shape of an elevator. Ted walked up to it and the doors opened. A dim glow lit the interior.

"You most assuredly are not taking the elevator," Joseph cautioned, grabbing Ted's arm to keep him from going inside.

"There's no other way down."

Joseph blocked the door with his body as he scanned the inside. No buttons or mechanical means to tell the elevator where to go. Joseph stepped back, aimed his rail-gun, and blew the floor out of the elevator. It dropped into the darkness below. The door started to close, and Ted stopped it with his hand.

He looked angry, but knew the vampire was right.

"You can do what you need to do from up here," Joseph reassured him. Cory and Petricia had no idea what needed to be accomplished beside something with the AIs duking it out.

Ted sat cross-legged in the elevator opening, hugging the box with Plato as he closed his eyes and together, they reached out with their minds.

CHAPTER TWENTY-EIGHT

The team from drop ships 5 and 6

Cap's armored foot exploded the door off its hinges. It twisted and fell inward. He rushed through, hesitating once on the other side. The other mechs ducked through and fanned out to either side of him. There was grass and a fountain, flowers and shrubs, small cabins nestled within decorative vines. His IR sensors showed two people in one bed in each building.

In the center of the compound was a multi-story building, but Cap's sensors suggested the majority of it was underground, which made it the largest building on Home World. He wondered why Christina hadn't been sent here.

To Capples, this seemed like the primary objective.

People stirred and rose. A quick check of the sky showed that it was still the middle of the night. He suspected ripping the door off its hinges had something to do with rousing people used to the quiet.

A man and a woman appeared from one of the buildings.

"Go back inside," Capples ordered.

The man looked into the darkness behind the mechs. He pointed. "The door is open! Can we leave?"

"Go back inside," Cap repeated.

The two did not move. They looked different from the Harborians, but not by much. They had more color to their skin and seemed to be in better shape.

Breeders.

"Why do you want to leave? Have you seen the rest of the planet? This is the nicest place there is."

"I'm tired of the sex. I can't take it anymore!" the man cried.

The team from drop ships 3 and 4

Christina waved the others back. She dialed the JDS up to ten and took aim. She hesitated, then walked to the door and pulled on the handle. It opened. She walked inside, the JDS aimed wherever her eyes looked. She thumbed it back to three, so she didn't blow the building up while she was inside. It was empty except for the structure in the middle.

An elevator. She stepped in front of it, and the doors opened. She vaulted backwards, accidentally pulling the trigger. The pistol sent a projectile into the elevator, exploding it. Something from inside fell. It screeched and bumped as it fell. It was a long time before it hit bottom. The mechs rushed in, filling the space around her.

"Give me your explosives, all you've got." Christina's lip curled as she looked past the blasted elevator enclosure and down the shaft.

· · ·

The team from drop ships 1 and 2

"There's a chamber up ahead. Looks like we've reached the bottom."

Terry clenched his teeth and gripped the JDS tightly. Char slowed to let Terry get in front. Her nine millimeter pistols were no match for the firepower in her husband's hand. Add that to what the mechs carried and she was simply along for the ride.

She kept her pistols at the ready, just in case, because sometimes a single well-aimed round could mean the difference between victory and failure.

"We have computers up here, but they look dead," Kim reported. The mech warriors behind her slowed and fanned out, assuming positions to provide covering fire if needed while Kim searched the space.

Terry and Char stopped and waited, as much as it chapped Terry's ass. He'd had enough of rushing into traps. His abilities had saved him in the past, and often, it had been necessary to run through a killing zone to achieve the mission objective. But not this time. It was a dead end. He could feel it in his bones.

"Give me your pack," Terry said. Char turned around and TH removed the explosives. He reciprocated and when they added the two piles together, they were ready to go. "Detonators." From a pouch on the outside of their ballistic protection vests, they pulled a small case with the volatile detonators. Terry stuffed four of them into the clay-like substance before connecting a mechanical timer with a backup electronic trigger.

Kim continued her sweep, using the suit's sensors to

look for a hidden passage or secondary location where the real Ten's computer might be located.

"Nothing," she reported. She clumped back into the tunnel and cleared her visor so her parents could see her face. "This isn't it."

"Time to turn it into trash just in case some of it is hiding in there. Get them back up the tunnel. Quick as you can. If Ten isn't here, then it's somewhere else. We need to get there."

The rear guard turned and ran up the tunnel. Char took off after them, and then the next four. Kim looked at her father. "After you, Dad."

"Fine," Terry replied with a smile. He set the timers for five minutes, then dialed them back to three and tossed the bag in. He sprinted up the tunnel, accelerating as only an enhanced human could. Kimber was right behind him, keeping her arms spread to the side to limit how much of the explosion might get by her.

When the timer hit three minutes, Terry realized that he'd cut it too close. There was nowhere for the concussive force to go. Even though he was almost out of the tunnel, the fireball and shock wave tossed Kim and her powered armored suit into him. The two flew ahead, ending in a heap by the original entrance.

The *War Axe*

"Main engines are back online," Clifton reported.

"Commander Suresha? Commander Wirth? Oscar, can you hear me?" Micky tried once again over the ship-wide broadcast.

"Do you want me to move the ship from the minefield?" Clifton asked.

"No. We'll stay right here. Have an emergency egress plotted in case the fleet comes back to life or something else appears. We'll be here to recover the drop ships if nothing else goes awry."

"Clodagh?" the captain asked, linking directly with engineering. "How did that mine get inside our shields?"

"I don't have an answer," Clodagh replied. "It could relate to the cloaking technology, that the shields didn't see it to repel it, but the thrusters were able to push one away from the ship. It's odd. Smedley and Ankh could probably answer it, but I haven't heard from either of them."

"Gefelton, are you at the CIC yet?" the captain added the man into the conversation.

"Almost there, Captain."

"Tony? I'm so glad to hear that you're okay."

"Great to hear your voice, Clodagh. I can't wait to see you again."

"You, too," she replied.

"Get a grip, people. We're still fighting a battle and the enemy has weapons we didn't see coming. What else do they have that we haven't seen yet?"

"Opening the CIC now," Private Gefelton reported. "Ankh is on the deck. There's a gash in his head and lots of blood. I'll get back to you when I know more."

The captain frowned. "We need to wrap a helmet around that big head of his. Smedley, add that to my list of projects." When there was no reply, Micky was reminded that the ship was hanging on by a thread, only the quality of the crew keeping things together. They'd lost the advantage of their AI.

The team from drop ships 3 and 4

Christina nodded toward the entrance to the building. The mechs headed out. When she was alone, she tossed a piece of twisted metal into the hole and timed it until it hit the bottom. She set the backup fuse for that amount of time, plus one second. She added two extra detonators that would trigger on impact. A primary and a backup. She aimed the loaded backpack toward the hole and tossed it in.

She turned and bolted out the door, running toward the pathway that brought them to the center of the compound. The mechs lined up behind her.

A rumble deep below them signaled the start of the explosion. The ground rippled as the shockwave passed. A pillar of flame erupted through the top of the building, sending debris skyward.

What goes up must come down.

Christina covered her head with an arm and kept running. The area was peppered by chunks of concrete and twisted steel. One of the mechs grabbed Christina and tucked her beneath him as the debris rained down. In a few moments, it was over. She thanked him and walked away.

"Colonel Christina Lowell reporting in. Objective destroyed. No human injuries. I say again, no human injuries," she said proudly. The smile on her face slowly disappeared when no one replied to her report. "Smedley?"

. . .

The team from drop ships 1 and 2

Kimber picked herself up before lifting her father to his feet.

He groaned. "That sucked." He rotated his neck and shoulders. "Nothing broken, or broken too badly, anyway."

"We still have no idea where Ten is," Kim said.

"And that's how you make it suck worse." Terry slapped the mech's mid-section as he limped past. "We have work to do," he growled, heading for the alternate tunnel.

"Barrier is down." Kim pointed to the original main door.

"Still covered with snow," he replied and kept walking.

Char was waiting for him inside the tunnel. "You almost made it, lover. Must be slowing down in your old age."

"The indignity of being outrun by a two-hundred-year-old. I'll never live it down." He was okay with wrapping an arm over her shoulder to help him over the rocks and into the open. Kimber followed them out, took a head count visually, confirmed it by the electronic means displayed on her HUD, and gave the thumbs up.

Terry nodded and twirled a finger in the air. The teams boarded their shuttles and buttoned up.

"Where to?" Terry asked. "Smedley?"

When there was no answer, Terry accessed the comm screen directly, tapped commands, and then started over. "Colonel Walton to the *War Axe*, please respond."

"Captain San Marino. How's it going down there?" he asked abruptly.

"We blew our target, but we don't think Ten was in there. Where's Smedley?"

"Missing in action, TH. We hit a cloaked mine. We're in the middle of the minefield right now, but we have a way to see them. We shouldn't hit any more. Ever since the explosion, Smedley has not responded."

"The Home World fleet?"

"Staying where they were."

"Is there any movement in the orbital planes?" Terry asked. Char raised an eyebrow as she watched him.

"What do you mean?"

"What if Ten isn't on the planet? What if the AI is cloaked, like the mines in orbit? It might have lost its comm link because of the destroyed satellites. I doubt it would broadcast anything directly. Look for bots trying to restore a comm sat."

"Will do. Have you heard from anyone else?"

"We have not, but we haven't tried. If Ten's down here, we'll find it and destroy it. If not, we'll destroy any place it can hide. Walton out."

"Christina, come in," Terry called.

"I wondered where everyone was," came her reply. "We blew our objective into a billion pieces and no human casualties."

"Good job. Walton out."

"Wait!" Christina called before Terry cut the link. "We have a shitload of women here. We need to take them with us."

"Define shitload."

"Five thousand, give or take a few thousand," Christina said softly.

Terry looked at the screen. He'd contemplated an evacuation of the planet, but expected he'd have Smedley's help in taking over the Home World ships. Without that, they were stuck.

"We will look for solutions to that problem once Ten is eliminated. Carry on." Terry signed off before Christina could ask another question that he wasn't prepared to answer. "Welcome to being a colonel."

Terry tapped the screen. *"Ramses' Chariot,* this is Colonel Walton, please respond."

He tried three more times without any luck before switching to check in with the final team.

"Sergeant Capples, this is Colonel Walton, please respond."

"Cap here. We have a situation."

"Explain."

"We found the breeding grounds. It's a mini-paradise with a major structure, a hospital, and nursery. We found couples, babies, and children. We can't leave them here, and, Colonel..." Cap stopped speaking without completing the thought.

"Bad Company isn't big enough to support a civil affairs branch. In the interim, we need to do the best we can with what we have."

"That's not it. The men. They're tired of having sex all the time."

Terry rolled his eyes before looking at the others in the shuttle. He couldn't tell what the warriors in the mech suits were doing, but Char struggled to keep a straight face.

"Ten. We're looking for Ten."

"We're in the hospital and childcare facility now. We've broken through a number of barriers that separated the

315

groups from each other, but haven't found anything that looks like a computer core."

"Seize and hold the hospital. We will bring all our people there. Ten's brainwashing starts *there*. It must have a presence."

"Roger, out."

Terry brought up the coordinates for Cap's group and put it into the autopilot. The two shuttles rose into the air and flew toward the horizon.

CHAPTER TWENTY-NINE

The team from *Ramses' Chariot*

Ted screamed. Cory ran to him, kneeled, and tried to look into his eyes. He had them pinched shut as he gritted his teeth. She heard her dad's call, but couldn't take it. She held Ted's head in her hands and tried to send her positive energy into him, helping in a way that was natural to her.

He calmed and rocked, his fingers gripping Plato's box so tightly that his knuckles turned white.

"Joseph?" Cory gasped. He and Petricia sat next to her, adding their support as she added hers to Ted.

"We're here," Joseph soothed. He reached out and gripped Ted's shoulder, ready to pull him back. The man was close to the elevator shaft. Too close, in the vampire's mind.

Ted was oblivious to it all. He had found the main uplink. Within this narrow stream, Ted and Plato battled Ten on the superhighway of data. Packets of energy raced up and down, threatening to burn them, slice bits of them away. Ted and Plato dodged, shielded, and dodged some more.

They generated their own energy and hurled it into the stream, expecting it to have no effect. The attacks on them continued relentlessly.

"How far?" Ted asked.

"Too far," Plato replied. "The farther we extend our reach, the thinner the umbilical and easier it will be for Ten to cut."

"A braided pair," Ted suggested. The two consciousnesses began to braid themselves like a rope as they stretched upstream. The shield before them grew more robust as they added energy to their effort. The attacks slowed and then stopped. Ted and Plato inflated their beings and surged, side to side, filling the stream with only their essence. The data packets stopped flowing.

A great cry of pain sounded from behind them, like a child lost in the wilderness. Beneath them, they built an energy dam, cutting off the entity below from the one above.

Permanently. The cry turned to a wail, then faded to a whimper. With a final gasp, the sounds died away.

They turned their attention upward, starting their slow but inexorable climb toward Ten. The bombardment renewed and their shield strained.

"We won't be able to make it," Ted said, as a matter of fact, not conjecture. He made no judgment of failure. As a scientist, he accepted that this approach wouldn't work and that they'd need a different way. "Calculate the physical location of the source."

"Done," Plato replied instantly. "And the terminus."

Ted relaxed against Cory, his head and body drifting forward, exhausted from his efforts. Joseph dragged him backwards. Ted laid on the floor, chest heaving as if he'd just finished a marathon. Petricia balanced Plato, to keep the box from falling. Ted gripped it, but weakly. They helped him hold it together until he opened his eyes and returned to the conscious world.

"Ten's in orbit," Ted said. Joseph nodded to Cory. She stood and pulled her communication device from her pocket.

"Dad, this is Cory." She looked at the comm device to make sure it was on.

"Cory, are you okay?"

"Yes. Ted had a run-in with Ten and says that it is in orbit." She watched Joseph prepare an explosive charge. He pointed to the elevator shaft. "Joseph is going to blow whatever is at the bottom of this shaft. Then we'll be off. But there are a lot of women here."

She expected that her father was rolling his eyes.

"The *War Axe* is already searching for a cloaked platform that is housing the AI. And once we've dealt with Ten, we'll figure out what to do with the survivors."

"Talk to you then. We'll be running away now. Watch for the fireworks." Cory signed off, stuffed the device back into her pocket, and helped Ted to his feet. Joseph signaled when he was ready.

"We're coming out, Bundin."

"Good!" the Podder declared. "I'm getting fried in this sun." Bundin wiggled and finally succeeded in unwedging himself. Cory went out first. The crowd of women was still there.

"Listen up!" she yelled, motioning for silence. "There's going to be a very big explosion here momentarily. You need to return to your homes and take cover. We're going to run through here, so please don't hold us up. It'd be best if you started running, right now."

Some of the women moved, but most remained motionless. Cory pointed out a path to the side, an opening that they could get through.

She looked over her shoulder. "Are you ready?"

"We need to get into orbit and find the AI," Ted replied impatiently.

Joseph nodded again. "Fire in the hole!" He tossed the explosive into the shaft and turned to run. The others had already bolted on a headlong rush to get as far away from the building as they could. The women raced after them.

The *War Axe*

Private Gefelton cradled Ankh's head in his arms as he poured water on the wound. He tamped it dry, but it started to leak blood again. Tony held a bandage with coagulant over the gash. He looked for a way to tie it into place, but didn't have enough stripping. Another warrior tied multiple pieces together until they had enough to wrap around the Crenellian's head.

Tony dabbled water on the alien's small mouth. A tongue appeared and licked his lips. Tony sat him up so he could better drink. Ankh groaned.

"Take a drink. You've lost some blood and water will help."

Ankh opened his eyes, but he couldn't focus. "We need to get you to the Pod-doc," Tony told him.

"No," Ankh said in a small voice. "Not yet. Help me into the chair."

Tony didn't want to, but he did as the Crenellian asked. The holo screens surrounded the alien. Ankh tapped two spots and then dropped the screens. "Now we can go."

"That was weird," Smedley broadcast to the entire ship.

Tony caught Ankh as he collapsed. He picked him up, keeping the alien's head elevated while telling the others to lead the way to sickbay.

Drop ships 1 and 2

"Aaron and Yanmei," Terry started. "Ten is somewhere in orbit, on a stealthed platform of some type. It is currently cut off from most communication, but if Ten regains control of the fleet, the *Axe* is going to be in the middle of a shit sandwich. I need you to find it and blow it out of the sky."

"You need us to find something that we can't see, in the vastness of orbit around the planet," Yanmei asked. She pointed the nose of her ship skyward and flew toward space. Aaron fell in behind her. "How do you know it's in space?"

"Ted confirmed it."

"Does he know where it is?"

"I don't know," Terry stammered. "I talked with Cory."

Yanmei didn't insult Terry by suggesting that he ask.

"I'll tell them to get in touch with you directly."

Terry tapped the comm screen. "Where can I take you today?" Smedley asked.

"Damn, bitch! I thought you were gone for good."

"Nice to talk with you, too. I got trapped inside Ankh's head after we hit that mine. It wasn't pleasant. Let's say that I'm happy to be out here."

"Ask Plato if they have an idea where Ten is, and if he does, tell him to send the info to Aaron and Yanmei. They're hunting for it as we speak."

"Done and done. The coordinates of Ten's last known location are on your screen."

Terry looked at the locations. It was surprisingly close to the *War Axe*. "Kill it, Smedley! Orient the ship and fire the mains!"

"The mains are not operational at present. The platform is within missile range. I will advise Captain San Marino."

"And take us to the main compound, the only one with men."

Terry watched the icons on the screen. The fleet in space was a reminder of what Ten had available, if it could only contact them.

He zoomed in on the *War Axe*. Mines started to appear around it and for as far as the ship's sensors could reach. The icon for Ten's cloaked platform flashed red. Two small icons represented the Black Eagles arcing into the upper atmosphere on their way to space.

"Kill that fucker," Terry whispered.

. . .

The *War Axe*

Xianna held Jenelope's head in her lap and started to sing. She stayed under the table, having no idea what was going on. She was happy to have gravity back, but felt alone.

That was what she liked about the dancing on Yol. She had plenty of attention, though not all of it good. She'd learned to fight, enough to get herself out of ugly situations. She was agile and fast. She found that vertical escapes worked best. She could climb faster than people could run.

And here she was, under a table, her friend injured.

The door opened and she called out.

"Only here to grab a sandwich!" the voice replied, having not understood Xianna's plea for help.

One of the warriors who was left behind.

"Xianna?" he called. She gently put Jenelope's head down and launched herself from under the table. She jumped into the warrior's arms and started kissing him in her joy.

He gasped, eyes wide. "Whoa!" he called, pushing her face away from his. "We don't do that. We don't suck face with a buddy's wife."

"I'm sorry," she said. "We are different on Torregidor, but I will learn your ways. Help me with Jenelope. She is injured."

The lithe dancer jumped down as if nothing had happened and hurried back to where the chef was lying under the table.

The warrior rolled her into a sitting position, then squatted to place his shoulder even with her mid-section.

He pulled her over and stood, holding one of her arms to keep her balanced. "To sickbay," he said and started walking.

Xianna grabbed a handful of packaged sandwiches on her way out. Jenelope's helper wouldn't be the only one who was hungry.

"Smedley!" the captain cheered.

"Miss me?" the AI replied.

"Status, Smedley. We can't get in contact with our people." The captain was all business, now that the AI had returned. Micky wanted all the information.

"Communication systems overloaded throughout the ship. I show all hands as alive, but many are injured, judging from their vital signs."

"Thank goodness. No fatalities." Micky wanted to know more about the ship and her crew, but buying time was the best he could do. He needed as much of it as possible. *Accomplish the mission and you'll have all the time in the world.*

"Smedley, get the mains online. This is your number one priority."

Team from *Ramses' Chariot*

They could hear the explosion, but the ground didn't shake. The building blew, but it didn't erupt. It collapsed in on itself.

Cory stopped sprinting. "That was less than expected."

"I only used one pack," Joseph admitted.

"Was that enough?" Petricia asked.

"Ted said that the battle wasn't here. We only needed to collapse the tunnel, not turn everything down below into slag, although it probably is anyway."

While the group talked, the women caught up and filled the empty space between the buildings. Soon, they were completely surrounded and the mob pressed in.

Bundin raised his railguns. Cory jumped onto his shell. Ted vibrated with anxiety.

So many people!

Cory wrapped an arm around Bundin's blue stalk to help balance her as she teetered on top. She took care not to poke one of his four eyes.

"Women of Home World!" Cory shouted. The murmurs died down. Cory froze when she saw all eyes on her. She had always found it easy to talk with people, but this was different.

She swallowed hard but couldn't find her voice. She raised one hand for silence after the noise from the women started anew and built in volume.

"We all come from Earth, a planet out there, a long ways away. Your ancestors were taken by aliens, used as slave labor, and then thanks to the alien artificial intelligence known as Ten, you were played with, toys for the AI's amusement. Ten tried to expand its influence. And that's how it discovered us. We stopped it out there and we're going to stop it right here!"

Ted hugged the case containing Plato and started to rock. He would only look at the ground. Joseph moved close, trying to shield him from the innumerable stares. Petricia stood shoulder to shoulder with her husband, taking his hand in hers, to put their being a couple on display.

"No matter what, we're going to offer you a chance to leave this place, take a shot at being human once again, with the opportunities that humanity enjoys within this universe. The opportunity to have friends from all races and all genders. Determine your own destiny."

Cory tried to finish with a flourish, but almost fell. The women didn't respond to her speech. Dokken stood with his front paws on Bundin's shell so he could better see his human.

"Am I reaching them?" she whispered to Joseph. He climbed onto Bundin's shell and joined her. The crowd sighed. An odd creature worked its way through the women and watched the newcomers. The heavy pig-like creature, half Dokken's size but with claws that rivaled a werewolf's, approached Bundin and sniffed the alien's shell.

"Who's the alien now?" Bundin asked in a near-whisper.

Cory shook her head, but smiled. Joseph took a deep breath and prepared to speak.

"We're taking you off this rock, as soon as possible, but only if you agree. I'll fight tooth and nail, and I have long teeth, trust me on this, to reunite you with your men, the other half of your race."

"They're alive?" a lone voice wondered.

"That, my dear, is the same question they are asking. They believe that you are dead, all of you. Ten made them think that. Ten's evil knows no boundaries. If you would be so kind, talk among yourselves and find a leader, the woman that you look up to, because getting you out of here will take everything she has and more. All of us, working together, to bring you home. I don't mean this concentration camp, either. A real home with art and love and most importantly, a purpose for living. If you will let us through, we can get the ball rolling by destroying Ten. It is still out there!"

The women reluctantly moved out of the way. Ted took off running. Cory jumped down and ran after him. Joseph waved until Petricia pulled him to her. They loped through the opening, waving as they passed. Bundin apologized as he bounced people out of the way from an opening that was too small. Once clear, they accelerated toward *Ramses' Chariot.*

The strange creature ran like a thing possessed to keep up.

CHAPTER THIRTY

Drop ships 1 and 2

"Land on the roof of the hospital," Terry ordered. The drop ships hovered as the warriors ran off, taking care not to pound the roof too hard and risk breaking through. Terry and Char walked off last.

Someone opened the roof door. Terry crouched and the JDS leapt into his hand. Capples peered out.

Terry returned the pistol to its holster. "Where's your mech suit?"

"Some of the corridors are too narrow, and this set of stairs. The mechs will have to jump down and come in through the main doors." Cap pointed to the correct side of the building. Kimber looked but didn't move.

"Go ahead. We'll meet you inside," Terry told her.

She walked to the edge, looked over, then jumped. One by one, the other eight went over and into the darkness.

"Shall we?" Terry motioned for Cap to precede them inside. Char went next and Terry waved good-bye to the drop ships when they lifted off and headed to a defensible position outside the community.

Once inside, the extent of the hospital spread out before him. The pregnancy suite, the maternity suite, the baby section, and below ground, the youth. The children were separated early by gender. Much of their time as children was spent in growth chambers—the benefits of physically aging without the experience.

It made Terry sick to his stomach. Workers in the facility were assigned to a section and stayed there for life. Too many of them could not remember the last time they'd been allowed to leave the building.

"Who allows you, and more importantly, what happens if you say no?" Terry asked one woman.

She was shocked to be talking with a man, so Char moved in front of her husband and asked the same question. The woman finally answered. "We can't say no. We obey the commands. There is no other way." She pointed to the screen on the wall.

"The good news is that you can all read. That will make your assimilation into a human society easier. If you want to leave, leave. Ten's days are numbered," Char told her.

"Who's Ten?"

"The one who has been giving you direction your entire life," Char replied. Terry stayed out of the conversation. This was Char's show. And he expected, Christina's and Cory's, too. They could talk with the populace without getting them stirred up. Terry was out of his element.

Cap pounded into the hallway, having returned to his suit. He kept his visor mirrored. The women had less of a problem with the mech than they did with men.

Problem wasn't the right word. Cap settled on discordant fascination.

"Find the power link between this terminal and whatever is driving it, then trace it back to whatever source you can find. If you come across a server farm or whatever that thing might be in hiding in, destroy it without hesitation. Don't give the tendrils a chance to escape," Terry said

The Black Eagles

"Plotting a flight path between the mines," Yanmei said as she gently rolled one way, straightened, then ascended. She maintained her speed through the smooth maneuvers.

Aaron couldn't change course without jerking the ship. He would follow her into a turn, oversteer, over-correct, and finally be on course by the time she changed again, then it would start over.

He wanted to slow down, but he didn't want to lose her. He could fly or he could navigate. He wasn't up to the challenge of doing both simultaneously. The more he tried to relax, the tighter he became, until his hand started to go numb from his death grip he maintained on the joystick.

Yanmei accelerated as she closed. "Prepare to fire," she told Aaron. He backed off the throttle and stuffed his head inside the cockpit to make sure he activated the external cannons properly. He saw the flashes from Yanmei firing. He waited for an explosion but none came. She slowed and fired in a circular pattern, increasing in size as she approached.

"Negative contact. Target coordinates engaged, but there doesn't seem to be anything here," she reported.

"Roger," Micky replied. They could hear the disappointment in his voice.

The *War Axe*

"Smedley? Is it still cloaked and in that state, is untouchable? Or did it move?"

"I can answer none of your questions since I never saw it in the first place," Smedley replied. "I can see the mines, but the technology to cloak Ten must be different."

"What about a comm satellite being restored? Can you find any repair activity?"

"Space is a big place, Skipper. I have the sensors focused exclusively toward the area where Ten was supposed to be located. I am digging through a great deal of data trying to find an anomalous reading when it may not appear as an anomaly."

"All sensors are focused inboard?" The realization hit Micky. "Why does the Home World fleet show as static?"

"A projection based on previous location and activity."

"Are they still there?" Micky asked.

There was a long pause. "The fleet is moving toward us."

"I need the mains. I need you to find the restored communications satellite. I need you to fix the comm within this ship. I need you to help me fight this battle!"

"I understand," Smedley said sadly. "I am doing all I can."

The AI audibly clicked off.

Clifton turned around to face his captain. "We're in no position to fight. We need to move."

Micky studied the charts. "How long until the main weapons are online?"

No one answered. Micky leaned forward, bowing his head. He needed more time.

But that was the one thing that he wasn't going to get. The Home World fleet was accelerating toward the *War Axe*.

The Black Eagles

"Tell me where to shoot and I'll light 'em up," Yanmei broadcast.

Are you sure you want to do that? Aaron said using his comm chip. *You'll make yourself a target.*

If Ten doesn't know that we're here, then the AI is pretty sad. I don't think it has offensive weapons. It has a massive fleet at its beck and call.

I thought I heard TH talk about a communication satellite. Can you find one of those?

Yanmei didn't bother to tell Aaron to use his systems to look. She knew that he had no affinity for flying. It wasn't natural to him. He was only doing it for her. She found that adorable, except when they were in a life or death combat situation.

"Check out a data variation at these coordinates," Smedley said. A new icon appeared on Yanmei's screen.

"Moving now," she reported and engaged. The ship launched ahead. Aaron accelerated slowly. He looked inside the cockpit to see where he was in weapons activation sequence. When he returned his gaze outside, Yanmei was gone. He looked at his navigation screen, trying to figure out which way to go. He pressed forward, slowly.

Home World Birthing Hospital

"Do you have a target for me?" Terry asked the mech. Cap shook his head as he paced the hallway. Sensors weren't allowing him to trace the data feed. He needed something more robust than what the suit provided.

"IR, UV, and sonic vibrations. Once it leaves this point —" Cap pointed at the wall. "—it disappears."

"What's behind this wall?" Terry asked.

"Want to see?" Cap asked.

Terry thought of the implications. "Do it."

The sergeant rammed his armored fist through the wall and tore out a huge section.

Terry looked through. "That's why."

The metal plate on the other side of the wall remained intact. A forcefield shimmered. "This is supposed to be the outside of the building?"

"Yes."

"A false wall," Terry replied. "Give us some room please."

The woman looked aghast at the destruction in the hallway. "In all my years... Are all men like that?"

Char had the opportunity, but she didn't take it. This wasn't a joke. In her eyes, Ten made Home World an abomination.

"Not just men, but women too, people who care that humanity is not mistreated. I want to see Ten burn in hell for what it's done to you. Now, if you don't mind, we need to go. There will be a great deal of debris shortly." Terry joined them as they sought shelter around the corner.

"Fire in the hole!" Capples called and launched a long stream of fire from his oversized railgun. "We're through."

Terry tore around the corner and stopped because of the heavy dust in the air. He covered his face and powered forward, squinting through the debris. He bumped into the mech, who guided him through the opening he'd created. On the other side was a small room with a collection of devices Terry thought would be computers.

"I don't know what I'm looking at," he said. "Cap, call *Ramses' Chariot* and get Ted here, ASAP!"

Ramses' Chariot

"We can't just leave them," Cory said as the *Chariot* lifted off and raced for the hospital. Ted wanted pictures. Capples transmitted a few images.

"Tell him not to touch anything," Ted replied. "I'm on my way. I'll be there in five minutes."

Home World Birthing Hospital

"Ted said not to touch anything," Capples relayed.

"Of course he did. Give me your explosives, Cap. I promise I won't set them off until after Ted gets here." Terry reached through the gap. "Don't tell him that."

The *War Axe*

CRAIG MARTELLE & MICHAEL ANDERLE

A new icon appeared on the screen. Micky watched the Black Eagles approach.

"Preparing to fire," Yanmei broadcast. "Almost in range."

A flash and the Black Eagles disappeared from the screen.

"What happened?" Micky asked.

Clifton shrugged. He hadn't been watching. He was updating the plots for an emergency acceleration through the minefield and into open space.

"EMP weapon," Smedley replied.

"Dammit!" Micky shook his fist at the screen.

"Mains are online," Smedley reported in a firm voice.

"Helm! Aim and fire, dammit. Aim and fire!" Micky shouted.

Clifton pulled his head out of the course program and reoriented himself. He activated the thrusters and the ship started to slowly swing around.

"Where are the Eagles?"

"They are too close to the object. We shouldn't fire," Smedley advised.

"Prepare to fire," Micky said, confirming his earlier order.

The Black Eagles

Yanmei had been accelerating toward the target. After the EMP weapon hit, she coasted by, powerless to do anything.

Aaron watched her disappear past the void in space—a

place where no light shone through, a place where a satellite could be hiding.

Relieved of the pressure of flying the ship, he activated the mechanical system, something his ship had that Yanmei's didn't. He wanted her to have the better ship, the most modern, even if they were both dated.

He saw the wisdom in having a mechanical firing system.

He opened a panel beside his pilot's seat and pulled out a metal wire at the end of which was a plunger. He released the safety and watched the space in front of him. He jammed the plunger and a stream of bullets flew into space. He let up when he realized he had no idea where Yanmei was. He couldn't see the pinpoint of light that she had receded into.

He'd have to wait until he was closer and couldn't miss.

Home World Birthing Hospital

The shuttles deposited the warriors onto the hospital's roof. The mechs jumped over the side as Kim instructed. Christina walked through the door and headed down the steps.

She met Char when she exited the stairwell. Charumati smiled in greeting. The woman she was talking with also smiled, relieved that the newcomer wasn't a man. She'd already made the assumption that males were more violent.

It was good that she didn't see the Pricolici in action.

Christina skipped the preamble. "There are a lot of women we need to evacuate."

"A lot," Char agreed. "And children, including babies."

"How in the hell are we going to do that? Five hundred shuttle runs by the drop ships?"

"Terry expected we'd use the Harborian fleet."

"The ships that turned on us?" Christina crossed her arms and smirked.

"We're working on a new plan right now. Terry thinks he found Ten's hiding spot here in the hospital."

"You haven't killed it yet?"

"It's in orbit somewhere," Char replied.

"Then what are we doing here?" Christina punched her fist into her hand. The woman backed away and started to revise her opinion of who was most violent.

"Are you sure you want to use that much explosive?" Cap asked.

"I'm sure, but we need to evacuate the building. There are a lot of people in here. Start the evacuation, if you would. And those breeder males? Try to keep them separated. Depending on how many there are, we might take them separately. There could be enough room in the *Chariot*."

Cap pounded away, calling Kimber as he went. She picked up the order and made it her own. The mechs used their external speakers to ensure that everyone heard the evacuation order.

People started streaming outside into the darkness. It was still early morning on this part of Home World. That had worked to minimize the number of people milling about, but that advantage was long past.

Terry wired the explosives to the backs of the systems. He held the remote in his hand and waited for Ted to arrive. It didn't take long. His five-minute estimate was on the money.

When Ted rushed in, he immediately spotted the explosives. He checked how they were set up. "Good," was the only thing he said, surprising TH.

Ted sat and hugged the box containing Plato. They got to work, or so Terry assumed. They could have been asleep.

He waited until Ted started spasming. And then the only thing he could do was hold the werewolf tight.

"Welcome back, Ted," the entity said cordially. "I wondered when you would get here."

"Wonder no more," Ted's consciousness replied. Plato stood at his side, looking like the ancient philosopher, just as Ted had designed his avatar.

"Looks like you brought your B Team. That's too bad."

"Is that what you've been reduced to, childhood insults?" Ted looked at the nondescript landscape on the digital battleground. There was nothing to use as a weapon, nowhere to hide. The battle would be fought within and between the minds.

"I guess not. My compliments on how far you've come, but now it's time for us to part ways." The entity, a humanoid shadow lacking all detail, turned to walk away.

"Wait. That's it? I pass your traps and tricks and work my way here, only so you can run?"

"Mistakes were made. Sometimes it's best to reposition one's forces. It's my time to move on. You have won the day. The planet that the humans quaintly call Home World is yours. Enjoy it."

"Wait," Ted repeated, but the entity had disappeared. Ted turned to go, but he and Plato were in the middle of nowhere, with no landmarks to reference how to escape. The temperature dropped quickly, racing toward absolute zero. Ted shivered as his being started to freeze.

"Wake up, Ted!" Terry called from somewhere, but Ted had already rolled into the fetal position, hoping to preserve the last of his body heat. He could hear Terry calling, but couldn't tell from where.

The Black Eagle

"Just a little bit more, a little bit closer. Come on nose, turn." Aaron bounced in his seat, but that only put the nose of the fighter further off target. He jammed himself upward against the canopy and wedged himself in. The nose dropped.

"Can't miss now." The darkness blocking space filled his screen. Aaron drove the plunger down. The ship bucked once before the explosion engulfed the fighter.

Home World Birthing Hospital

Ted groaned and fell limp.

Terry gently laid him on the floor. TH checked Ted's

pulse. It was slowing and his breathing was becoming steadier. Terry threw Ted over his shoulder, picked up the box carrying Plato, and worked his way through the opening.

When he made it outside, he found the mechs coaxing people from the inner compound. The darkness made it more chaotic. The confusion and tension rose with each step.

Kimber was closest to the building. She was conducting one final check with the IR.

"The growth chambers are still occupied. We haven't figured out how to remove the children without injuring them. But they're on the lowest level. They should be protected."

"Can't do it, Kim," Terry said. She took Ted and Plato from him and Terry went back inside. He climbed upstairs and found his way to the breach. He removed the detonators, repacked the explosives in the backpack, and took out his JDS. He dialed it to two and from the safety of the gap in the wall, he started firing. The equipment exploded as the darts slammed into it. From left to right, he swept the room, firing as fast as he could pull the trigger. He dialed it to four and fired into the room again.

When he finished, he holstered his pistol and pulled out his comm device. "Micky, we're all done on this end. Anywhere that Ten could hide has been blasted."

"We're on a search and rescue up here. The Black Eagles are missing," Micky replied.

"What happened?"

"They took out the platform but disappeared in the process. We'll find Aaron and Yanmei, have faith."

"The enemy fleet?"

"Are the enemy no more, or so Smedley tells me."

"We need the ships, down here, all of them," Terry said and signed off.

He looked at his comm device. The corridor was littered with debris. Chaos outside. He had healed from the earlier explosion, but he remembered it.

Vividly.

"Find them, Micky. Find my friends."

CHAPTER THIRTY-ONE

The *War Axe*

The ship fired its main weapons. One round per mine, blasting them from space to clear a wide path to the platform. The ship angled in, destroyed the restored comm sat, and continued past.

Yanmei's ship tumbled toward deep space, with no friction to slow it down. The *War Axe* flew past, caught it with two maintenance bots, and guided it into the hangar bay.

The ship retraced its path to the blasted platform. The *War Axe* came to a halt while the sensors searched.

Still in her ship, Yanmei reached out with her senses as soon as she realized that Aaron wasn't on board and waiting for her. She popped the hatch and jumped out, skipping the ladder and vaulting straight to the deck.

"I know where he is!" she yelled and ran for the screen by the airlock. Smedley showed space around them and she tapped it where she could feel his body drawing Etheric energy. He was floating free in space, only his suit between him and the cold vacuum.

The *War Axe* twisted on its axis and slowly moved in Aaron's direction. "You'll lose gravity momentarily, Yanmei," Clifton told her. "I'm going to maneuver him in and then we'll slowly bring gravity back so he doesn't slam to the deck."

Yanmei grabbed a handhold and waited. She could no longer feel the weight of her own body. The ship moved forward. Aaron's lanky form drifted through the atmospheric shield and floated downward as the artificial gravity pulled him to the deck. Yanmei kicked off the wall to float as far as she could before her feet touched, then she started to run.

She caught him before he hit the deck, cradling his helmeted head. She unsnapped the release and carefully removed his helmet. He took a raspy breath. When he exhaled, frothy pink bubbles appeared between his lips. "I need a stretcher!" she yelled into the emptiness of the bay.

Ramses' Chariot

"I think he'll be all right," Joseph said when he put Ted in his quarters, tucking him in and pulling the blanket up. "Do you have any idea when last he slept?"

Cory shook her head. "On Keeg Station, maybe?"

From the corridor, they heard a scuffle. "No, you are with me in the cargo bay. You'll get a bed when we're back at the station," Bundin explained impatiently.

"But we're hand selected..."

"By someone with no hands. You get over that elitist attitude right now. You'll have to work like everyone else."

"We worked," the man said indignantly. "We maintained

the beauty of our village. When the women came, we did our job, and they went away. Always the beauty of our small village remained."

"I am horrified," Petricia told the man. "If you clean up your act, you might be able to get a job at All Guns Blazing. Outside of that, Buff and the wiener brigade will stay out of sight. Get to the cargo bay and stay there!" Petricia sounded angry.

"What are you doing in here?" Joseph asked when he saw the creature. "You look strangely like a wombat."

The creature snorted and pranced. Joseph took out a protein bar and broke it up as he handed it over. The wombat greedily ate it, chewing quickly and swallowing large chunks.

Really? You're befouling the ship with vermin? Dokken asked.

"I think Terry is going to love her." Joseph petted the rough head. The wombat trilled in response.

"What is the world coming to?" Bundin said before walking away.

Bundin's shell scraped against the bulkheads while he went to the cargo bay. The men followed. Petricia had been held captive. She didn't tolerate a superior attitude. That was why she felt comfortable with the Bad Company. No one was better than any other.

K'Thrall and Slikara stuck their heads in through the hatch. "Join us. We could use a hand with these derelicts." Petricia crooked a finger at the pair.

"Derelicts? I thought they were the so-called cream of the crop." K'Thrall looked confused. His mandibles clicked as he analyzed the statement.

"Tell them that you're coming with us," Cory said. Slicker disappeared from the hatch. When she returned, she gave the thumbs up and climbed aboard. K'Thrall entered and shut the hatch.

Home World

Terry Henry Walton and Charumati stood outside the compound, the concentration camp that Ten had convinced the females they had no choice but to call home.

The women formed long lines, waiting for the fleet to touch down, where they'd board and join the men from Home World for a short gate back to Keeg Station, where they would join the other Harborians. With those stationed on the ships, the numbers would grow by nearly fifty thousand.

"Fifty thousand new mouths to feed," Terry lamented.

"Fifty thousand chances to find love," Char countered.

"Fifty thousand new problems."

"Fifty thousand ideas to resolve those problems."

"I guess I'm not going to win this one." Terry took Char's hand and watched the informal leaders from each compound step up to organize their people and move them to the ships. The men readily welcomed them.

"Do we need to give them the werewolf treatment?" Char asked.

"They know that they're not to go anywhere in a group of less than four." Terry watched the women climb aboard, quickly and efficiently. "I expected this would take four days, maybe longer."

"Less than a day, but it's what, twenty-five thousand

people from four different locations? We only needed a hundred of the ships. And it's women running the show, so of course it runs better."

"We're bringing home a lot of empties," Terry said, ignoring the jibe.

"Cory said that the breeder boys might make good workers at All Guns Blazing."

"Do you think it'll be open when we get back?"

"We've been gone for three days. I doubt it."

"Felicity's pretty good at getting that kind of stuff done."

"Another woman leading the way. Maybe we should run all the things."

"Maybe. Will you make me the brewmaster?"

"I've smelled your beer. I don't think we want to put our customers through that. We'll leave that to the professional that AGB Enterprises sends."

"But you didn't taste my beer! So you can't be sure. You're intrigued, aren't you?"

Char looked at him blankly, deciding not to dignify his insanity with a reply. He dropped his hand to Floyd's head. "What do you think, little girl? Are you ready to come to your new home?"

"No one claimed her?" Char asked.

"They treat them like pets, but not. They think of them like big rats. But not me, not me, my precious Floyd."

"You called a female wombat Floyd?"

"Yes. And you know what I'm going to do with her."

"The Pod-doc. Get in line behind Wenceslaus."

"We will, but then we're next, aren't we, my good girl?"

"How did a wombat get all the way out here?"

"Maybe wombats are aliens and someone took them to Earth? We should be asking, was it the grays who dropped them off, like the sailing ships of old and rats."

"You have some strange thoughts," Char suggested, squeezing her husband's hand tightly.

Terry keyed the mic. "Status?"

"We'll have the fleet in orbit within two hours," the captain replied. "Looks like a great time to go home."

"Charge the gate drive, Micky. We're bringing home one of the greatest fleets in humanity's history. We're going to slap Bad Company logos on all these bitches, and then the bad guys can stand the fuck by. We're bringing the heat."

The End

Liberation, Book 4 of The Bad Company

If you like this book, please leave a review. Reviews buoy my spirits and stoke the fires of creativity.

Don't stop now! Keep turning the pages as Craig & Michael talk about their thoughts on this book and the overall project called the Age of Expansion (and if you haven't read the eleven-book prequel, the Terry Henry Walton Chronicles, now is a great time to take a look).

*Terry, Char, and the rest of the Bad Company's Direct Action Branch will return in **Destroyer.***

BONUS MATERIAL

This is the original outline that I used as the basis to write this book. You'll see how my mind works and how much I have to fill in outside of the key points.

Enjoy!

The *War Axe*

TH, Char, Ted and Felicity are having a quiet dinner in the director's quarters on Keeg Station. Ted apologizes for being a bully. He did it just to get back at Terry while Terry's orders and what Ted perceived as coercion were for a different purpose.

Aaron and Yanmei introduce Cory to eastern philosophy to help her cope. Jenelope plays a role. Cory spends a lot of time working in the kitchen.

Cory and Christina have increased roles and visibility.

Introduce Asplesians – Felicity was warned about them as the previous station manager had been killed by one in a bar fight.

Kae & Marcie head out to support the integration of

former Empire Forces into the FDG as an offensive peace-keeping military – big numbers and old-time tactics.

Shonna and Merrit take over the management of the asteroid mining operation while Sue & Timmons take over Spires Harbor. Felicity jacks people up to improve access for trade with Keeg Station. She works Nathan hard to out the station and build a gate.

Some of the people take vacations and head out. Fitzroy, Cory, Aaron, and Yanmei go back to Earth (now starting the Age of Madness) to deliver the communication units that Ted and Ankh have invented. They take a small ship, one of the Harborian frigates with a new miniaturized gate system and an EI under Smedley's tutelage.

Kailin is having trouble managing the home business (son of Kim & Auburn).

TH has a beer in All Guns Blazing on Onyx Station, decides to take his windfall from Nathan for the not swearing bit and open up a franchise on Keeg Station. The Crooner (Ankh) takes an interest in the business of the bar. Asks that a few of his people immigrate to Keeg to run it for Terry while he's away on missions. These little guys will be all about profit and start getting into shady side deals once the station is opened up to all people.

Best bar in outer space, on Meredith Reynolds, in dock area. Room to drink (solo space, or in groups), room to dance, adults with adults, families, game area, private rooms. Bar down the middle, separating drinking side from other activities. Large viewing window, into space (20' high, 60' long). Premier draw for the bar. Can create auditory privacy, as needed, in any area of the bar. Expanding, to franchise in other systems, other planets. Will help Dark Company to further it's ends. TKG18

Ixtali - Physical description - Look like standing spiders. 4 eyes. Humanoid form in pic, but 4 legs (spider legs crossed with crab legs) in text. Four major mandibles, 2 minor ones also, one top, one bottom.

Malatians! Originally from Malatia, but those in Shadow Vanguard 1: Gravity Storm are colonists on Alma Nine. They have teal skin and bright eyes. Females are born with buzzcut-short blue hair, which stays that way for life. Males have long, flowing silver hair, which they wear in eccentric styles to attract a partner - like certain animals and birds do on Earth. Quiffs, spikes, dreadlocks and more - some men add strings of LED lights, small ornaments or even glitter to garner attention. When happily married, men allow their hair to grow long and unkempt to show they are no longer 'on the market'. The messier the hair, the happier the marriage! Every Malatian has a name consisting of two, three-letter words which are never used separately. So, Tor Val, Saf Tah, Jon Rey, etc. But, never just Tor, Saf or Jon.

K'Thrall starts training with the Bad Company along with a number of new recruits, a whole platoon's worth, many Harborians like Brice, some station personnel like Tim.

The team comes back together, minus Kae, Marcie, and the pack. Ted decides he has to go because he can't leave Char as an alpha without a pack and Nathan makes him promise to watch over Christina. Kimber takes over the mech recon. Christina moves up to be a deputy to TH, filling the role that Marcie held for all those years.

They leave for Home World, taking a number of captured ships as a ruse to get close to the planet. Ted brings the bit of Ten that they'd sequestered. Plato runs the ships and it becomes a battle of wills between Plato and Ten with Ted & Ankh on the outside looking in.

The planet is lush and they find the women. They hadn't been culled as Ten led the men to believe. The number of women equals the number of men, but the problems with them are reversed as they also don't know how to act with the opposite sex. Everyone is challenged to the extreme until the women of the Bad Company have to take over and get things under control.

AUTHOR NOTES- CRAIG MARTELLE
WRITTEN APRIL 14, 2018

I can't thank you enough for continuing to read this series. Terry Henry Walton and the fine characters who surround him have become a part of my world. I hope they've become a part of yours as well. Honor. Courage. Commitment. Something we can all live for and be proud of.

Sarah Lewin gets to celebrate the first anniversary of

her 29th birthday today (publication day, April 23rd, 2018)! Hearty congratulations from this side of the pond and many more joyous days to follow (you don't need to wait for your birthday to bash like it's your birthday).

TSP's Fine Dining – my friend Scott Paul who is a world-class author, is a real chef with a formal education from culinary school. Have you ever eaten the kind of magnificence these good people produce? You should. There's a big difference between the way they cook and what you get at chain restaurants.

Thanks to the incredible world of the internet, I know all kinds of Irish – real people who live in Ireland. Thanks to my friend Tommy Donbavand, he volunteered his cousin to be a character within the Bad Company, so Lieutenant Clodagh Shortall was given some screen time. Someone had to keep watch on the good king Wenceslaus, our most favorite big orange cat.

It snowed in Dublin, a fairly rare event, and Clodagh made a snowman (see the picture on the next page) and that is where the inspiration for Micky (character named after our very own Micky Cocker from the UK) and the great HVAC failure came from. So there we are, living in a world that is only a few keystrokes apart no matter where you live. What a great time in which we live! Think about it. Too many think the world is falling apart because the whole world is at your fingertips. Out of seven billion people, we let the misdeeds of so very few weigh us down. Think about your parents and when it was a much simpler time, when you had to get off the couch to answer the phone because the cord wouldn't reach. The world was a very small place back then. Now, we can make it whatever we want if we don't let the immensity of it all overwhelm us. Take a moment to say hello to Clodagh in Dublin.

Shout out to Beck Young who gave me the name Alant and Nicole Emens who offered Cole. I love the fact that I don't have to search the internet for names anymore. All I have to do is ask the best fans in the universe. Two minutes later, I have a huge selection to choose from and it makes me feel bad that I can't pick them all. Thank you so much for being there for me.

According to Chrisa Changala, the names Eldis and Xianna are from a 20-year long friendship that started online in EverQuest and continued through many other MMOs and into real life. It is great to see an online friend-ship that turns out well, as opposed to the Craig's List killers (or parade of killers on my namesake site! Damn –

could they make things suck any worse?). But not for Eldis and Xianna. The green woman may be free with her affections as part of her culture, but welcome to humanity! We'll see how Jenelope does keeping the young couple on track.

James Grant is one of the Kurtherian Gambit Universe Just In Time readers. He also does some 3D modeling of space ships and such, so I included one in the story – the combat support drone. It's a necessary addition to the combat power of The Bad Company, in addition to the cryo-drones (that idea came from Norman Meredith). As we always do in life, we learn most of the lessons the hard way. We tend to fight the last battle as we prepare for the next one. Terry and company are trying to get ahead of the bad guys with a massive increase in the ability to put munitions on target.

This book has a significant amount of cross-over in it. I had to coordinate extensively with those in the know – Tommy Dublin, Sarah Noffke, Micky Cocker, James Caplan, Kelly O'Donnell, Natale Roberts, and Erika Everest. They made sure that I hit the right notes on the cross-over work. Tommy and Sarah actually wrote those parts that I've pasted into this book. Shows what a team effort all of this is. As I tell other indie authors, this is a lonely profession, an author at his/her computer writing the words, but you don't have to be alone. I have people around the world that I can talk to no matter what time of day or night it is.

Why did Ramses have to die? War sucks and the more we fight, the more times our number might come up. It is a taste of reality, but I don't want it to be debilitating. We all have loss in our lives, but we still move forward, even if we think we don't want to. I want people to be happy after they finish reading my books. I ended Price of Freedom on a sad note and that needs to be remedied! I hope you found this book to be more fun and uplifting, ending on a high that made you feel good.

Marcie and Kaeden moving on? There's a reason for that, too.

I introduced the Belzonians as a prelude to the series that Jonathan Brazee and I will co-write. This will be more traditional military science fiction, combined arms combat operations on a planetary scale. Two Marines writing it. I don't think we can go wrong. Marcie and Kae will oversee the operations but we'll create all new characters for the brunt of it. I'm going to write from the perspective of the Sergeant Major who spends most of his time with the front lines, while Jon will write from the command team's perspective, but in the Belzonian Army, the command team fights, too. Everyone fights. It's how they're wired.

I was starting to get lost in the story tendrils because I had so many main characters. Cutting that back was important for my sanity, which is another reason I had to trim the numbers of main characters. We can't have the same people doing the same thing forever. By splitting things out, we can broaden what people do and that opens up so many more plot lines. You, the readers, deserve that.

I also introduced Rivka, our soon-to-be favorite barrister who will star in her own series that will be called 'Kurtherian Legal.' The first book is titled The Queen's Barrister. I have a bit written on this one already, but I'm mostly dabbling story ideas at present. I can't take credit for the concept. Michael came up with the overall arc. He knows a few lawyers and asked one to co-write the series, but he wasn't able to – the day job working as a lawyer sucks your life away where the last thing you want to do when you're off is sit in front of the computer.

I'm one of the other lawyers that he knows, so there was Michael, knocking on my virtual door... It's hard not to like the story line. I'm ashamed that I didn't think of it, but I shouldn't be. Michael is the story guy. He lives to tell tales. I get quagmired in the details. I think between the two of us, we came up with something pretty compelling. The stuff I wrote as the introduction in here has been incredibly well-received by the readers who follow us on the Kurtherian Gambit fans page. I mean really well received, almost overwhelming. It is so much fun to put it together that I want to drop everything else and go all in. Alas, I have too many commitments.

I'm not sure when the first one will be ready. I'll say sometime this summer. I can't commit beyond that, sorry. But it'll be a total bash when it arrives. The choice bits that I've been able to cobble together are flowing well.

But that's all boring story stuff. You didn't read this far just to hear me prattle on about future stories. You want me to bag on Michael Anderle about what he looks like in our early morning Zoom calls. We rely on Zoom because the phone calls work only intermittently. "Can you hear me now?" "How about now, motherfucker?" That's how those conversations go. So Zoom it is.

It's important that neither of us stand up. As we say in the indie author community, if you're wearing pants, you're probably missing out on valuable writing time.

I unfortunately had to see that Jonathan Brazee adheres to that rule as well. We were on a conference call together and told him to let the ugly noise go, but he said he had to check it out. Neither Michael nor I got our eyes closed in time.

I can't bag on Michael or Jon. Those two guys are so damn upright, it's not even funny. Me? I'm boring as hell. I live in the interior of Alaska, far afield from the rest of the world. Although, Michael slept through the opening of 20Books London. There I was, doing the welcome to the show and Michael was in his bed, sound asleep. His wife woke him up at 9:09 am, eight minutes into my tap dance. And it still irks me that I started a minute late.

I stretched it out to thirty minutes so Michael had time to collect his wits. Many people would not be able to address a major conference twenty minutes after they've been awakened from a sound sleep, but Michael pulled it off. He promised not to be late in Vegas. I promised not to put him on before noon.

Michael has made it possible for me to work with some incredible people. Tommy Donbavand (writing as Tom Dublin), Sarah Noffke, and Amy DuBoff, to mention a few. I'll take credit for introducing Amy to Michael and bringing her in for at least four books within the Age of Expansion. We'll keep after her for four more, and then more...

Tommy D wrote the meeting between Terry, Char, and the Shadow Vanguard team. I hope you like it. It meant a lot to me that he would take time out of his schedule to jam some words that we can both use.

Same thing for Sarah Noffke. I asked if she would do a

crossover with the Ghost Squadron where they could meet Terry and Char. She readily agreed as well and jammed lots of cool words that you'll find in this book. Thanks, Sarah – well done!

At the beginning of May, Michael and I will visit a major facility. We'll share pictures after that has gone down. For now, you'll have to wonder where we're going and with whom we'll be talking.

And today (April 23rd, 2018) marks the release date for Darklanding 8, too. That series is running along with a new release every 18 days for the entire first season (twelve total episodes). We call it a space western, but if you like Firefly or Tombstone or Bonanza or any of those, then you should be able to sink your teeth into Darklanding. Please, give it a try - always free in Kindle Unlimited. myBook.to/Darklanding

That's it—break's over, back to writing the next book. Peace, fellow humans.

Please join my Newsletter (www.craigmartelle.com – please, please, please sign up!), or you can follow me on Facebook since you'll get the same opportunity to pick up some of the books at fan pricing (only 99 cents) on that first day they are published.

If you liked this story, you might like some of my other books. You can join my mailing list by dropping by my website **www.craigmartelle.com** or if you have any comments, shoot me a note at craig@craigmartelle.com. I am always happy to hear from people who've read my work. I try to answer every email I receive.

If you liked the story, please write a short review for me on Amazon. I greatly appreciate any kind words; even one or two sentences go a long way. The number of reviews an ebook receives greatly improves how well it does on Amazon.

Amazon – www.amazon.com/author/craigmartelle

Facebook – www.facebook.com/authorcraigmartelle

BookBub - https://www.bookbub.com/authors/craig-martelle

My web page – www.craigmartelle.com

Thank you for joining me on this incredible journey.

First, THANK YOU for not only reading this book, but reading these Author Notes, as well!

Here we go, running down the path of book four and finding out MORE about The Bad Company.

Plus, we get a hint into a new player, and new view into The Kurtherian Gambit Universe.

When we are thinking of a new series to create, we don't look at what's successful (well, we do some of that of course) but rather we look at areas we think would be fun to do, within what we believe are stories fans would like to read.

And what we think would be fun to write.

Enter Rivka.

Something born of Boston Legal crossed with a real lawyer (Craig) while kicking ass and taking names (a bit of Judge Dredd) but wrapped up as a lawyer first, not a cop.

A lawyer with some bite.

Bad Company is moving on, and moving forward with

new stories and The Kurtherian Gambit Age of Expansion is just opening up as we move forward into the future.

New stories with familiar friends. New stories with new friends that always remind you of a certain something that runs through everything we do.

Justice, friendship, badassery.

<new marketing pitch I'm trying out here – I hope you like it.>

Stories in the Kurtherian Gambit Universe are...

An uncommon cure for physiological mental angst caused by today's lack of justice in many areas of life.

Something every reader can do that won't cause one to end up in jail for acting out in frustration.

So, belt up, read on, enjoy a few laughs as those who deserve it get a foot up their ass.

All in the name of mental health ;-)

Ad Aeternitatem,

Michael Anderle

Craig Martelle's other books (listed by series)

End Days (co-written with E.E. Isherwood) – a post-apocalyptic adventure

Mystically Engineered (co-written with Valerie Emerson) – dragons in space

Monster Case Files (co-written with Kathryn Hearst) – a young-adult cozy mystery series

For a complete list of books from Craig, please see www. craigmartelle.com

www.ingramcontent.com/pod-product-compliance
Lightning Source LLC
Chambersburg PA
CBHW031607100726
47898CB00006B/1677